The Jester
and the Kings

Also by Marek Halter

The Book of Abraham

The Jester and the Kings

A Political Autobiography

MAREK HALTER

Translated from the French by
LOWELL BAIR

ARCADE PUBLISHING · NEW YORK
Little, Brown and Company

First English-language Edition

Library of Congress Cataloging-in-Publication Data

Halter, Marek.
    [Fou et les rois. English]
    The jester and the kings : a political autobiography / Marek
Halter : translated from the French by Lowell Bair. — 1st English
language ed.
        p.   cm.
    Translation of: Le fou et les rois.
    ISBN 1-55970-001-7
    1. Halter, Marek. 2. Jews — France — Biography. 3. Jewish–Arab
relations — 1949– 4. Refugees, Jewish — France — Biography. 5. Israel
–Arab conflicts. I. Title.
DS135.F9H34313 1989
944'.00492402 — dc20
[B]   89-6753
                                                                     CIP

Published in the United States by Arcade Publishing, Inc., New York,
a Little, Brown company.

10 9 8 7 6 5 4 3 2 1

Designed by Jacques Chazaud

MV PA

Published simultaneously in Canada by Little, Brown & Company (Canada) Limited

The author is grateful to *The New York Times* for permission to reprint his letter to
Yasir Arafat of August 30, 1988. Copyright © 1988 by The New York Times Company.

PRINTED IN THE UNITED STATES OF AMERICA

For Clara

Contents

The Jester
and the Kings

1

In the Name
of Memory

W e had been talking for hours. There were about fifteen of us packed into the clay hut. Two of the
Palestinians, sitting cross-legged on the beaten-earth floor,
unthinkingly caressed their submachine guns. Around us, the
sounds of the refugee camp — Sabra, on the outskirts of Beirut — blended into a vague murmur. The intensity of our voices
and eyes was heightened by the calm, shadowy light.

Revolution is made of discussion as much as action, of patience as much as violence. We could probably have gone on
talking for more hours, without making any progress. No matter
what I said to further the idea of a meeting with the Israelis,
·they immediately rejected it: an imperialist plot. Maybe it was
because they had an uncertain command of the language we
were using — a mixture of French and English — or maybe it
was simply an expression of their conviction, but they said
"you" to me whenever they meant "Israel." Our discussion
was going nowhere.

"I'd like to know," I said, raising my voice, "whether you're fighting against the Israelis or the Jews. If it's the Israelis, you'll have to settle your differences with them, and sooner or later you'll have to talk with them. But if it's the Jews, then you're fighting against me, a Jew who lives and works in Paris. And I want you to know that even though I struggle for peace, I'm not a nonviolent man. If you attack me, a Jew, I'll do everything I can to wipe you out before you wipe us out. I'll put bombs in your houses and I'll fight you wherever you are, constantly, without mercy."

In that part of the world, words are worth their weight in dynamite. The silence that followed was tense and heavy. The Palestinians were evaluating me, their eyes suddenly uncertain.

"We have nothing against the Jews," one of them finally said. "They're our cousins. It's the Zionists we're fighting against."

"What's a Zionist?" I asked. "An Israeli? Or a Jew who supports Israel's existence?"

"It's the same thing."

"What if the Jews affirm Israel's right to exist but are still critical of its government's policies?"

"We'll fight them all."

"Because they're Jews?"

"No, because they're Zionists."

A young boy brought in another tray loaded with cups of coffee. Near us, in the middle of the camp, a few bursts of submachine-gun fire made me start.

"It's nothing," said a Palestinian, "it's just our fedayeen practicing."

Suddenly they all began talking at once, telling me about their struggle. Slogans, dreams, and despair. They spoke of Jaffa, Haifa, and Jerusalem as if they, children of exile, had been born there. Why was it that I understood them so well, that I even understood their attachment to the submachine guns they held between their legs like penises, when they didn't understand me, even though I was so much like them and had been exiled so many times?

I told them about the child I had been in faraway Poland; the scattered corpses lying at the corner of Smocza Street and Nowolipje Street in Warsaw, where we lived; the nights and days spent in a basement where I could do nothing but count whistling bombs. And the day when, standing on our balcony with wooden marbles clutched in my childish hand, I saw three Germans in an open car chasing an old Jew and trying to lasso him while he ran in front of them with his long black overcoat sweeping the pavement. They came back a few minutes later, dragging the little old man's body, wrapped in his bloody coat, at the end of their rope. I thought I screamed, but I now realize that my voice never left my throat; the scene is engraved in my mute memory, but my scream still resounds in my head. When the car had disappeared, I threw my marbles at a German patrol passing under our balcony. They bounced off the soldiers' helmets with a terrifying *bing!* and then rolled into the gutter. My mother, on her knees, had to beg the booted and helmeted soldiers who invaded our apartment. "He's so little," she said, "he didn't know what he was doing! He didn't mean to drop his marbles, they just slipped out of his hand. He didn't do it on purpose!"

I talked to the Palestinians in the refugee camp a long time. The Gestapo, the yellow star, the barbed wire. Fear and rage. Hunger. I talked a long time and they heard me out. What I said left them perplexed. More coffee was brought in. This time we drank it in silence. Outside, a group of children were playing with wooden submachine guns and shouting, "Death to Israel! Fedayeen! Fedayeen!"

From the way the Palestinians looked at me, I realized they were wondering who I was and what I wanted. What they knew about me — a forty-year-old painter who used money from the sale of his paintings to finance a political magazine on the Middle East — wasn't enough to let them classify me as either a friend or an enemy. Especially since, even though they sometimes accused me of being an Israeli spy, or an American or Russian one — what "false beards" they made _me_wear! — to them, being Jewish meant only practicing the

Jewish religion, and it therefore hadn't occurred to them that my actions and my presence in their camp might be explained by the fact that I was a Jew.

Actually, they had consented to let me visit them only because I was a leader of the International Committee for Peace in the Middle East, because certain political and trade-union forces in various parts of the world had given me their support, and because newspaper articles about me justified their curiosity. They also knew that I often came to Israel and that I was inalterably opposed to the destruction of the Jewish state. All this irritated them, but at the same time it made them respect me.

It was in struggling for Israel's survival that I discovered the Palestinians' existence. Ever since then, I have upheld the legitimacy of their claims, not only because it seems to me essential but also because it is the best guarantee of the Jewish state's physical and moral survival. In that region, which some call Palestine and others Eretz Israel, there is room for two independent states; since justice cannot be shared, the land must be shared.

I still had so many things to tell them, explain to them, that I didn't know how to go about it. The creation of Israel had been both the fulfillment of an ideal and the result of a necessity, and it had also been an attempt to remedy an irremediable wrong. They had to understand that. The thought of Israel's disappearance revolted me, and my feeling of revolt had the same taste as the one that had seized me in my childhood, soon after the end of the war, when I discovered that while Jews were being killed in gas chambers, people in Paris, New York, and Buenos Aires had calmly waited in line in front of movie theaters. I wanted to blow up the Louvre, the Metropolitan, all museums. Why museums? Probably because they assure us that we are civilized. But I was a child at that time. Today, I would do it.

"How many Jews were killed by the Germans?" asked one of the young men with a submachine gun.

"Six million."

"How do you know that? Maybe it's only Zionist propaganda."

I have heard that objection in all Arab countries, and it always infuriates me. As if we were envied for those deaths.

"I didn't count them myself," I said, "but at Auschwitz I saw a mountain more overwhelming than Mount Hermon, horrifying as an atomic mushroom cloud, a mountain made of hundreds of thousands of shoes taken from children whose bodies were cremated, and I saw —"

"That's not our fault," a Palestinian interrupted irritably.

"True, but you still ought to feel solidarity."

"Solidarity?"

He was astounded.

"You ask for solidarity and understanding," I said, "but solidarity doesn't go in only one direction. What was done to the Jews is everyone's affair, just as the famine in Africa is now everyone's affair."

From somewhere close by, another burst of gunfire.

"We die six million times a day," said the same Palestinian.

"But *you're* still alive."

2

An Uncommon Childhood

I was born in Warsaw. A million inhabitants, including four hundred and fifty thousand Jews, with their restaurants and newspapers, their cinemas and theaters, their rich and poor, their beggars and thieves, their political parties, their language — Yiddish is my native language.

Sometimes my mother would take me to spend a few days with an uncle by marriage. The village where he lived, near Warsaw, was called Grodzisk Mazowiecki, and it was like all other Jewish villages in central Europe. The people lived on practically nothing, the streets had a good smell of fresh bread and pickled herring. In the village square, the men commented on the day's main event with broad gestures. Women wearing colored scarves that hid their hair did their families' washing in narrow courtyards where little children played. Outside, laughing adolescent boys chased each other, their earlocks dancing to the rhythm of their running feet. In the bustle of the market, amid the shouts of newspaper sellers and the cries of poultry, I remember an old hunchbacked Jew who had been waiting forever for someone to buy his three shriveled tomatoes.

That warm, lively world, transplanted from the Middle East to Central Europe, with its morals, customs, and prayers, its culture and laws — that world no longer exists. Those who regard the Jews as Europeans unjustly imposed on the Middle East don't know any Jews except members of the tiny elite who share their tastes and careers. They have never been in Grodzisk, my nostalgia. They have never met the people.

My father was a printer, like his father, his grandfather, and his great-grandfather. He taught me the trade as soon as he could, so that the chain wouldn't be broken. He was a good and simple man who liked people and books — he looked at himself in them, as in a mirror. He wasn't religious, but he followed tradition, and every Friday evening my mother lit the Sabbath candles. He was a socialist, and politically active, I believe, in the Jewish printers' union. He was proud that he could speak a little French: he had spent a year in Paris after going there clandestinely in 1935 to attend the funeral of Henri Barbusse, whose books he knew by heart.

Foggy memories, sketchy, superimposed images. One face is clear, however: that of my father's father, Abraham Halter. A tall figure, carefully combed white beard and earlocks, eyes both cheerful and somber, a broad forehead beneath a square skullcap. He personifies all the richness of that vanished world.

Deeply religious, he was on close terms with the famous rabbi of Gur and often went to his home for scholarly discussions. But he was also sympathetic to the Bund, the Jewish socialist party. I remember how, when I went to bring him home on Fridays, he would clean the print shop, cover the machines and typesetting tables with sheets of white paper, wash his hands and forearms, then pray with the other workers, who were pious, bearded Jews like him.

I also remember how we gathered for Passover on Nowolipje Street. When he left the synagogue, very late, the rest of us had all been in the apartment a long time. He slowly climbed the stairs, coughing at each landing to announce that he was coming. We children stopped chasing each other, our parents quickly straightened our clothes, and everyone sat down around the big table. When the patriarch finally opened the door, he saw his whole family and his face brightened. He took off his coat, sat down on the cushions reserved for him, and said, "Good holiday!" Passover then began.

A mixture of authority and gentleness, of reserve and interest in others, he was equally in his place when he presided over the family table, read his prayer book in the synagogue, or paraded behind the red flag of the Bund on May Day. I was later told that during the revolt of the Warsaw ghetto he, Abraham Halter, jumped from his balcony onto a German tank, with a grenade in his hand.

I think he liked me. He had wanted me to bear his father's name, Meir-Ikhiel — which a Polish clerk at the city hall turned into Marek. He taught me to play chess. I was three years old and already terribly impatient. Whenever he saw that I had stopped following the game, he would take me on his lap and talk to me about Warsaw. Warsaw. . . . Since the day, after the war, when I walked among the ruins of the city, on the bank of the Vistula, Warsaw has been in my memory only as an album of charred photographs. Sometimes one of them comes to life. Then, while sirens wail and bombs whistle, Jews begin running, houses burn, women cry, gray-green uniforms invade the street and pass by us, back and forth, while we wait in line for a piece of bread. One day, in front of our door, they caught an old, white-bearded man whom my mother had tried to save from a raid; they took him by the feet and dragged him down the marble steps, and his brain left yellowish streaks on them when it leaked through the crack in his skull.

When, long after all that, we came to live in Paris, how I envied the casual unconcern of my fellow students at the Ecole des Beaux-Arts! Most of them had memories only of ordinary days, full of friendly meetings, affection, vacations — innocence. They had, of course, known the German occupation, rationing, anxiety over this or that family member, but not the earthquake that had uprooted us and delivered us, defense-less, to the unknown.

The last time our family was all together had been shortly before the war, when cousin Hugo came. I had never heard of Hugo before, and after he left I never heard of him again. He came from Germany with a knapsack and several days' growth of whiskers. My mother ran a bath for him and he stayed with us awhile. He slept on the sofa in the dining room. I don't remember his face, only his name, his whiskers, and his knapsack.

When my father had assembled the whole family, Hugo de-scribed what was being done to the Jews in Germany. He often spoke of Hitler, and added each time, "Cursed be his name!"

"The Germans," he said, "will soon be in Warsaw. You must either organize yourselves or leave. You don't have much more time."

But leaving would mean abandoning everything, without even being sure that Poland was going to be occupied. Maybe Hitler wouldn't dare to break the agreement he had made at Munich with France and England. And maybe Hugo was ex-aggerating: the persecution of German Jews was more remi-niscent of czarist pogroms than of the Spanish Inquisition, and Jews were used to pogroms.

The uncles and cousins agreed on collecting money and food: the Jews in Germany had to be helped. But as far as we were concerned, the danger didn't seem imminent.

When they were all gone, Hugo took me in his arms and said, "Did you see those Jews, Marekel? If they don't change, they're all going to die. Remember this: we have to change. Persecution isn't inevitable."

I didn't understand what he meant, but I knew he was the one who was right. He left the next day, leaning forward un-der his knapsack. A few days later, war broke out.

First there were three weeks of bombings, with just enough respites between them to let us dream. So when we believed the Russians were coming to our rescue, people began dancing in the streets. No one was more capable of hope than the Jews of Warsaw. In accordance with the Soviet–German pact, the Red Army occupied part of Poland, but Warsaw was in the area marked out for German control, and the bombings continued.

One day a terrified aunt came to tell us that my grandparents' apartment house had been cut in half by a bomb. My grandfather had been praying in a back bedroom. After the blast, he had found himself alone on the fourth floor of a building without a façade, as though in a stage set. I laughed a long time. My mother looked at me sternly, but I couldn't help laughing — and that may have been the last laughter of my childhood.

The Germans occupied Warsaw. Heavy, obsessive fear gripped the city. I knew serious things were happening, and I kept thinking of what Hugo had told me: if the Jews didn't change, they would all die.

My Aunt Ruth died, of an illness that had nothing to do with the Germans, but she did die. To me, it was as if Hugo's predictions were beginning to come true.

"What's death?" I asked my mother.

"Your aunt is dead; that means you can never see her again."

"What about you?"

"I'll never see her again either. No one will."

Another time, at the corner of our street, some hungry people were cutting up a horse that had been killed by a bomb blast.

"Doesn't it hurt him?" I asked.

"Of course not, since he's dead."

I didn't want to be cut up in little pieces, like the horse. I didn't want to be invisible, like Aunt Ruth. I didn't want to be dead.

Warsaw was adjusting to its new life. Jews were pressed into service to clear the streets. Special brigades of the German army patrolled the city. They still stopped only men: the youngest ones to send them to "work" in Germany, the oldest ones for their own entertainment. They were especially amused by the religious Jews' beards and earlocks: they set fire to them. Once I saw a man whose face was in flames. As soon as the Germans abandoned him, some of the neighbors rushed to him with blankets. It was too late; his face was nothing but a swollen mass of burned flesh.

That whole period now appears to me as a long, confused night pierced by sharp images, precise memories of faces, spoken words, moments.

Most of those images are of people carrying bags, packages, and suitcases, a succession of wanderers looking for a home. Our family was increased by a crowd of cousins I didn't know. They had fled from a village whose name I have forgotten. Their houses had been burned. They had been able to save only a few belongings, which they carried in wicker baskets closed with string.

Then, with bundles slung over their shoulders, men began leaving the city, some to go into the Soviet zone, others, like my father and my uncle, to join the underground Resistance, whose first groups, composed mainly of pro-British nationalists, were beginning to be organized; the Communists didn't join them till after the German invasion of the Soviet Union. But Jews weren't liked in the Resistance either, and many were murdered by Polish peasants and even partisan fighters.

As for those who went to territories occupied by the Red Army, they met various fates. Some soon came back to wait for peace with their families; they had been told that the war would quickly be over. Others, not accepted as refugees, were allowed to stay in the Soviet Union only if they became Soviet citizens, thus cutting themselves off from any possibility of return. If they refused, as many did, they were accused of spying and sent to Siberia. It was a cruel punishment, but it saved the lives of some of them.

A month or two after my father had left, soldiers came for my mother and me. She cried, and I cried at seeing her cry. I didn't want us to be put among those people who left with their bundles and never came back.

They took us into a big room. Now, as words revive those

moments, I *am* in that big room, even though I remember nothing about it, except that it was huge. Two Germans are holding me in front of my mother. She is pale, her hair is disheveled, her eyes are red. A spotlight blinds me and makes me cry. I close my eyes with all my might. I hear only voices: "Tell us where your husband is and your son will be given back to you."

My mother says she doesn't know. I'm slapped once, then again. I hear a scream. I'm not the one who screamed, I'm sure of that, so it was my mother. I keep my eyes closed. I don't want to see. I don't want to know.

I don't know how long it all lasted, or what my mother said to the Germans to make them release me. I never asked her.

I didn't open my eyes again till I felt the cold outside air on my face. It was dark. My mother was squeezing my hand. A military car took us home.

We lay down on the only bed we had left, and we said nothing.

In Warsaw a wall already surrounded what was going to become the ghetto. The gates were still open, but few people went through them. "Where is there to go?" asked a lady who lived with us and said she was our cousin.

Those who had money could buy bread, sugar, and a few vegetables "on the other side." But the prices demanded of Jews were so high that they soon stopped buying. For a time, the richest ones thought they could pay to be sheltered by Poles in Warsaw and its environs, but word soon spread that most of those who tried it were stripped of everything they owned and then turned over to the Gestapo. In the border areas, Poles traded us chunks of bread for sets of silverware, a little flour for furniture.

Their hostility isolated us as surely as that wall whose gates we were afraid to go through. Those who left had no assurance that they could ever come back, and most people felt that if they had to die in one place or another, they would rather stay with their families.

But on November 17, 1940, the gates of the ghetto were

sealed shut. Jews who lived in other parts of the city or in neighboring villages had been given a few days to join us. Again, images of people pushing carts and baby carriages overloaded with mattresses, clothes, pots, packages, all the wretched odds and ends of the homeless.

It was cold. We heard children crying in the streets. Hunger, fear. I wanted to share something with them. But what? We had nothing left. I cried too. The people living with us put their hands over their ears. Only an old cousin ignored me, calmly praying in his corner. "He's lucky to be deaf," said the lady who was also a cousin. I clearly remember how her voice sounded when she said, "They're going to their death" each time she saw a group of men being taken away, heading for Germany. Her tone was perfectly even, as if she were saying what time it was. "You're hungry," she used to tell me, "but don't worry, you'll get used to it. People get used to everything."

My mother and I lived alone in one little room of that apartment which no longer seemed to be ours. I was nearly five. There were other children in the building, and they made dolls with rags and pieces of wood. I didn't want to play with them. The grown-ups told us to play, but something wouldn't let me do it, probably my confused feeling that grave events which I didn't understand were happening. As Hugo said, we should have changed if we didn't want to die.

My grandfather Abraham had taken refuge in the basement of his building. It was said that he had begun studying the Cabala. Like many of his contemporaries, he had a pressing need to understand the designs of the Almighty. On the Sabbath, the synagogues were filled. So too, on Sunday, was the church on Leszno Street, the only one in the Jewish quarter that was still functioning. Children of converts to Christianity — Jews nevertheless, in the eyes of the Nazis — came there wearing the yellow star, to seek a little comfort from the priest, who also wore the Star of David.

My mother and I moved into my grandfather Abraham's apartment. He showed us the basement where he now spent most of his time. I later learned that the first issue of the clandestine newspaper *Yediess* had been printed there, and that my grandfather had worked on it.

It was in the basement that he liked to read the Bible to my mother and me, especially certain verses of Exodus, which he embellished with Rashi's famous commentaries, to give us courage and hope.

One evening when the three of us were there, sitting under the lamp, we heard footsteps on the stairs, then a knock on the door, and finally a few words in Polish. My grandfather stiffened, but my mother stood up and opened the door. It was my father's friend Janek, a printer like him, and a Catholic. He had come to take us away. My grandfather refused to go with us. We left without saying good-bye to anyone but him. Without baggage.

Through an underground passage, we went to the basement of a neighboring building, where several of Janek's companions were waiting for us, and after wandering a long time through the sewers we finally succeeded in leaving the enclosure of the ghetto. It was dark. Janek led us to a railroad track that crossed a long open space, at the end of which we came to a motionless freight train. In front of one of the cars stood my father. He was with my aunt and her husband and several people I didn't know. A little later I saw Janek try to give money to a railroad worker; the man refused it and Janek gave him more.

The train soon left. We were in a cattle car, hidden under a pile of straw that the cows were eating. The train stopped at every station. Each time, the doors would open and powerful lights would sweep across the inside of the car. I huddled against my mother and she put her hand over my mouth to keep me from talking, but I knew we were hiding and I wished I could stop the beating of my heart, which seemed to me as loud as church bells. There were shouts, the locomotive whistled, the train started off again, and I went to sleep.

The last time the train stopped, the doors were opened wide and men came in, grabbed us, and threw us out. I was daz-

zled by the lights and bewildered by the loud voices. Along
the platforms, German soldiers were running behind dogs.

"Are there any Jews on the train?" bellowed a loudspeaker.
"Jews have been reported on this train!" And the voice repeated, "Jews on the train . . . Jews on the train . . ."

"Jews? Poles? *Ausweiss!*" said an officer, pointing his pistol
at my father's chest.

"Have you got a light?" Janek abruptly asked the officer.

Janek was tall, and strongly built, like an Aryan in a propaganda poster. The officer was surprised. After a moment of
hesitation he put his pistol back into its holster and turned to
take out his lighter. Just then a hand gripped me by the arm
and pulled me under the cattle car. I heard shots. People began running in all directions. Pandemonium. My parents, my
uncle, and I ran a long time, across fields, through forests.
Like a broken record, I kept repeating to myself, "When I grow
up, I won't allow this, when I grow up . . ."

I don't remember how long we kept going. I remember only
that we walked at night and hid behind thick shrubbery during the day. Janek did his best to bring us food. He wanted
to take us to England, where he intended to join the free Polish army.

One morning, in a forest, we found ourselves face-to-face
with a patrol of Red Army paratroopers. The young mus-
tached officer first took us for spies and wanted to shoot us.
Then he saw me crying and noticed my mother, who was
pregnant. He decided it would be better to escort us to Moscow and turn us over to the authorities.

In Moscow we were given a mistrustful reception, but we
were saved by the Soviet mania for demanding that everyone
write the story of his or her life. My father wrote his, and it
happened that only the day before there had been an article
in *Pravda* on prewar Polish publishers, in which my great-
grandfather, who had published the first revolutionary tracts
in Yiddish, was quoted at length. The Soviets believed in ge-
netic determinism: they welcomed us with joy.

And, with a commendable desire to preserve us from the

danger of the bombings that Moscow was undergoing every day, they sent us to a *kolkhoz* (collective farm) near Novuz-ensk, at the edge of the Kazakh steppes. A long train trip across an empty landscape: all the inhabitants of the former German Volga Republic* had been deported to Siberia.

We stayed on the kolkhoz for a year. I sorted potatoes: big ones with the big ones, little ones with the little ones. The people were poor and friendly; the small houses were half buried in the ground. The infinite horizon began at our door. There were also camel caravans, which my father sometimes accompanied for several days. My sister, Berenice, was born there. We called her Bousia, and she cried all the time.

The potatoes were meant for the army and the large cities. Hardly any were left for us. I always managed to hide a few of them in the padded lining of my coat: we had nothing else to eat. One day, unexpectedly cold weather froze a mountain of potatoes; the kolkhoz sent them to the front anyway.

We were also short of fuel and clothes. The dried cow manure that we used for cooking potatoes gave off very little heat. My father went to the Party section leader to explain our situation.

The section leader was a fat, likable man with a big mustache frayed at the ends. He brought us all together in the room that served as his office: my parents, my uncle, his wife and her sister, my aunt Zosia and her husband, and two other families who had come from Poland before us.

This section leader knew that my father had tried to enlist in the Red Army but had been rejected because of a cavity found in one of his lungs. He himself suffered from the same ailment. Cold wasn't good for them. But the kolkhoz was poor,

---

*In 1924 the people of German descent living in the Volga region, some of whose ancestors had come there more than a hundred and fifty years earlier, were made members of an autonomous republic, with the city of Engels as its capital. But Stalin did not trust "his" Germans, even though they were Russianized and Communists, and in 1941, when German troops were advancing toward the Volga, he decided to abolish the German Volga Republic.

and the country was at war. He couldn't even promise us any clothing for the winter, because he didn't know where he could get any. He looked at us, all squeezed together in the little room. Suddenly he smiled in his mustache.

"Go to a warm part of the country," he said. "You may not be rich, but at least you won't be cold. I'll take care of the tickets and the *propuska* [travel permit]. Think it over and decide where you want to go."

He left us alone for a few minutes. As soon as he was out of the room, everyone began proposing a name. On the big wall map of the Soviet Union we looked for a place to continue our lives. The map was old and its colors were faded, but the country had never seemed so vast to us before.

"Why don't we go to Tashkent?" I asked.

No one else had said that name. I had just read *Tashkent, the City of Bread,* by Aleksey Tolstoy, and I wanted to remind the others of my presence. After all, I was six years old, and I worked, and I had my contribution to make.

"Tashkent — that's not a bad idea," someone said. "It's always warm there."

And so we left for Tashkent, the capital of Uzbekistan. The whole kolkhoz accompanied us to the station. They all kissed us good-bye, and each of us was given a little bag of flour: our wages for a year.

That year had actually gone by quickly for me, with my potatoes and my little sister's crying. I was melancholy. I had learned that word from the people of the kolkhoz: "A real Kazakh is melancholy," they often said. I wasn't a real Kazakh, yet I was melancholy. Would I change when I became an Uzbek?

It was a tiresome trip. The train crawled along and the distance was enormous. After a few days we settled into our railroad cars as though into houses. Each family isolated itself with boxes and crates, and decorated and arranged its space. We had nothing else to do.

Things became complicated when our train was diverted toward the Caspian Sea: the direct route was reserved for mil-

itary transportation. We went into an area of frequent bombings. At the first alert, the train stopped in the open country-
side. Messerschmitts dived at us. We scattered into the fields,
but the planes came after us with their machine guns firing.
We ran in zigzags, like rabbits. The uproar — engines, explosions, gunfire — was so loud that Bousia forgot to cry.

When the Messerschmitts flew away, what was left of the
train was in flames. We waited, without moving, till it had
finished burning. Then we began walking along the track.

It was night by the time we came to a station. My father
found some hot, boiled water and we each took a few sips of
it. Then I went to sleep on the floor. In the morning I was
awakened by loud voices. Standing on a bench, the railway
transport officer was doing his best to calm the people who
had filled the station: they were all trying to make themselves
heard and pass in front of the others, as always happens when
the authorities decide that only a few can go to what is regarded as safety.

There was only one train for Asia and it was already packed
with technicians and their families on their way to start up the
evacuated factories of the occupied regions. By squeezing together a little more tightly, they had been able to make room
for a few more passengers. The order was that in deciding
who would be saved, priority would be given to Party members and intellectuals — those whom Lenin had called "engi-
neers of the soul."

Everyone was jostling, gesticulating, shouting, trying to get
closer to the transport officer. Angry cries and desperate wails
rose to the metal roof, bumped against it, mingled, amplified
and distorted each other, and fell on our heads like wounded
birds.

My mother had a membership card from the Union of Soviet Writers; while we were at the kolkhoz, some of her poems
had been published in newspapers. We were therefore among
the few people who left that station, which, we learned later,
was bombed the next day.

It took us about a week to reach Kazalinsk, and two more weeks to arrive in Tashkent. The first few days of the trip were especially difficult. Every two or three hours Messerschmitts would dive at the train, and it would come to a sudden, jolting stop. We then scattered over the steppe, chased by the planes. When the alert was over, we got back into the train and it went on for another two or three hours, till the next alert. Again the steppe and the chase. Each time we lost a piece of the train, and each time we checked to see if someone had failed to come back. Like my aunt Zosia's husband: the train was already moving again when we realized that he was no longer with us.

As we approached the Aral Sea, the alerts became fewer. Once, during a stop, we even made a fire and drank some hot water for the first time in days. By the time we got to Kazalinsk, our long train had been reduced to only a few cars, and they were in pitiful condition.

At last we reached Tashkent. For two days the train stayed a few kilometers away from the station, waiting for we didn't know what authorization. My father and I walked into the city to get water for Bousia. Tashkent was as it had been in my book. I liked the look of the men in their colored caftans and embroidered skullcaps. The women, however, with their black veils, frightened me a little.

We weren't allowed to stay: there were already too many refugees. We were given a propuska for Kokand. Farewell, Tashkent . . .

I now know that, with its light and its minarets, Kokand, a city of Uzbekistan, in Soviet Central Asia, looked like Marrakech. In the morning, we were awakened by the calls of the muezzins. On one side of the valley were the Tien Shan Mountains and the Pamirs; on the other side, the deserts of Kara Kum and Kyzyl Kum.

A dozen of us lived in one room and slept on the beaten-earth floor. I don't remember how, but someone had unearthed a jar of peaches in syrup. More than a luxury, a dream. We cut one of the peaches into thin slices so that everyone could taste it, and we kept the rest for New Year's Day, as a wondrous offering to those who would survive till then.

Every day after work, hungry and tired, we looked at the jar of peaches displayed like a sacred object on the only shelf in the room. For us it was a symbol of another time and another world, both a memory and a promise. One evening my aunt pointed at the shelf.

"One of the peaches is gone!"

All faces immediately turned to me, since I was the youngest.

"Are you the one who took the peach?" asked my mother.

"No."

"You're lying!" she said.

And she slapped me.

For the first time, and all at once, I realized the injustice and misery of the life we were leading. I was seven years old, and I was never a child again

Tens of thousands of refugees were crammed into clusters of flimsy wooden buildings around the city. The only food we had was what UNRRA* could give us, and it wasn't much. We saw living skeletons stagger along the streets and suddenly collapse. They were piled into high carts, taken to the edge of the desert, and left there. One day my little sister's turn came. My parents were both in bed with typhoid fever, in an elementary school transformed into a hospital. I had put Bousia in a child-care center. She died there. Of hunger, I was told. She was two years old.

Kokand. . . . A donkey was trotting in front of us, shaking his rider, who was trying to get away from us. We ran barefoot. The ground was burning hot, having been heated since

---

*UNRRA, the United Nations Relief and Rehabilitation Administration, was an organization for helping refugees in Europe and the Far East, founded on November 9, 1943. It stopped functioning in 1947 and was revived two years later under the name UNRWA (United Nations Relief and Works Agency) to help Palestinian refugees.

dawn by a sun that seemed to multiply, as though with mirrors, the snowy peaks of the Pamirs. Two bags of rice bounced against the donkey's sides. Rice. Rice was salvation. "Find some rice," a nurse had told me, "if you want to save your parents."

I was the one who caught the donkey. A knife cut into one bag, then into the other. Streams of little white grains. My companions and I filled our caps, as though from a fountain. The donkey's rider didn't make a sound. He was afraid, and his only thought was to get away.

The men were at war, the women worked in the evacuated factories of occupied Byelorussia. We children did as we pleased in the city. We were called hooligans. We raided places where black-market business was concentrated, we robbed the apartments of the richest bureaucrats, and at night we even attacked passersby.

I had become a hooligan by chance. One day when I was on the way to the hospital with a basket of food for my parents, I was attacked by a group of boys my age. I was furious.

"Seven against one — that's easy!" I shouted. "All seven of you, to steal what I was taking to my sick parents! Go after rich people, you sons of bitches!"

"You're right," one of them said, "seven against one is too easy. We'll fight you one at a time, starting with me."

We fought for a long time beside the basket. He was stronger than I, but I was more tenacious. Finally, bruised and exhausted, we fell in the dust together. The others laughed. We talked. They went to the hospital with me, to make sure I hadn't lied to them, then they told me to meet them that night.

They took me to Kalvak, an open space in the lower part of the city where gangs gathered to settle scores, tell jokes, sing together, celebrate their exploits, and pass judgment on "traitors."

Behind their knives, those gang members were tender-hearted boys who dreamed of another life, another society. They didn't talk politics, didn't criticize the system, and respected the guide of the peoples of the Soviet Union, Iosif Vissarionovich Stalin. But they considered it unjust that factory managers should have more privileges than their parents, who were workers. And in the stories they liked, friendship took precedence over self-interest, justice triumphed over treachery, heroes risked their lives for honor.

That evening at Kalvak, I don't remember why, I began telling the story of *The Three Musketeers* to my new friends. Other groups joined us. By early morning, my fame was established. I became *Marek cho khorosho balakaiet*, "Marek the good storyteller."

Tough boys of fourteen or fifteen treated me as an equal and they all wanted me in their gang: I didn't steal any better than the others, but I was able to tell stories that lasted all night — stories by Victor Hugo, Alexandre Dumas, Gogol, Sienkiewicz.

My father couldn't get used to the idea that I was a hooligan. But he told me later that when he had left the hospital and begun working at night, he was often spared by gangs that were about to attack him: "Leave him alone, he's Marek's father."

I was eight and a half years old when the leaders of a Communist youth organization, the Pioneers, accepted me for membership. I soon became head of the local section. They were glad to have redeemed a hooligan with a talent for organization, and I was glad to have been finally accepted somewhere. Ever since I had begun drifting on the stream of exile, this was the first time the current hadn't pulled me away from shore. I was proud, too; I was a Soviet citizen. Our soldiers were fighting the Nazism from which my family had fled, and they were dying for my freedom. And at school the other boys had told me, laughing, that our Russian teacher was in love with me. She was twenty and blond. I was flattered like a man and apprehensive like a child, though actually I was neither a man nor a child.

But my position as head of the Pioneers, my parents' recovery from their sickness, the victories of the Red Army, the long, troubled looks our teacher gave me — all this formed a whole, and for the first time I was happy.

One day, during a meeting of the leadership of the Kokand Pioneers, I proposed a program of festivities for the anniversary of the October Revolution. My comrades were opposed to it.

"We're in Uzbekistan," one of them pointed out to me, "and you don't know our problems."

They were impregnated with Uzbek nationalism, Great Russian domination angered them, and it was hard for them to accept being led by a Polish Jew.

"And what republic are you from?" another one asked me.

"I'm from the Soviet Union."

"The Soviet Union is made up of republics and autonomous regions."

I tried to answer, but all I did was make them laugh at the stuttering that suddenly takes possession of me whenever I become irritated. I broke off the discussion. After all, maybe they were right: I wasn't an Uzbek and I wasn't in my home country. Stalin had tried to create a Jewish autonomous region, Birobidzhan, in the Siberian taiga. He had moved thousands of Jews there by force, but the only thing Jewish about Birobidzhan was a sign in Yiddish on the railroad station where newcomers arrived. Can a homeland be imposed on a people who have not found historical, mythical, or cultural roots there?

Palestine, however, was part of my history. I had heard talk about it in my earliest childhood, and I had rediscovered it in the poems of Pushkin and Lermontov. I had also found it in the old atlas that my Russian teacher and I turned up while rummaging in her attic. I was struck by the names of cities unknown yet familiar to me: Jerusalem, Safad, Tiberias, Jericho, Jaffa. They were inexplicably dearer to me than the cities I knew and liked: Kokand, Tashkent, Samarkand, Bukhara.

Then why not a Jewish republic in Palestine? I raised that question in an article reporting on our meeting, published in the newspaper of the Pioneers of Uzbekistan. Since the exodus of the Hebrews, I wrote, there had not been an independent state in Palestine. The country was occupied by the British? The Jews had to struggle against that imperialist occupation. Another people also lived there? A binational socialist state had to be created. The Jewish problem would then be solved, and socialism would be implanted in the Middle East. I didn't realize that my Soviet education was making me reinvent Zionism.

My article wasn't received as well as I had hoped. The Soviet Union was not yet interested in the anticolonialist struggle of the Jews in Palestine, or in converting the Arabs to socialism. And the British were allies — they had, in fact, just routed Rommel's army. What was left of my theory? The idea that it was impossible for the Jews to solve their national problem within the framework of the Soviet Union.

The editor of the newspaper was fired, and my parents were ostracized. Their friends, thinking they were responsible for my ideas, expected us to be deported soon and were afraid to talk to them. After having a stormy confrontation with a Party leader because I refused to engage in self-criticism, I was replaced as head of the Kokand Pioneers by a young Uzbek. That seemed only natural to me.

We weren't deported. My parents resumed normal relations with their friends, and I with my hooligans.

For some reason the Party decided to redeem me again. I was included in a delegation of Pioneers from Uzbekistan who were going to take part in the victory celebration in Moscow. We had learned about the victory one morning and we didn't know what it meant. All those red flags, those patriotic songs, those tearful eyes — it didn't make sense to us; the war was part of us. Only when we saw the first men discharged from the army, most of them wounded, did we really understand that the war was over.

I don't remember much about Moscow: the shapes of the buildings, the width of the streets, the color of the Moscow River. I remember only the people, the crowd, the festive atmosphere. Tears and laughter, accordion music, Red Army songs blaring from loudspeakers. Delegations from all over the country, wearing the national costumes of their republics. Soldiers too, great numbers of soldiers, some of them wounded, either walking on crutches or leaning on their comrades' shoulders. Near the statue of Pushkin, one of them was telling how they had taken Berlin.

Pravda had published a list of heroes of the Soviet Union, by nationalities, and the Jews were cited among the first. So that victory was also mine. I was the equal of the others, and happy like them.

At the last moment I was chosen to give Stalin a bouquet from the Uzbekistan Pioneers. He looked like the pictures of him that I had seen on public buildings and in my history textbook. He was greeting the crowd in Red Square with what seemed to me a familiar gesture.

I was placed on the speakers' platform with about twenty boys and girls. One by one, we gave Stalin our bouquets. He said a few kind words to each of us, and the crowd applauded. When it was my turn, I was so overcome with emotion that I had to be pushed forward. Stalin took my flowers, ran his fingers through my hair, and said something that I was too perturbed to hear.

For someone who doesn't know what Stalin meant to tens of millions of people, someone who didn't share the veneration that surrounded him, who didn't feel the thrill produced by his calm voice when everything seemed to be giving way before the Nazis' tanks — "There will be a party on our street too!" — who didn't escape from the ghetto to bring flowers to the "architect of victory" — for someone like that, it will be hard to understand the pounding heart, and the anxiety, and the pride of the child I was then.

Back in Kokand, everyone wanted to know what Stalin looked like, what he had said to me, how he had been dressed. I really didn't know what he had said to me, and he looked like his pictures. But I had seen him, and I had been part of his glory.

Before I had time to take much advantage of my experience, I learned that we were leaving again. An agreement between the Soviet government and the provisional government in Lublin* allowed Polish nationals to return to their country. So we were going back to Poland. And when the minarets of Kokand, my friends' faces, and my Russian teacher's tears had disappeared in the smoke of the locomotive, I was as sad as I had been two years earlier when we left the kolkhoz. Yet I knew that I was no more an Uzbek than I had been a Kazakh.

On the way, our train was attacked by Polish peasants. They threw stones at us and shouted insults: "Dirty Jews! Go somewhere else! Get out! No Jews in our country!"

We settled in Lodz, the Polish Manchester. We had to organize self-defense groups against anti-Semitic demonstrations. For example, when Jewish children left school at the end of the day, we went to protect them from organized gangs that tried to attack them. It often led to fierce battles fought with sticks and broken bottles. Once I was even stabbed.

Since it was becoming more and more distressing for Jewish children to go to Polish schools, as soon as the government authorized the opening of a Jewish school I enrolled in it. It was named after the Yiddish writer I. L. Peretz. I and the other students spent much of our time in discussion. I especially remember something our history teacher told us: "I don't expect you to know the dates of events, but to try to understand why they happened."

I was eager to understand. I was at the age when one begins to forge convictions on the basis of a mixture of experience and knowledge. Furthermore, Marxist dialectic gave my questions a set of coherent answers. Anti-Semitism didn't surprise me, but I wasn't resigned to it. While the Jews in Palestine were fighting against British imperialism for a Jewish and, we hoped, socialist state, I felt that I was taking part in the

*In opposition to the Polish government in exile supported by the Allies, with its headquarters in London, Stalin created a provisional Polish government, officially proclaimed on July 22, 1944, in the liberated Polish city of Lublin, under the presidency of a socialist, Osóbka-Morawski.

struggle where I was: I became one of the leaders of Boro-chovist Youth,* a far-left Zionist organization.

One day, in collaboration with other Jewish groups, we organized a march in Warsaw for the inauguration of a monument to the memory of those who had fought in the ghetto. Trains and special trucks brought in the remnants of the more than three million Jews who had lived in Poland — seventy-five thousand who had survived death camps and underground warfare, only two and a half percent.

It was a beautiful day in May. The sun glittered playfully on the broken windowpanes of the few façades that were still standing. A passage had been cleared through the devastated streets. We walked in silence through the cemetery that Warsaw had become. I remember that silence, broken only by the sound of our footsteps and the flapping of flags — red flags and white-and-blue flags. On both sides of the street, Poles who had come from the intact parts of the city watched us pass. They seemed surprised that we weren't all dead. Some of them spat into the dust. "They're like rats," we heard someone say. "You keep killing them and they keep coming back." We clenched our fists. We were under orders not to answer. Silence.

I was in the group at the head of the march, carrying a big red flag that was too heavy for me. When I saw those people looking at us from the ruins of our houses — stairs, sections of walls, blackened chimneys — I felt like singing the song of the Jewish partisans:

> *From the land of palms*
> *And the land of white snow,*
> *We come with our misery,*
> *Our sufferings.*
> *Never say*
> *That you are on your last road.*

*Named for Ber Borochov (1881–1917), the ideologist of proletarian Zionism.

The leaden sky
Hides the blue of the day.
Our time will come,
Our footsteps will resound.
We are here.

And our footsteps resounded, and we were there. Marching beside me, a young Jewish officer in the Red Army fired a burst from his submachine gun into the air. Policemen came up to us and made us stop. "That was our memories exploding," the young Soviet officer told them sadly, and we resumed our march through the rubble.

We also took part, with Communist Youth, in demonstrations against Stanislaw Mikolajczyk, the prime minister who had parachuted in from England, to which he returned when old Boleslaw Bierut regained power. Anti-Semitism didn't disappear, contrary to what we had tried to believe, but I was no longer afraid to fight: I was eleven years old and had a pistol.

The Communist bloc began supporting the Jewish national revolution in Palestine. Soviet and Czech officers taught us how to live clandestinely, how to organize street fighting, how to use the weapons they gave us. We even had a training camp in the Carpathians. It was an old castle, with superb parquet floors, where we went for one-month periods: accelerated courses in Marxism, Hebrew, the history of Palestine; handling weapons, making bombs, long hikes in the mountains.

It had been less than two years since I wrote the article published in the newspaper of the Pioneers of Uzbekistan, and history had already changed. I was again in the current of events. For how long?

The proclamation of the State of Israel was celebrated by the Polish government. To Jews of my parents' generation it seemed miraculous. Not to me. That affirmation of our identity seemed normal to me — maybe because I had a pistol in my pocket.

Years earlier, my father and I had been walking together at night, on an empty street in Kokand. We were thin and hungry. Suddenly, a gang of hooligans surrounded us. They wanted money. My father didn't have any.

"So, you dirty Jew, you live in our city and you don't even have any money?"

My father was butted on the jaw. He began bleeding and the gang ran away, laughing.

For a long time I resented his failure to fight back. To me he was no longer the authority I respected, feared, and loved. But afterward, whenever he smiled with his mouth a little tight on one side as a result of the blow he had received, I was angry with myself for not having at least tried to defend him.

I realized much later that my father's attitude was an expression of a culture. Before the war, when a Polish prince, riding through a village that belonged to him, stopped and beat a Jew with his riding crop, the Jew never rebelled. All he did was look at the prince condescendingly and say, "Poor man . . ." And he was genuinely sorry for a man who had to beat someone to assert his power. The only power the Jews accepted was the power of the mind. They admired people of knowledge, those who knew the Bible, the Talmud, the sciences and literature. That was probably one reason the revolt of the Warsaw ghetto began so late.

The Jews have often been accused (by Hannah Arendt, among many others) of some sort of "traditional passivity," caused by rabbinic culture, with regard to the Nazis. And in their postwar works, Jewish historians have often given primacy to the two crucial months of April and May 1943, when the uprising in the Warsaw ghetto took place. It is as if Mordecai Anielewicz's fifty to sixty thousand fighters were expected to save the lost honor of six million of their brothers and sisters who supposedly went off to be slaughtered without putting up any resistance.

In a world where violence answers violence, it was inevitable that the revolt of the Warsaw ghetto would be regarded as the sole, exemplary manifestation of the Jews' courage in the face of adversity. Actually, however, the ghetto fighters left us one example of a recurrent kind of behavior in Jewish history, behavior in which faithfulness to the basic principles of Judaism may prove to be more precious than life, and in which the ideal heroic figure is not necessarily a man with a weapon in his hand.

Let us remember. . . . On October 2, 1940, Ludwig Fischer, governor of the Warsaw district, ordered the creation of the ghetto, the quarter to which all Jews living in Warsaw would be transferred. More than four hundred thousand people, cut off from the outside world, were confined in an enclosure that was to become a vast "living cemetery." But instead of giving in to despair, the Jews immediately began creating a network of mutual aid to provide for the needs of that enormous population. German officers and enlisted men came with cameras, sometimes with their wives, to see and take pictures of those "subhuman" people.

At this time the Jews entered the first phase of their resistance: they decided to talk to the Nazis. Teams of men who spoke German struck up conversations with the soldiers in the hope of shaking their convictions. It is hard to imagine the courage, the vast amount of courage, needed for a condemned man to strike up a conversation with his executioner. But six months later Himmler issued a special order forbidding German soldiers to go into the ghetto and speak to the Jews of Warsaw.

The Jews then went into the second phase of their resistance: testimony. Emmanuel Ringelblum's archives show that starving people, knowing they were condemned to death, found enough strength in themselves to contribute to the memorial work he had undertaken by gathering documentation on everyday life in the ghetto. Their work to break the silence that the Germans tried to impose on them, their acute awareness of having to transmit their story to posterity so that history would continue — these are ways of resisting whose scope and boldness are not inferior to those required by the sacrifice of life.

And when Emmanuel Ringelblum and his collaborators were deported, other Jews finally took up arms. Without faith. Because they had no choice: *B'ein breira*, as they say in Hebrew. The uprising was the third and final phase of the resistance of the Warsaw ghetto.

A child of war, I was brought up in respect for that tradition, for that culture which esteems faithfulness to the ancient moral law as highly as the commandment to safeguard life, even at the cost of violating the law. My friends and I, all Zionists, felt that if we had to take up arms to defend our national identity, we would do it — but only after first talking and negotiating with those who refused to grant us that right.

I was eleven then, and I had a pistol that never left me. Had I become a man, an armed man among other armed men?

Some time earlier, my father had put advertisements in the newspapers asking our surviving friends to get in touch with us. Among those who answered were Daniel, a playmate of mine from the ghetto, and his mother. They had been separated at the beginning of the war and had had no news of each other since then; they were reunited in our home.

Daniel and I went walking in the street. It was evening. I told him about the kolkhoz, Kokand, Moscow. Then he told me what had happened to him. First, he had been part of a contingent of several thousand Jewish children whom Germany, glad to be rid of them, allowed to leave Poland at the request of the Jewish community in Palestine. But Britain, the mandatory power, refused "for security reasons" to let them enter Palestine. Then Daniel found himself, with hundreds of other children, on a train to Auschwitz. In his car there were only two German soldiers to guard dozens of children. Daniel vainly tried to persuade the others to kill the guards. They were afraid. When he jumped from the moving train, only one of them went with him — and was killed by the fall. Daniel was taken in by a Polish peasant who brought him up as his son.

We were still recounting our wartime adventures on Kosciuszko Boulevard when a group of Poles stopped us.

"Glad to be back, little Jews?"

They began hitting us. We defended ourselves as best we could, but we were greatly outnumbered. They beat us for a long time.

A police patrol picked us up and took us home. I had to spend several days in bed.

I was sick again when Daniel and all my friends in Borochovist Youth left on the *Exodus*, the ship overloaded with Jewish refugees that unsuccessfully tried to land in the Promised Land. If it hadn't been for a case of pneumonia with complications, I would have been with them.

The *Exodus* was stopped by the British navy. The Jews defended themselves and were interned in camps on Cyprus. Barbed wire again. Some of them, including Daniel, were able to escape and arrived in Palestine just in time to take part in the 1948 war. Two of my friends died in it. One of them was Jerzy, a little cigarette seller in the ghetto. He was sixteen, the other only fifteen.

We learned that my uncle David, who had moved to France long before the war, had survived the German occupation and was living in Paris with his wife and daughter. Besides us, he was the only survivor of the family. He sent us visas and a work contract for my father.

Another train. Borders, customs, police. Interrogations: "Why are you leaving Poland? Do you have permission to take out all those books?" Prague, a sad, beautiful city. Finally Paris, the Gare de l'Est. Uncle David was waiting for us. He lived on the Place des Fêtes.

Everything was new and exciting to me — the smell of the subway, the crowd that swept me along on the boulevards, the displays of fruit and vegetables, the lighted signs, the nougat sellers, the sidewalk stalls, people selling political newspapers. Nothing had prepared me to live in a society of abundance and ideological pluralism.

Since early childhood I had known only the rigors of Nazi and Stalinist totalitarianism. Now I suddenly discovered the benefits of a democratic society. First of all, freedom. Freedom of speech, which makes it possible to express political opinions even in street demonstrations without risk of being sent to the gulag; freedom of assembly; and so on. But what surprised me most was probably the absence of lines in front of stores, the elegance of display windows, the refinement and stylishness of clothes and objects.

I had great difficulty getting used to all that, and I seemed incapable of learning French, the symbol of my disorientation.

One day, I don't remember how, I met a girl who spoke Polish and was learning pantomime with Marcel Marceau. Once I went with her to one of her sessions. Around Marceau, a whole group of young people were getting ready for a show. Unable to communicate, I followed their example and painted my face.

The interplay of colors and forms was a revelation to me, and a sudden passion. On a little street in Kokand I had come across a painter meticulously putting the finishing touches on a landscape, and that memory had left me with mixed feelings: I was filled with admiration to see that the visible could be translated by another visible, but also with uncertainty, since I saw that visible differently. In Paris, it was quickly decided: I would be a painter.

To buy canvas and paints, I worked at night in a Yiddish print shop. During the day I either painted or spent hours in front of Uccello's battle painting in the Louvre. Then I enrolled in the Ecole des Beaux-Arts.

But I felt I also had to go on being a militant. My political choice hadn't changed: support for the Jewish state, which was still threatened, and struggle for justice all over the world. Members of Borochovist Youth in France contacted me. I joined them and soon became one of the leaders of the movement. We had a double goal: to prepare young people to go to Israel, and (this distinguished us from other left-wing Zionist groups) to struggle for a new society where we were.

We took part in various actions of Communist Youth in France. In the 1949 May Day parade in Paris, representatives of two liberation movements were greeted and applauded: the Algerians, behind a portrait of Messali Hadj, and we with our red and blue-and-white flags. I was even congratulated by Maurice Thorez and Marcel Cachin, leaders of the French Communist Party. The Soviet Union fervently supported Israel, the Party collected money to send ambulances there, and the kibbutz was held up to a whole generation as a model of communal life.

It was during this time that I met Clara. She was a wholehearted Borochovist and, like many of our comrades, extremely pro-Soviet. They listened skeptically to what I told them about the Soviet Union: the terror constantly aroused by the political police; the climate of denunciation and individual insecurity; the internment camps; "construction sites" like the one I saw between the Syr Darya and Amu Darya rivers, where thousands of prisoners, not knowing why they were there, worked as if they were in the time of the pharaohs, digging an endless canal across the hot sands of the Kyzyl Kum desert. I was a socialist in very fiber of my being, and that made me all the more repelled by what was being perpetrated in the name of socialism. My friends told me — already — that criticizing the Soviet Union could only play into the hands of imperialism. They admitted that the Soviet government might occasionally make "unfortunate mistakes," but insisted that they were insignificant, compared with Stalin's victory over Nazism.

I went to Israel for the first time in 1951. When, after five days at sea, I saw Mount Carmel and the city of Haifa appear in the distance, shimmering in the heat, I was so deeply moved that I wept. If it hadn't been for the sickly reluctance to show emotion that has always afflicted me, I would have kissed the dusty ground, like most of the people who got off the ship with me, and as Judah ha-Levi* had done long ago.

Yet I already knew I wouldn't stay there. The fight in which

---

*A Jewish poet and philosopher who lived in Spain during the time of the caliphs. According to legend, when he arrived in the land of Israel for the first time, he bent down to kiss the ground, and a Muslim who happened to be riding past beheaded him with one stroke of his sword.

I had taken a modest part, for the establishment of a Jewish state and recognition of a Jewish national identity, had ended as far as I was concerned, now that the State of Israel existed. And though its future still seemed uncertain to me, because of the hostility that surrounded it, I was sure its courage would be equal to the difficulties it was going to encounter, and for me, within myself, our old problems were solved. Now I was like others, and what interested me more than anything else was painting.

In Israel I wandered at random, spending a few months here and a few months there. I had discussions with young Arabs in villages. Unlike Max Nordau, the old Zionist leader, I wasn't surprised that there had already been inhabitants in Palestine. I felt that someday a Palestinian state would exist beside Israel, in the territory temporarily usurped by King Abdullah. I was even convinced that it was through the Palestinians that the ideas of the Jewish socialists would penetrate the Arab world.

When I came back to Paris, it seemed to me that the future was rather bright and had a good chance of matching my hopes for it. The Jews had finally taken their fate in hand and the world was full of promises. I was completely at peace with myself.

"Why are you telling us all that?" asked a Palestinian.

"Because people have to know each other if they're going to understand each other. It's time you knew who the Israelis are, where they come from, what they want and what they don't want anymore. I'm not an Israeli, but I know who they are, just as I know who you are."

There was a silence.

"Are they afraid of death?" someone asked.

"They've taken a liking to life," I said.

"And you, what do you know about death?"

3

The Race
against Death

I n Kokand I had been friends with an old Uzbek who told
stories. In the afternoon he used to sit on a bench in the
Park of the October Revolution and wait for evening. Whenever I could, I sat beside him. We would talk awhile, and then,
as though giving me a gift, he would tell me a story.

"Listen to me, *moi malchik* [my child] . . ."

It sometimes seemed to me that he invented his stories as
he slowly told them in his soft voice. I liked them. There was
always death at the end of them.

One day he pointed with his cane to an old building with
jutting towers, which at that time held Japanese prisoners
of war.

"You see that castle, *moi malchik?* It used to be the castle of
the Khan of Kokand, a very powerful khan, brother of the
Khan of Samarkand. They say his people loved him. And they
say that every night when he went to his private rooms, his
faithful guard, who was also his trusted companion, went all
over the castle to make sure the sentries were at their posts.

"One night when he was making his usual rounds, the guard saw Death prowling in the castle.

" 'What are you doing here?' he asked.

" 'I've come for your master,' replied Death.

"The terrified guard went to wake his master, told him of his encounter with Death, and advised him to hurry off to stay with his brother, the Khan of Samarkand. Trumpets were sounded, horses were saddled, and the khan and his entourage galloped into the night.

"After a few weeks, comfortably living in his brother's castle and caught up in all the festivities given in his honor, the Khan of Kokand completely forgot about Death. His faithful guard, however, continued to watch over him. One night he again met Death, prowling in front of the castle.

" 'Why are you here?'

" 'I've come for your master.'

" 'But you were supposed to take him in Kokand!'

" 'That reminds me to thank you,' said Death, 'for making him come here to Samarkand, because this is where I was meant to take him.' "

When he had finished his story, the old Uzbek sat in silence.

"How did the guard recognize Death?" asked the child I was then.

"You know, *moi malchik*, when Death is there, you recognize him right away."

Years later, when my mother called me at the end of one of those cold, damp winter days in Paris, I went to the Rue Boucry and immediately recognized him: Death was there.

My father was lying in the room that had been mine for a long time, at the back of the apartment. A heart attack, the doctor had said.

When I came in, he opened his eyes and smiled at me confidently, as he always did when he saw me. He had always believed that I, his son, could take care of anything. It had been that way at his work, in the print shop where he taught me the trade, or when he found himself in difficulty with the government bureaucracy that he both mistrusted and respected.

I called some friends of mine who were doctors. They were still caught in a traffic jam when my father's heartbeat and breathing stopped and his pulse vanished. The mirror I held in front of his nose and mouth remained unclouded.

With my mother's help, I applied hot compresses to my father, then began massaging his chest with all my strength. I heard his bones cracking under the pressure of my hands. After a few moments I felt his heart move. A rattle came from his throat, then another. He opened his eyes and silently looked at my mother. Then at me. His lips moved, soundlessly at first, then words came from his throat.

"What's going to happen?"

Why didn't I wait before answering? I knew he wouldn't die without getting an answer. Why didn't I think of anything to say except what's usually said?

"You'll see," I answered quickly, "everything will be all right."

My father smiled sadly, nodded, and ceased to live.

The last time I had seen Death from so close up, I had been in Buenos Aires, a youth of eighteen. I had gotten permission to paint a corpse in a morgue. To tell the truth, I wasn't feeling very self-assured when I came at nightfall to the morgue of the La Boca hospital, in the old waterfront quarter, with my permit, my box of paints, and my easel.

The guard seemed surprised. He read the piece of paper I handed him, probed me with his little nearsighted eyes, and finally asked, "You're a police painter?"

Instead of launching into a long explanation, I nodded. He prepared a corpse for me, put it on a table, and left me alone. I went to work.

Suddenly the guard's voice made me start.

"Have you finished?"

Absorbed in my painting, I had forgotten the time and where

I was. I looked at my watch: seven in the morning. The inert body and my painting were bathed in yellow electric light.

I don't remember having felt curiosity or compassion for the dead man in whose company I had spent the night. I know only that he had red ears. A yellowish body with red ears. I knew nothing about his life or how he had died, I knew nothing about his plans, I didn't know what there was to regret.

My father's body lying in front of me was the body of someone I loved, someone who had still been living, talking, and hoping only an hour before. I knew his hopes and plans, and it seemed unfair and sad to me that he hadn't been able to carry out his plans and make his hopes come true, or at least try to do it.

Having death brush against you is enough to make everything change its meaning. A Hasidic legend says that the Angel of Death always carries a bag full of eyes. When he mistakenly takes someone's soul before his time, he gives him back his life and, with it, a new pair of eyes.

Death has been following me since my childhood, through time and space, cities and borders. Death lurks in the hollow of my past, and bursts out in dark flowers. I hate my past, the past I drag along with me like a peddler's cart; sometimes its weight holds me back, and sometimes it threatens to carry me along with it. I hate the past that keeps me in its shadow, clings to my gestures, controls my dreams, laughter, and tears. I hate the past that devours my life, hides hope from me, and speaks to me of death. And I hate death. I hate death, I hate death.

"What do you know about death?" the Palestinians in the Sabra refugee camp asked me. They were willing to give their lives for their freedom, they told me enthusiastically. But the idea of death, my own or anyone else's, has never made me enthusiastic. The Angel of Death has given me a new pair of eyes and I don't want people to die anymore.

What could I have told them about death? I think that my constant awareness of it is what keeps me moving, acting, and impassioned. The feeling of time passing is painful to me; in art, love, and politics I race with time, as if I had a chance of winning. What can I oppose to the time that haunts me?

As a child, I regretted not being a grown-up so I could "do something" against injustice and misfortune. Ever since I have been old enough to struggle, I have struggled. The more I struggle, the more my powerlessness overwhelms me.

Between the Arabs and the Israelis, where circumstances have placed me, I run a great deal. Today Beirut, tomorrow Tel Aviv, day after tomorrow Cairo. I try to persuade both sides to make peace. I meet with heads of state and terrorists, people who live in the limelight and people who live underground. I appeal to consciences and refer to political programs. I don't know how many times I have boarded airplanes that took me nowhere, organized meetings that accomplished nothing, arranged appointments where I found myself alone. I don't know how many hours I have spent trying to convince people who didn't want to be convinced, how many nights I have spent writing texts without knowing who would read them, if anyone.

Has all that done any good? Have I advanced the cause of peace by even one step? Those who, like me, take it upon themselves to "do something" are familiar with that feeling of loneliness, and sometimes of bitterness. I like to believe that some of the ideas that seem to be produced by the pressure of events are actually ideas that people like me have expounded at length to the belligerents, preparing them to accept them. Yes, but how can we know?

More often, I think of myself as a court jester, a buffoon who is received by powerful figures because his goodwill is touching, his efforts are entertaining, and his naïveté is refreshing. Sometimes he is asked for advice, and perhaps, without his being aware of it, for information. But if the buffoon stresses his mission a little too much, if he asks to be taken seriously, he loses all the good qualities that were attributed to him.

I can't resign myself to either cynicism or indifference. My memory is Jewish. It still carries all the inner and outer reasons that propelled me into this adventure on a spring day many years ago.

4

Doing Something

M ay 1967. Clara and I had married ten years before. She, the Catholic writer Maurice Clavel, and I were driving out to the country. When we were stopped by a traffic jam on the highway, we listened in silence to a radio news broadcast: "The president of the United States, Lyndon Johnson, has sent an aircraft carrier into the Red Sea. . . . Two more Soviet submarines have gone through the Bosporus, heading into the Mediterranean." War was imminent in the Middle East. Egyptian divisions were advancing in the Sinai. Israel had ordered a general mobilization. Heads of state were making bellicose declarations, and Akhmed Shukeiry, leader of the Palestinians at that time, was promising to throw the Jews into the sea — or at least those who survived.

The traffic jam finally eased a little, and we were able to move forward in slow, patient lines, like cars of an endless train. Feeling dazed, we acted as if the traffic jam and the war were both misfortunes that we had to resign ourselves to accepting. War! In the Middle East, people were getting ready for it, friends of ours were probably going to die. Explosions, flames, screams, corpses . . . I felt as if I were reviving my familiar nightmare.

"Now that I'm a grown-up," I said.

Clara and Maurice looked at me without surprise. They understood what I meant. Clara suggested that we go back to Paris. I turned off the highway at the next exit.

In Paris my anxiety became even more painful. The war hadn't begun yet, but here there was already fierce fighting between pro-Israeli and pro-Arab factions. *Le Monde* published an article by the Middle East specialist Maxime Rodinson in which I was alarmed to read that the reason the Israelis hadn't yet attacked was that they were afraid of being defeated. His numerical account of the opposing forces seemed to show that he was right.

I was afraid for Israel. If there had to be a war, I wanted it to win it. I had no hostility at all against the Arabs, and I felt that the muezzins' calls in Kokand had made me close to them forever, but I couldn't accept the idea of the destruction of the Jewish state.

I have no experience of the Spanish Civil War. I was born too late. I am always stirred by stories and pictures of it, partly because of love for the arid mountains of Ronda, the scorched browns of Toledo, the Jewish quarter of Córdoba, and the poetry of Machado, but especially because of the unique solidarity created by that war. Tens of thousands of men and women who had never been to Spain before went there to die for her. Surely the prospect of making peace between Israel and the Arabs, and assuring Israel's survival, deserved that same kind of devotion. My idea, of course, was not to go and die for Tel Aviv. But my ancestral faith in the power of words and logical discussion made me think that putting pressure on both sides would be enough to make them stop fighting and recognize each other — provided there were enough of us saying the same thing, and in the same voice.

A few exhibitions and prizes and a certain amount of traveling had enabled me to meet many people, some of whom had become my friends. I had to call them and rally them. I was full of fervor and impatience.

The three of us began making phone calls: Clara from our home, I from the bistro across the street, Maurice Clavel from his home.

It was later hard for me to explain to my Arab friends that our "mobilization" hadn't resulted entirely from Israeli propaganda, that the speeches of Arab leaders — they spoke of destroying the Jewish state and wanted to "eradicate the Zionist cancer in the Middle East" — had reminded us of a past that was recent enough to stir up fear in some of us and pangs of conscience in others. "Never speak of rope in the house of a hanged man" is also an Arab proverb.

We formed a group of sixty intellectuals, all distressed by the situation and our own powerlessness. We had to decide what to do. Claude Berri, who had just finished his film *The Two of Us*, proposed calling on French families to take care of Israeli children as long as the war lasted. The rest of us rejected that idea, first of all because it wasn't a way of preventing war, and also because we were sure that Israeli parents wouldn't let their children leave.

Finally we decided to publish an appeal.

I called Günter Grass in Berlin and Heinrich Böll in Munich; they encouraged me to go on, and so did Italo Calvino, who was passing through Rome, and Primo Levy in Turin, and, in spite of the time difference, Elie Wiesel in New York. They all agreed to sign an appeal for peace, and so did the writer Fernando Arrabal, the cartoonist Tim, Clara Malraux, Jean Lacouture, and Marguerite Duras, who gathered in our studio.

This was our first group action, and I was disappointed. Did "being a grown-up" amount only to signing appeals? Were we going to mobilize once again the names we were used to reading in *Le Monde*, the *Washington Post*, the *New York Times*, and *Die Zeit*, under declarations concerning Vietnam, Spain, or Latin America? But we wanted to make ourselves heard, to say what we felt we had to say — that war was not inevitable — and this was the best way to do it.

We were almost the only ones, at that time, to talk about the possibility of peace: nearly everyone else was thinking only of supporting one side or the other.

Once the text of our appeal had been dictated over the phone, an embarrassed silence fell over the studio. After all, it was only a public statement and we realized that something else had to be done. Someone, I don't remember who, suggested that we go to the scene of the conflict ourselves.

The idea slowly took shape: to charter a plane, fill it with the best-known representatives of everything that mattered in the West, and land between the enemy lines. In the nineteenth century Leo Tolstoy had imagined a similar action in *War and Peace* (without, of course, the use of an airplane). And in 1914 Gabriele D'Annunzio had tried to carry it out, this time with an airplane. We were excited. We could already see ourselves in the desert, between the Israeli and Egyptian armies. What an image! Captivated by the idea of going there, Eugène Ionesco came out of his personal nirvana every few minutes and, like a character in one of his plays, gently nodded his round head, rubbed his hands together, and asked, as if he were chanting a refrain, "Well, when are we leaving?"

Clavel proposed that while we were waiting for all the preparations to be made we should go to see General de Gaulle. It was late when Clara called the Elysée. A presidential secretary answered the phone.

"A delegation headed by Maurice Clavel," said Clara, "would like to visit the president and give him a memorandum concerning the Middle East, signed by a hundred and twenty-eight eminent people in literature, science, and the arts."

The voice asked Clara to cite a few names. She cited them. The voice asked for our phone number.

The Elysée called us the next morning: we had an appointment with President de Gaulle at two o'clock on the afternoon of June 6.

At the beginning of June, events moved quickly. Israel was encircled. Moshe Dayan became minister of defense. On the fifth, war broke out. When our first surge of emotion had passed, we called our friends and decided to go through with our visit to the Elysée. As for chartering a plane, that was out of the question now.

Potbellied, magnetic, General de Gaulle received us standing behind the presidential desk. After greeting Ionesco, whom he knew, and me, whom he didn't, he addressed Maurice Clavel to tell him that he had spoken on the phone with Alexey Kosygin that morning, and that he could assure us that the Russians would remain neutral. He was convinced that the Arab–Israeli war would be limited to the Middle East, that the great powers would not intervene. In our state of near-panic, this was important information.

De Gaulle, of course, was right: the great powers remained neutral. And two days later, on June 8, 1967, there were these headlines across the front page of the *New York Times:* "Israelis Rout the Arabs, Approach Suez, Break Blockade, Occupy Old Jerusalem; Agree to UN Cease-fire; UAR Rejects It." Below, a photograph showed Jewish soldiers praying in front of the Wailing Wall.

How many Jews in France and elsewhere, having long been engaged in the struggle of the left and having lost all contact with Judaism, were waked up at that time! They were the "Jews of June 5," as they were called by Fernand Rohman, a philosophy professor who joined us later and became one of the pillars of our organization. In saying that, he was speaking first of all about himself: after being in the French Resistance during World War II, he had been active in Jean-Paul Sartre's movement, joined the new left and the United Socialist Party, and supported the Algerian National Liberation Front in its fight for decolonization; he had even begun legal proceedings to remove the *h* in his name, which he had come to regard as symbolic of a Jewish identity that he no longer felt. In June he dropped the proceedings.

The Israelis won the war in six days. Their victory aroused in many parts of the world an enthusiasm that was sometimes dubious, and it gave rise to marked uneasiness in intellectuals. Many of those who had sided with Israel, when they thought the Jewish state was threatened with destruction, now had the feeling that they had been deceived. A large part of the European left and the American radicals rose up against Israel, as if the victory were unforgivable. As for the far left, it openly declared its opposition to the very existence of the Jewish state.

Those strangely sectarian radicals and humanists who always end up disappointing our hope, but who still share our dream of a free and just society, have often been analyzed, criticized, and judged. Many, at that time, were painfully torn. Did they have to betray Israel if they wanted to go on saying they belonged to the left? I remember all those meetings in New York, Los Angeles, Montreal, Paris, Rome, Geneva, Brussels: hundreds of people, most of them students, who kept interrupting each other to reproach us for the dilemma in which they found themselves, as if we were responsible for it.

Each day we received dozens of letters. Some of them touched me more than I can say. "Because I don't want to seem suspect," wrote a woman student at the Sorbonne, for example, "I'm afraid to say that I have a brother in Israel." The heavy, clanking machine of totalitarian thought has no concern for individual problems.

And our phone kept ringing. Always the same thing, always the same questions. Could one, because of Israel, forget one's friendships and take up a position that would put one on the side of the most hardened conservatives? Or should one abandon Israel?

I later spent part of my time with the leaders of political parties, with Palestinians I met in Beirut or Cairo, and with Israelis in Tel Aviv or Jerusalem, trying to make them understand that I saw no contradiction between my adherence to universalist principles and my support of Israel's existence, or between support of Israel's existence and criticism of its policies, or between affirming the Israelis' right to a state and affirmating that same right for the Palestinians. The International Committee for Peace in the Middle East was established on that basis.

At the end of 1967 I was often asked why the committee we had created didn't take a political position, didn't advocate action capable of influencing world opinion and perhaps bringing the Israelis and the Arabs together. For my part, I was reluctant to become involved in all that because I knew it would take up most of my time and strength, to the detriment of my work.

Chekhov says somewhere there are three kinds of people: those who eat others, those who are eaten by others, and those who eat themselves. I probably belong to that last category. I knew that whatever my decision turned out to be, it would leave me with a bad conscience. And, knowing that, I felt I might as well forge ahead.

Our goal, of course, was not to create a political party, with an ideal as its ultimate purpose, and action limited to day-do-day strategy. Our main objective was peace in the Middle East.

With the friends who were always coming to our apartment, we tried to find a means of expression. In France alone, we had been able to mobilize tens of thousands of names. In the first phase, we had to take full advantage of the media, publicly state our objectives, put out a magazine to promote our ideas, interest eminent people in other countries. In short, convey the idea of a new force for exerting pressure on the conflict in the Middle East.

"Do you want to create a lobby?" I was asked one day.

"No. Lobbies are pressure groups in the service of political or economic forces. That's not what we are. We're going to get involved and stand up for our ideas. We'll be attacked, and therefore respected. Only then can we make contact with political parties and unions. And, with the support of some of them, we'll go to the Middle East."

I was convinced that we had a chance of succeeding where diplomats and soldiers had failed: in setting up favorable conditions for dialogue between Arabs and Israelis. Clara and I decided to begin with Israel and the occupied territories.

5

Golda Meir — First Meeting

I like the drive up to Jerusalem, the slow approach to the city that the Samson road makes through the Judean hills, before going down toward Bab-el-Wad, the valley praised by so many poets, which is lined by wrecked armored vehicles covered with flowers in memory of the fighting in 1948. After Bab-el-Wad the road rises again and then, suddenly and unexpectedly, the city appears. At first I see it in black and white, light and shadow, as in the picture in the old atlas I had in Kokand. Then I put colors into it, the colors of my latest paintings. Jerusalem is always faithful to me, and always new.

This time, however, the friend who was driving us, the Israeli writer Amos Elon, turned left after the town of Ramla and drove past a sign that said, "Attention: border."

"It's shorter by way of Latrun," said Amos.

After being squeezed between their narrow borders for twenty years, when the Israelis broke through their pre–June 5 boundaries they felt as if they had regained their freedom. At the time when we arrived there, Israel was being lulled by

Naomi Shemer's song "Golden Jerusalem," and the whole country was plunged in sweet euphoria. No overflowing of joy, but deep relief. To the almost technical satisfaction of having won that war "elegantly" were added that of the return to Jerusalem — an ancient promise — and faith in imminent peace.

"Now the Arabs will have to talk with us," we heard again and again.

My skepticism irritated most Israelis. One of the few who shared it was Moshe Sneh,* with whom we had dinner. In his view, Israel now had an unhoped-for stroke of good luck: the chance to control a large part of the Palestinian population. It should take advantage of it to offer the Palestinians self-determination; their freely elected leaders would then talk with Israel.

"Why doesn't Levi Eshkol understand that?" Sneh said. "In a few years it will be too late."

I agreed with him; victorious Israel's recognition of the Palestinians' national rights would have a strong psychological effect on the Arab world.

"You ought to say that in the Israeli press," Sneh suggested. "If it came from me, they'd be suspicious. It's important for the Israelis to know the views of a large part of the international left, the part that doesn't want Israel to disappear."

I took his advice: my opinions, stated in answer to questions from the writer and journalist Hezi Carmel, were published in *Ma'ariv*, at that time the largest Israeli evening newspaper.

Night was falling when we came to the Jaffa Gate, at the entrance of the Old City. We went in on foot. The iron curtains of the shops were lowered, and the few Arabs we met didn't hide their hostility. I asked one of them, in French, the reason

---

*Former head of the Hagana, general secretary of the Israeli Communist Party, who died in 1972.

for that unusual calm. After a moment of hesitation, he explained that the shopkeepers were on strike as a protest against the Israeli occupation. I realized that Amos Elon had begun speaking English to his wife, Beth: it is easier to be a conqueror than an occupier.

Victor Cygielman, a journalist friend, told us in this connection that, having been called up as a reservist, he was put on duty checking Arab cars coming from the occupied territories. At the end of the first day, his captain congratulated him.

"But how," he asked, "can you distinguish Arabs from Jews so quickly?"

"By the Jewish look in the Arabs' eyes," Victor answered.

After being dominated for so many centuries, were the Jews now going to dominate others? It was an agonizing question that some Israelis were asking themselves at that time. But the answer seemed clear to them: the territories conquered in the course of the war were only a medium of exchange for peace.

Israel's behavior with regard to those territories reminds me of an old Jewish story. In a Lithuanian village, a Yekeh — a Jew of German origin, not very quick-witted — wants to sell his cow. He takes her to the market. A peasant comes up to him, looks at the cow, and asks, "Is she young?"

"No," says the Yekeh.

"Does she give much milk?"

"No."

"Does she eat a lot?"

"Oh, yes!"

The peasant walks away, the scene is repeated with another peasant, and the cow is still unsold. Then a Litvak — a Lithuanian Jew and therefore a clever man — pats the Yekeh on the shoulder and says, "Let me do the talking and I'll show you how to sell a cow."

An interested peasant approaches.

"Is she young?" he asks.

"Very young," replies the Litvak.

"Does she give much milk?"

"Enormous amounts of milk."

"Does she eat a lot?"

"Almost nothing."

"Then I'll buy her," the peasant decides.

But the Yekeh steps forward and says, "Just a minute. Since that cow has so many good qualities, I'm going to keep her."

The occupation of the territories was one of our concerns. Clara decided to go to them and record some interviews for the first issue of the magazine we planned to put out. Although Amos Elon tried to dissuade her from going alone, by bus, in two days she was able to make contact with a whole group of young Palestinian leaders: Abdel Jawad Saleh, mayor of El Bireh, who was later expelled by the Israelis and became one of the ten members of the Palestine Liberation Organization's leadership; Jemil Hamad, editor of *El Fadje,* an Arabic newspaper published in Jerusalem; Raymonda Tawill and Dr. Kilani of Nablus; and several notables such as Sheikh El Jaabari, mayor of Hebron; Hamdi Kenaan, mayor of Nablus; and Anwar Nusseiba, former minister of King Hussein of Jordan.

During that time I went to see Shimon Peres. We discussed my forthcoming trip to the United States. He offered to recommend me to some of his friends. He was trying to call them when Yitzhak Korn, a Labor member of the Knesset, interrupted us. He wanted to know if I would attend a meeting of the Labor Party's fact-finding commission.

In spite of the changes that had taken place in Israeli society, a residue of the pioneers' socialist and egalitarian sentiments still remained, all the more deeply rooted because their dreams were one justification for the creation of the State of Israel. The hostility of the left was therefore felt painfully, and, Korn told me, the members of the commission would be glad to have a chance to question me.

In the little conference room on the seventh floor of the imposing building of Histadrut (the General Federation of Labor), about twenty people were gathered, including Golda Meir, who had arrived, sick and fatigued, leaning on Korn's arm. Golda Meir became widely known in 1948, when she was appointed Israel's first ambassador to the Soviet Union. From

1956 to 1966 she traveled all over the world as the Israeli foreign minister. Only two years after our meeting she became head of the government. At the time of that meeting, however, she held no official position, and she had come only because, she said, she had been interested by my interview in *Ma'ariv*. She reminded me of one of those Eskimo statuettes consisting of a rectangle supported by two thick, straight legs and surmounted by a head with heavy features. Her eyes were magnetic, but it wasn't till much later that I discovered their color.

Despite the gaps in my Hebrew, I tried to give a brief, clear summary of the positions taken by the European left with regard to Israel, but Golda Meir asked me abruptly, "Why have the left-wing intellectuals abandoned Israel? Did they feel guilty about being on the winning side, since they prefer to weep for the dead?"

We have often reproached those intellectuals for their inconsistency regarding the Arab–Israeli conflict, and now she was turning me into a spokesman for the left that exasperated her, though the Israelis had been trying for years to establish friendly relations with it.

She was launching into a series of questions when I interrupted her to say that she was both right and wrong.

"I know I'm right," she retorted, lighting a cigarette, "but I'd like to know why you think I'm wrong!"

"You're wrong," I said, "in trying to generalize too much."

I realized that I had unintentionally begun speaking Yiddish to her. The others looked at me, smiling, and seemed to be keeping score.

I resumed my summary, trying to differentiate the many positions of the European left, and the many currents that agitated and divided it. I granted Golda that some intellectuals had had strange reactions during the war: like the editor of a leftist Catholic magazine who, having signed a statement in favor of Israel just before the war, later complained that he had been "manipulated."

"No one forced you to sign that statement," I pointed out to him.

"Of course, but how would I have looked if the Egyptians had occupied Beersheba and massacred thousands of Jews?"

Nevertheless, I said, most of the leftist intellectuals were not anti-Israeli.

"They're willing to let us survive!" Golda remarked.

"Real support," I went on, "isn't blind support. I'm afraid of *tzetzerniks*."

"What's that?"

"It's Koestler's term: *tzetzerniks* are professional admirers. In Polish and Lithuanian villages before the war, they used to cluster around a great rabbi, rock back and forth to the rhythm of the prayers, and admiringly murmur, *'tze-tze'* as soon as he opened his mouth."

"What have they got against us, those intellectuals who support us?" asked Golda.

"Not recognizing, for example, the Palestinians' right to self-determination."

"But that would mean the end of Israel!"

I tried to demonstrate the opposite: if the Palestinian problem wasn't solved quickly, Israel would risk having to fight other wars. Palestinian nationalism would someday have to be expressed within the framework of a state, and it would be better for that state to be created in peace and with Israel's consent, rather than in war and against Israel's wishes.

"Where would that Palestinian state be?"

"Beside Israel."

"But Jordan is beside Israel!"

"Between Israel and Jordan is the West Bank. And Jordan itself," I added, "will someday have to be part of a Palestinian state."

"King Hussein is the only Arab leader willing to make peace with us — you can't expect us to help the Palestinians overthrow him!"

"I don't think you should help them to do it, but I don't think you should stop them, either."

"For their own good?"

"For Israel's good too."

Golda found me sincere but naive.

"I think she likes you," Korn told me after the meeting. "She doesn't often listen calmly to the kind of ideas you were expressing."

As Golda was about to leave, she changed her mind and asked me why I had decided to do what I was doing, and why someone as young as I was could speak Yiddish so well. I told her about my childhood — Yiddish was the first language I heard at home — and tried to make her understand how all that was connected.

She listened without a word or a gesture, looking at me with those penetrating eyes set into her heavy face. When I had finished, she was silent for a moment, then asked me to tell her more about our escape from Warsaw. I described how my father's Christian friend had come for my mother and me in the ghetto, how we had had to walk all those kilometers, and how I had developed the feeling of revolt that had never left me. She gave me another long look, then stood up and took my hand between both of hers. She said she was glad to have heard me and asked me to call her soon.

Stories like mine never left her indifferent, but I think it was Yiddish that really established contact between us. It is a language in a class by itself, with a flavor that is practically untranslatable, a language that puts people at ease, in which an intonation changes the meaning of a word, and in which I always recognize the fraternal song of the persecuted. It is said that Hebrew is spoken, but Yiddish speaks itself.

When I saw Golda Meir again a few years later, she was prime minister of Israel.

6

Eléments

W e went back to Paris. The harvest had been good. We had made many contacts, in both Israel and the occupied territories; we had brought back recordings of conversations and interviews, ideas for articles, data for reflections. We had enough to fill two issues of the magazine that seemed to us more and more urgent and important to publish, though we had no money for it.

During that period our group met at least once a week. We decided to have our political program published in the press, which charged us nothing for printing it, and to send delegations from the committee all over the Middle East.

That program resulted in an avalanche of letters and countless phone calls: hundreds of people wanted to help us. How could we put them to work? How could we best make use of all that goodwill?

The Middle East was the subject most often debated in the press, by political parties, and, of course, among our friends. Driven by external "demand" as much as by our own passion, we tried to take a position on every event and gave an impression of extraordinary vitality.

Some of our initiatives set off violent reactions. One was our letter to Yehia Hamuda, successor to Akhmed Shukeiry as head of the PLO. Hamuda had made a declaration that contained some highly positive points: he went so far as to accept "a Zionist state, if such is the will of the majority of the Jewish population in Palestine." We took that opportunity to write him a letter suggesting a meeting between him and a group of Israelis, a meeting that might lead to mutual recognition, the first condition for a settlement of the Arab–Israeli conflict. After sending our letter to Yehia Hamuda by way of the Lebanese ambassador in Paris, we published it. It provoked a vehement response from the Arab League, and also from several leaders of the Jewish community.

For the first time, however, we received messages of encouragement from Israel, as well as from Beirut and Cairo. Michel Rocard, national secretary of the Unified Socialist Party, sent us a long letter telling us how close the "concerns" of his party were to those of our committee.

The time had come to carry out our plan for a magazine of our own. Certain daily and weekly newspapers were open to us, but we didn't want to take advantage of them. We soon agreed on the magazine's name — Eléments, which Clara had thought of; it was the title that best expressed the meaning of our endeavor.

We had a name, but we didn't realize how many problems still remained. We had to decide on the format, the layout, and the paper, set up a budget, find a typesetting shop and a printer, work out the details of distribution. All eyes naturally turned to me.

I remember what the painter Yves Klein said one day to a flabbergasted collector in Montparnasse: "We painters are lucky people: we sleep when we want to, eat when we can, and tell everybody to go to hell."

"And when do you work?" asked the collector.

At this point I chimed in: "We never work. We paint only when we feel like it."

Because they have no fixed schedule, painters often give the impression that they do nothing. So my friends took it for granted that I should be the one to take care of everything.

I proposed Clara as the editor. Clara Malraux agreed to be the managing director of the publication. We already had more than enough copy for the first issue.

There are two ways of being valuable to an organization: knowing how to mobilize people, and being able to make them work. I belong to the first category; our friends were mobilized, but I did the work myself.

First of all, we had to get money. I have never understood how to raise money for political causes. It must be a matter of upbringing: my father used to say that in our family we had always earned money only by the sweat of our brow. I can't imagine what made him prepare a child so badly for life in a society based on money.

A few days later, in New York, where I had stopped on the way to an exhibition of my paintings in Los Angeles, I asked Robert Silvers, editor of the *New York Review of Books*, if he thought I might be able to get financial backing for *Eléments* in the United States.

Two secretaries were typing in his office. He sat behind piles of books and newspapers, in his shirtsleeves, with a pencil behind his ear, lighting one cigarillo after another and crushing each one out almost as soon as he had lit it. He was curious about everything and spoke French almost without an accent. He wanted to know about our positions on the conflict, our contacts, our prospects. Then, with typical American directness, he asked, "Where have you been getting your money so far?"

I told him that so far most of the magazine's expenses had been met by money from the sale of my paintings — I wasn't a writer then — and that contributions from my friends barely covered our phone bill.

"Do you know Martin Peretz?" he asked me. "He may be able to help you with your magazine. He's a professor at Harvard, and a rich man, and seriously concerned about the Arab–Israeli conflict. I'll call him right now."

And he called him right then. Peretz agreed to meet me in Cambridge in two days.

"While I'm there," I said, "I'd like to see Chomsky too."

Silvers, who didn't know me beyond Amos Elon's recommendation, also arranged for my meeting with Noam Chomsky.

When one comes to the United States for the first time, one has the feeling of having been there before. Each scene appears to be from a familiar film. The students strolling along the halls at MIT seemed like actors in a movie — and the fact that I could hardly understand what they were saying added an extra distance between those imaginary actors and the spectator I had become. All objects, down to the bundles of trash tied up and placed on the sidewalks, seemed to be copies of contemporary American art. Part of the American genius is the ability to reproduce reality in all its details: landscapes, people, things, situations. I think Americans have a sense of reality because they can grasp it; they aren't afraid of it, they feel strong enough to confront it. Europeans, however, take refuge behind an idealized reality, or, more precisely, an ideal of reality. They have enough culture to create concepts, but not enough strength to grasp their everyday aspects. Faced with an event, Americans wonder how it happened; Europeans wonder why.

Noam Chomsky invited me to sit down in a broken old armchair and we talked about the committee's action — in French and in Hebrew, which he still remembered from a stay in a kibbutz. Then he took me to a nearby restaurant where we had sandwiches and coffee, that American coffee which looks like black tea and is served to you as often as you want it. Professors and students spoke to him in passing, and he answered with a word or a gesture. With one of them he had a conversation that I couldn't follow. While it lasted, I was someone looking at myself, sitting in one of those restaurants so often depicted in American films and novels, an actor playing the part of Marek the visitor, in a film being made by a director I didn't know.

Then Chomsky said to me, "It's futile to imagine any kind of peace as long as Israel rules the occupied territories."

And I realized that he dazzled and irritated me at the same time. I admired his rhetoric and clarity, and also his calm and kindness. But what troubled me most was his unfailingly clear conscience. Like any self-respecting American university professor, he liberally sprinkled his speech with such phrases as "I think . . ." or "It seems to me . . ." but with him it was only a stylistic device, because he was actually certain of being right.

Noam Chomsky reminded me of Albert Camus, but as his opposite. After long efforts in favor of Algerian independence, and without ever ceasing to believe in it, Camus was so appalled by the horror of the National Liberation Front's attacks against the civilian population that he finally said, "If I had to choose between justice and my mother, I would choose my mother."

The atmosphere was quite different in Martin Peretz's functional, comfortable office at Harvard. Friendly, nervous, always in motion, with his hair falling down over his glasses, he began by asking me a rapid-fire series of questions. We communicated a little in French, a little in English, and a great deal by gestures. He wanted to know whom I knew in Israel, and what kind of relations I had with the left and the establishment. He promised to call me two days later in New York.

"Take care," he said to me as he showed me to the door.

"*Zol men zein gezund* [May we all be healthy]," I unthinkingly answered in Yiddish.

"Ah, you speak Yiddish! When I think how we suffered for an hour! Sit down again."

His Yiddish was colored by a slight American accent. We had coffee and were finally able to understand each other.

When I was back in New York, Robert Silvers called me.

Chomsky had suggested to him that he take advantage of my visit to revive an American peace organization, the Committee on New Alternatives in the Middle East, which had stopped all activity because of differences of opinion among its leaders. I agreed to a meeting with several representatives, which took place on the second floor of a Chinese restaurant. I was introduced to the writer Peter Weiss; Paul Jacobs, an editor of the magazine *Ramparts,* who had made a special trip from San Francisco; Stanley Diamond, an ethnologist and a professor at the New School for Social Research; and Allan Solomonof, a young man recommended by Chomsky to work full-time for the committee.

Despite the absence of left-wing parties or groups, American intellectuals were, like us in France, torn by the problem of the Middle East. Supporting Israel, or simply asking the American government to guarantee its security, put them in the camp of those who also supported the American intervention in Vietnam. Actively opposing that intervention placed them among those who advocated isolationist ideas — "Let the Israelis solve their own problems!" — or Third World doctrines that condemned the "Zionist state." And so, as in Europe, many Jewish intellectuals had moved away from the left, because of its anti-Israel position, and were slowly drifting toward the right.

I suggested that they broaden their committee by taking in everyone who had joined ours on an individual basis, and by coordinating their activities with our committees in other countries. They enthusiastically accepted my suggestion: the prestige of the American intellectuals who supported us would strengthen our position in Europe, and, likewise, their own position in the United States would be strengthened by support from the European intellectuals. They also accepted the idea of an English edition of *Eléments.*

When I went back to my hotel, I found a message from Martin Peretz asking me to have breakfast with him the next morning.

I told him about the decisions that had been made the day

before. He drew up a list of eminent people to be mobilized, then wrote out a check for a thousand dollars.

"My first contribution to *Eléments*."

That afternoon I gave Martin Peretz's list to Allan Solomonof. Friendly and straightforward, he sat down on the floor.

"I'll be surprised," he said, after looking over the list, "if these people are willing to belong to your committee." I suggested sending a copy of the committee's program to all the people on the list. It seemed to me that they could then make up their minds more on the basis of the arguments presented than as a result of their feelings for this or that person.

"Personal animosities," Solomonof remarked, "are often stronger than political programs."

He was right.

When I came back to Paris, I had Peretz's thousand-dollar check and what was left of the money from the sale of my paintings in Los Angeles. I hurried to the printer.

It is said that one day the famous rabbi of Berdichev came to pray in the synagogue of a little village. Before turning his thoughts to God in the Holy of Holies, he went over to a poor peasant standing in one corner of the synagogue and asked him to lend him a ruble. The peasant, happy to have been chosen, took out his only ruble and handed it to him.

After his prayers, the rabbi gave the ruble back to the peasant and thanked him warmly. That night the peasant lay awake wondering why the great rabbi had needed a ruble in order to pray. Early the next morning he hurried to him and said, "O great rabbi, I gave you my ruble wholeheartedly, but I'd very much like to ask you why you needed it."

"It's quite simple," replied the rabbi. "I had something to ask of God, and you always talk differently when you have money in your pocket."

I am tempted to believe in the point of that story: now that I had some money, the printer gave me a price only half as much as the one he had quoted before I went to the United States. I must have talked differently.

The first issue of *Eléments* was received with passion; criticized as much as it was praised, it divided readers into two camps. We took in hundreds of subscriptions in the first two weeks; especially encouraging were the requests from booksellers in Beirut, Tel Aviv, and Cairo.

During that time we also received the first answer to our requests for visits in the Middle East: Histadrut invited us. We formed a group composed, among others, of the writer Jean-François Revel, the physicist François Englert, and Pierre Verstraeten, professor of philosophy at the Free University of Brussels and spiritual son of Jean-Paul Sartre. We left ten days later.

In the meantime there was a strange episode.

7

The Mysterious
Liu Kuang-ya

The Argentinian writer Bernardo Kordon came to see us during a brief stay in Paris. He wanted to know how I was doing with my painting: he hadn't seen any of it since my exhibitions in Buenos Aires in 1954. He said he was delighted with my development and seemed to appreciate my political drawings. We also talked about the Middle East. Clara and I explained what we were trying to do. He showed great interest, listened attentively, and questioned us about our relations with the various left-wing parties.

"Have you had any contact with the Chinese?" he asked us abruptly.

"No," I said. "But since you're a friend of Mao and go to China every year, maybe you can get us some introductions."

I was already imagining what a triumph it would be for the Chinese if, leaving the United States and the Soviet Union each to back one side in the conflict, they succeeded in having the Israelis and the Palestinians sit down together at the same table. My enthusiasm must have been contagious, because

Bernardo, who was going to have lunch with the Chinese ambassador the next day, promised us he would talk to him about it. He would call us, he said, immediately after lunch.

We waited a long time, in the grip of that mixture of hope and apprehension that seems to stretch out the hours. Bernardo didn't call till the end of the afternoon. He was very excited.

"I'm calling from the embassy," he said. "It's all settled."

He asked us to give the embassy copies of articles written by members of the committee, and of the appeals we had published. He would call us the next day, before leaving for Argentina. He seemed very proud.

He woke us up the next morning: the ambassador had called Peking and delegated Liu Kuang-ya, a top-ranking embassy official, to keep in touch with us.

"Liu Kuang-ya," said Bernardo, "will see to it that you get all the help you need."

That same day, Clara called the Chinese embassy in Paris and got through to Liu Kuang-ya without difficulty. He told her that he greatly appreciated our endeavor, was already familiar with what we were doing, and considered it very important. He wanted to meet us. He proposed Friday, March 15 — but where? Clara suggested that he come to our apartment. He laughed, then said that for our first meeting we could come to see him at the embassy.

On March 14, the day before our scheduled meeting, we received a letter written on the letterhead of the embassy of the People's Republic of China in the French Republic: "In our recent telephone conversation, I had the honor of making an appointment with you for Friday, March 15. Because of an unexpected development, however, I will not be free on that day. I am therefore taking the liberty, to my regret, of sending you this letter to suggest postponing our appointment to a later date. Please accept my apology." And it was signed Liu Kuang-ya.

Two days later, Clara again called the embassy. After a moment the switchboard operator said she was sorry, but Mr.

Liu Kuang-ya was unavailable, because he had gone away for two days.

We waited three days, then Clara called back. This time the switchboard operator connected her with someone who was not Liu Kuang-ya and who, after listening to her explanations, advised her to call back the next day.

She did. The operator connected her with another stranger. This one claimed he had never heard of Liu Kuang-ya.

"Are you sure he works at the embassy?"

Clara said she was sure. The stranger asked her to wait. She waited. When he picked up his phone again, he informed her that no one by that name worked at the embassy.

"Maybe he did work there," Clara insisted, "but had to leave his post and go back to China."

The stranger politely offered to go and make inquiries if she would wait a little more.

"No," he said when he came back, "I'm sorry, but no one by that name has ever worked at the embassy."

Clara was too bewildered to say anything.

"Are you sure he was supposed to have worked here, at the embassy of the People's Republic of China?" asked the stranger.

Clara told him that she had in front of her a letter from the embassy signed Liu Kuang-ya.

"Yet we've never heard of that gentleman here!"

"That's odd," said Clara.

"Yes," said the stranger, "it *is* odd."

And he hung up.

8

Ben-Gurion

Clara, having gone to Israel a few days before us, was waiting at Lod airport with a delegation of trade unionists and the schedule of a well-filled week. Histadrut had put two cars at our disposal, in which we were going to drive all over the country from six in the morning till past midnight.

Like many other intellectuals, Pierre Verstraeten traveled with books under his arm, and he kept checking their contents against reality. His remarks set off discussions that were sometimes fruitful but often acrimonious. It was almost as if he did it deliberately.

Although our driver, Ami (the name means "my people" in Hebrew), was used to all kinds of visitors, he was amazed at our behavior. He had never seen anything like it, he said. "You're in a country that you claim you want to become acquainted with, yet you spend all your time arguing, without even looking at the landscape!"

It seemed to me that Israel had changed in a few months.

The country had been enlarged by the occupied territories, whose Arab population evidently didn't want to revolt; after the severe recession that had preceded the Six-Day War, business was good again; the song "Golden Jerusalem" had been replaced by a song that said, "Sharm al-Sheikh, we're coming back to you for the second time." With their inimitable art of adjusting to the situation, and without any qualms of conscience, the Israelis were settling into that state of neither-war-nor-peace, which, though it resolved nothing, at least let them hurry back toward what they called normality.

Most Israelis felt that the European left, with its misgivings and reservations, had sided with the enemy. So the arrival of a delegation from the International Committee for Peace in the Middle East aroused general curiosity. Everyone wanted to see us: the Matzpen (far left), Lyova Eliav, Abba Eban and Yitzhak Ben-Aharon (the doves of the Labor Party), Uri Avnery, representatives of the two Communist parties, and even Moshe Dayan and Moshe Kol, ministers currently in office, as well as the Palestinians of the occupied territories.

One morning we arrived in Gaza. The commander of the Khan Yunis military region was waiting for us: a burly, red-haired man, born in Israel, whose Belgian wife had taught him to speak French with a Namur accent.

"War is war, and we didn't ask for it," he said as he drove us toward one of the eight refugee camps in the Egyptian enclave of Gaza. "But being the occupying power is really dirty work."

"This is no worse than the *favelas* in Brazil, the slums in the Bronx, or the shantytowns in Aubervilliers," said Jean-François Revel, genuinely surprised.

"Your Brazilian *favelas* don't justify these camps," said Pierre.

"I'm talking about facts, not justification," said Jean-François, "and this isn't like what we were led to expect."

In front of a long clay building was a line of women, old men, and children.

"Help from the UNRWA," the commander told us.

We went closer. Inside, behind a counter, a few people in white coats were handing out rations of flour and rice. Flies. Three big fans laboriously raised a few slow waves of air.

Sitting off to one side, on a stone, I saw myself again as a little boy, waiting in line like that for rations like those. One day my ration cards were stolen. I was afraid to go home. I knew what hunger meant. My father found me asleep on a bench in the little square near the lower part of town. A friend who cleaned out the headquarters of the UNRRA took pity on us, gathered the flour and rice left on the counter, and gave it to us. My mother boiled it, and we ate it in silence. The sand mixed with the flour crunched between our teeth, and our throats were filled with a taste of dust. One of my cousins couldn't finish eating; he went out, and I heard him vomit behind the house.

In Gaza, I didn't feel like taking part in the discussions that my companions had begun with the Palestinians. A school-teacher was acting as their interpreter. More and more people were gathering; there aren't many diversions in a refugee camp. The commander wanted to join the group, but François Englert told him, "They wouldn't talk in your presence."

The Palestinians stated their grievances, not only against the Israelis, but also against their own representatives.

"We want to go home," said a young man.

"Where is your home?" asked Jean-François.

"In Jaffa."

"In Tel Aviv too," said another.

"How old are you?"

"I'm eighteen," said the first one, "and he's twenty."

"So you were both born in the camp?"

"Yes."

"Why haven't you ever left here?"

"Where would we go?"

"To Egypt, for example."

"The Egyptians don't want us."

"And if a Palestinian state were created in the West Bank

and Gaza, would you be willing to live in Gaza, Nablus, or Jenin?''

"No."

"Why not?"

"Because we want to go back to Jaffa."

They all began trying to talk at once. Under the pressure of the crowd, the counter finally collapsed. A soldier managed to get to us in the midst of the tumult and asked us to leave: he was afraid the situation might degenerate into a riot. We extricated ourselves with difficulty. Near our cars, under the noses of the commander and the soldiers, some boys handed us anti-Israeli leaflets. We left the camp, silent for once.

"I hope I'll see you again soon," said the commander. "You can come to my kibbutz."

A year later he was killed when his jeep was blown up by a mine.

After leaving Gaza, we headed for Hebron, where we had an appointment with Sheikh El Jaabari and a group of eminent Palestinians. In the car, Pierre Verstraeten reproached me for not having talked to the refugees.

"You didn't even come near them!"

"I understood them," I said.

"You mean you sympathized with them?" François asked a little mockingly.

How could I explain?

"No," I said, "I *was* them."

"And maybe you're also a Vietnamese," François said with a touch of sarcasm.

"It happens that I was once those Palestinians spending hours waiting in line for inadequate rations, and I was the Vietnamese who hide for weeks in a basement, counting bomb explosions, and I was the emaciated Biafrans with their bellies swollen by hunger . . ."

I was becoming agitated. Jean-François intervened.

"That's why this war is different from the others. Many Jews who have come to Israel have the same memories as Marek, and when they sympathize with those Palestinians it's never, as it sometimes is with us, in a paternalistic way. They *are* those Palestinians. The tragedy lies in the fact that those young men in Gaza want Tel Aviv, but that Tel Aviv is the only place in the world where Jews don't feel like Palestinians."

Again I saw myself as a child, digging in the frozen ground in search of an overlooked potato and dreaming endlessly of white bread dipped in hot chocolate. It had become an obsession. I was reminded of the day when a package arrived from UNRRA: we had finally received some powdered chocolate and a box of moldy cookies. I made hot chocolate in our biggest pot and put the cookies in it to soak. It smelled as good as in my dreams. I carefully put the pot on the table and stood for a long time with my nose above it, like a little old man trying to recapture his childhood. When I began eating, I was sickened almost immediately. My stomach, tightened by constant hunger, could no longer handle that much food. I cried, I had the hiccups, and I felt as if I couldn't go on. I forced myself to keep trying, but I had to abandon half of the chocolate and cookies — I wasn't able to swallow my dream.

Should I tell the others about that experience to justify my attitude? The Talmud says that when Rabbi Yochanan ben Zakkai lost his son, his three closest pupils came to console him. The first one said to him, "Adam also lost his son, but he overcame his grief."

"Don't you think I'm already sad enough," said Yochanan, "without being reminded of Adam's grief?"

The second pupil came in and said, "Don't be in despair. Think of Job, who lost all his sons and daughters in one day."

"Isn't my own despair enough," said Yochanan, "without your trying to make me share Job's?"

Finally the third pupil, Rabbi Eliezer, came in and said, "You had a son; he studied the Torah and the Prophets, and he left our world without sin. I understand your grief, but bear in mind that you did everything you could for him."

"My dear Eliezer," said Yochanan, "you, at least, console me as men ought to be consoled."

All suffering is unique for the person who suffers. Telling about my life, making my memory bleed, would have been useless, except to explain my reactions in Israel–Palestine, and that wasn't the purpose of our visit. Our uncomfortable silence lasted till we came to Hebron.

We were approaching the big public square, from which a staircase leads up to the tombs of the Patriarchs, when a dull explosion shook our car. Ami slammed on the brakes. All windows and all the iron curtains of shops seemed to close at the same time. The crowd of Arabs holding baskets, packages, and bundles ran in all directions, like a terrified herd. The car was pushed and bumped. Within two minutes the square and the street were deserted.

"It was probably a bomb," said Ami. "We'd better go back to Jerusalem."

He was beginning to turn the car around when I stopped him.

"No, we have an appointment with El Jaabari and there's no reason not to keep it."

Then, from the corner of the square where our car was stopped, armed soldiers took up positions on rooftops; a helicopter landed in a whirlwind of dust to pick up the wounded — a little girl and a workman, both Arabs — and take them to a hospital; armored cars full of soldiers blocked all exits from the square; a dozen Arabs were made to stand against a wall with their hands up, waiting to be questioned one at a time by two Israeli officers seated at a table that suddenly appeared out of nowhere. From where we were, we couldn't hear the questioning. But at one point, one of the three Arabs still standing against the wall said something, and one of the soldiers guarding them immediately kicked him in the ass — and that kick marked our stay in Israel.

I was deeply upset by seeing those armed Jewish young men guarding Arabs with their hands up. As my old friend George Wald, a Nobel laureate at Harvard, wondered some time later, "Is that the price the Jews must pay to have a right to a nation?"

Sheikh El Jaabari was alone and was evidently surprised to see us in spite of the bombing. He seemed preoccupied with it, knowing it was aimed more at him than at the Israelis. But his Arab sense of hospitality soon came to the fore. He invited us into his living room, where a servant brought us coffee. He was dressed, as usual, in a black caftan over a white shirt, with a turban on his head, and his pale fingers moved along a string of big amber beads.

We asked questions, but he remained distracted. We were unable to get the conversation under way. Every few minutes someone came in deferentially and informed him of the situation in a low voice. We stood up to leave. The sheikh then smiled for the first time, asked us to forgive him, and invited us to sit down again.

The events we had witnessed in Hebron gave rise to a stormy discussion during dinner. It started again the next morning when Yigal Allon, deputy prime minister and minister of education, came to have breakfast with us. The white collar of his shirt contrasted with his suntanned skin.

"War," he said, "eventually warps the people who fight it, and that's one more reason the Arabs and Israelis should make peace as soon as possible."

"Are you willing to give back all the occupied territories for peace?" asked Pierre.

Allon had his plan. He described it to us, and it left us rather skeptical. Would the Arabs agree not to exercise full sovereignty over the territory they recovered? Was peace possible without a solution of the Palestinian problem? Allon was aware of the difficulty, but he felt he could overcome it within the framework of a separate peace treaty with Jordan. He seemed excited, and he finally told us that Israeli commandos had blown up high-tension pylons on the other side of the Suez Canal. (It was said at the time that he had taken the initiative in that operation.) Since he had to go to a cabinet meeting, he left us with our questions unanswered.

During the day, we were to visit Masada, the stronghold that Herod had built at the edge of the Judean wilderness, overlooking the Dead Sea, and in which the last Jewish rebels of the Roman Empire had held out for two years before killing each other to escape from slavery. Then we were to have dinner at Beersheba before going to see David Ben-Gurion, who had been living at Kibbutz Sde Boker since his retirement from politics.*

I was scheduled to meet Abba Eban in Tel Aviv, so I let the others leave without me, intending to rejoin them in Beersheba. A woman pointed out Ben-Gurion's little house to me. A sentry led me without formality or ceremony into the room where "the Old Man," wearing the khaki trousers and blazer of the Haganah era, was already talking with my friends.

"Here's Theodor Herzl!" he exclaimed, seeing my black beard. "Welcome. It seems to me that we've seen each other somewhere before."

"Yes," I said, "in the Knesset."

"That's right," he agreed, obviously trying to call up a memory, "but when?"

"Don't you remember? I'm the big portrait . . ."

"You're talking about the portrait of Herzl!"

Ben-Gurion burst out laughing. Even his laugh had an inimitable accent, a mixture of Polish Yiddish and a Middle Eastern intonation.

"Have you come to settle in Israel?" he asked.

"No."

He pointed to the others.

"And they haven't either?"

"No."

"We need people from the left here."

"But they're not Jewish."

"We don't need only Jews. And as far as socialist experiments go, we're practically the only ones who have accomplished something important. The kibbutz represents the only real success of socialism."

---

*Ben-Gurion came to Palestine in 1905, founded the State of Israel in 1948, and was prime minister for the last time in 1963.

He asked me to sit down beside him, and while Pierre was taking pictures he posed with "this young Herzl." He laughed again.

"Two such different generations!"

"Do you believe," asked Jean-François, "that there will be peace in the near future?"

"Yes, because I think Nasser also realizes how important it is. He's an intelligent and practical man: he must know that there are better things to do than make war. Look here, in the Negev, around this kibbutz, and you'll see how much land there is that needs to be reclaimed."

"Are you willing to give back the territories now occupied by Israel?" asked Pierre.

"For peace?"

"Yes, for peace."

"For peace, my young friend, I'm willing to give back all the territories, and we can easily come to an agreement even over Jerusalem."

Ben-Gurion was apparently glad to be talking with us. He became more and more lively, telling stories and laughing often. Sometimes he sank into distant memories — he had come to Palestine in 1905! — so deeply that he forgot we were there, and sometimes, suddenly emerging into present reality, he analyzed the current situation for us with uncommon intelligence and open-mindedness.

"Are you in favor of creating a Palestinian state?" Clara asked him.

"When the United Nations decided on the partition of Palestine in 1948, we accepted it immediately. That meant that we accepted a Palestinian state next to ours. It wasn't easy, believe me, but I had to point our guns at our own brothers, members of the Irgun, who didn't want to give up what they called the historical fatherland. It was the Arabs who, by opening hostilities and annexing the West Bank and Gaza, prevented the creation of a Palestinian state."

Ben-Gurion stopped for a moment and a faraway look came into his eyes, then he went on:

"In April 1936 I had a long discussion with George Antonius.* He was a great Arab nationalist and a very intelligent man. I asked him why the Jews and the Arabs couldn't unite in struggling for the liberation of the region. Together, we would have been very strong. He answered that it was a good idea, but that in no case could liberation simply lead to the creation of a Jewish state, because the Arabs regarded that land as theirs and would fight to keep it.

" 'But, my friend,' I said, 'the land is almost empty: marshes in the north, desert in the south, and a sparsely populated strip along the coast.'

" 'That's true,' Antonius said, 'but people don't struggle for their own generation. Their sons and grandsons will need that land.'

"I told him that for us Jews, Eretz Israel was the only possible country, the only country where we have our historical roots, whereas the Arab nation has vast stretches of territory. He didn't agree: he felt that each part of the Arab nation had its own identity and wanted to live independently. He also didn't agree when I said that the existence of a Jewish state in Palestine wouldn't threaten Arab civilization and its freedom. He was afraid that the arrival of hundreds of thousands of immigrants trained in Western technology would eventually turn the Arab population into a pool of cheap labor.

" 'Why not have confidence in the Arab nation?' I asked him. 'Don't you believe in its human, intellectual, and economic potential? Once it was liberated, why couldn't it quickly reach our level?'

" 'It's a problem of education,' he said. 'Many of the Jews who come here are university graduates, while most of our people have barely come out of the desert. By the time they catch up with you, you'll have established a strong state that will dictate conditions of coexistence with us. As far as we're concerned, Arab and Jewish aspirations are incompatible.'

"Needless to say, I didn't agree. I believed we could struggle

---

*An ideologist of Arab nationalism, author of *The Arab Awakening*.

together to liberate ourselves, then work together politically and economically for the good of our two peoples. I made him understand that the return to Eretz Israel wasn't just a whim for us, but a question of survival, a matter of life and death. I warned him that we would come here whether or not there was an agreement between us, and that if we had to choose between pogroms in Germany or Poland and pogroms in Eretz Israel, we would choose pogroms here.

" 'But why should we fight?' I finally asked him. 'Wouldn't it be better for everyone if . . .' "

Ben-Gurion stopped talking, ran his fingers through his disheveled white hair, and looked at us as if he were wondering what we were doing there. He frowned, then relaxed: he was regaining a foothold in reality.

"If you go to see your friends in the Arab countries," he said, "tell them that here in the Negev I'm still asking them the same question I asked Antonius more than thirty years ago."

The guard was gesturing to "the Old Man." I went over to him. He told me it was late and that the doctor had ordered Ben-Gurion not to stay up so long. I said we would leave. Ben-Gurion looked at me reproachfully, reluctantly stood up, and showed us to the door. While we were walking to the car, through the cool desert night, we saw his stocky figure in the doorway of the wooden hut. It seemed to me that he was waving to us.

In 1973, through the mediation of Shimon Peres, Clara was able to record a conversation with Ben-Gurion at his house in Tel Aviv. He was very ill and greatly weakened, and didn't even recognize her. The doctor had asked that Clara go there alone: he was afraid the sight of two people might unsettle Ben-Gurion. So I stayed outside, on one of the benches.

Later, it was painful for me to listen to Clara's recording. She had to repeat her questions several times, and then he either answered beside the point or didn't answer at all. Those unintelligible grunts, coming from a man like him, make me feel sick at heart. But then he had a few moments of lucidity, perhaps his last.

"What would you have done if you had been a Palestinian?" Clara asked him.

"I can't answer that, because I'm *not* a Palestinian."

"What do you think the Palestinians need in order to make themselves capable of creating their own state?"

"Like the Jews? A Ben-Gurion!"

He died a few months later.

9

May 1968

The rest of the group went back to France the day after our visit to Ben-Gurion, but Clara and I stayed a few days longer. I left on May 7, 1968. At Orly airport I got into my car and began driving home. The police stopped me near the Place Denfert-Rochereau and directed me toward the Boulevard Arago. When I tried to turn left to take the Rue Saint-Jacques, I was stopped by another police roadblock. I parked the car and, curious, went to see what was happening. Near the Panthéon, the street was blocked by a compact mass of policemen. Helmeted, dressed in black, standing motionless behind their round shields, they were like medieval knights drawn up in battle array. A little farther on, the air was saturated with the harsh smell of tear-gas grenades, and hundreds of young people were running in all directions. Then I heard someone calling me through the smoke.

"Marek, come and help us!"

It was my friend Dany Cohn-Bendit, the leader of the 1968

student revolt in France. He began handing me paving stones, and I passed them on to a young woman in blue jeans and a yellow blouse. And so I found myself building one of the first barricades of that famous month of May.

The faces of the Arabs and Israelis I had met only the day before suddenly seemed remote. Here, in the excitement of the moment, I was engaged in nothing less than an attempt to change the world — another dream of my childhood.

During the first days of the student uprising, I walked around the Latin Quarter — with crates, overturned benches, and empty cases from tear-gas grenades scattered over the ground — like Pierre walking around the burning city of Moscow in *War and Peace*. I couldn't help admiring the beauty of the spectacle. Young people singing revolutionary songs with their fists upraised, red flags, barricades — images as strong as those of Eisenstein. My throat was also tightened by a memory that comes back to me at every demonstration when a crowd carrying red flags sings in a single voice about revolution on the march. It is a distant memory. On one May Day in Warsaw my mother brought me out onto the balcony of our apartment so I could see the parade. After a long wait, I saw what seemed to be a sea of men and women, with their flags making red waves. My father walked beside my grandfather at the head of the printers' union, composed mainly of religious Jews with beards and skullcaps. . . . When the mounted police charged them, they sang the "Internationale" and the "Marseillaise," and I was overcome with emotion as their voices rose up to me.

It seemed that May 1968 would never end; it was a constant celebration in which people didn't fold up their flags when it was time to go home and sleep, in which days were improvised without rigid schedules or plans drawn up by a distant staff. We discussed each decision a long time. Athenian democracy had conquered the Boulevard Saint-Michel. At every street corner there were groups commenting, explaining, persuading. If only the slogan of that time, "Talk to your neighbor," could be in effect all over the world!

But in fact noncommunication is the rule. One day in New York I went to see Henry Geldzahler, whose word on contemporary painting seemed to be law in the United States. I was received in the Metropolitan Museum by a fat little gentleman with a goatee and big round glasses. An immense office, decorated with big paintings by American artists. He invited me to sit down beside a low aluminum table and asked me to show him my work. I handed him transparencies of my paintings and albums of my drawings. He glanced over them and handed them back.

"I'm not saying whether they're good or not, but they don't interest me."

"Why not?" I asked.

He looked at me in surprise.

"I don't have to give you any explanations."

At that point I left the man whose opinion was so important. A few days later I was in Brussels when a police patrol stopped my car. I was asked for my papers. I handed them over and asked, "Why?"

The policeman shrugged.

"What do you mean, why? I don't have to give you any explanations."

"Violence," Elie Wiesel said to me one day, "begins where words end." I have always felt the blind pressure of the law as a kind of violence. And each time I have to show my papers or give explanations, account for my existence in one way or another to people who feel they don't have to give me any reason for their attitude, I have an urge to kill. Yes, it seems to me that I could kill at those moments. Unlike Kafka's K., I wouldn't have spent hours, days, and years waiting in front of the door of the law; I would have blown it open. I remember the laughing Germans who, when I was a child, aimed their flashlights at my face and asked, "*Jude?*" Should I tell the truth? Lie? Or ask, "Why?"

In May 1968 sensible people were amused by all our speeches, but, after all, maybe it was because we talked so much — because we communicated — that there were almost no victims.

"We took the floor, as well as the Bastille," Clavel wrote as a comment on my drawings.

The square courtyard of the Sorbonne was always full; it was the great forum of direct democracy. People came there out of conviction or curiosity, and, caught up in this or that wave, they often stayed. The classrooms were turned into dormitories. In that molten mass sprayed with the revolutionary music that constantly poured out of two loudspeakers, Jews and Arabs confronted each other with their problems and passions.

An enormous Al Fatah stand soon appeared, followed by a stand of the Zionist socialist students. Between the two, Jews and Arabs from all over the city finally found a place where they could have discussions. Amos Elon, sent to Paris by his Tel Aviv newspaper, could hardly believe his eyes.

"The Sorbonne students," he said, "seem to be more interested in what's happening in the Middle East than in what's happening here!"

Claude Lanzmann, a collaborator of Jean-Paul Sartre and the future producer of the film *Shoah*, came one evening with Simone de Beauvoir. They were both outraged by the anti-Israeli virulence of the Al Fatah stand. Since Claude was beginning to be agitated — he quickly becomes violent — I suggested that we go to the Occupation Committee and ask to have the two mutually hostile stands closed down. As usual, there was no one at the headquarters of the Occupation Committee. Claude left, furious.

He came back two days later, this time with Judith Magre. He pulled me out of the group of students I was talking with and warmly hugged me. I have seldom seen anyone change his mood and feelings so quickly and drastically. This time, when we went to the Occupation Committee, we found one of its leaders, a thin young man with an aggressive expression.

"Who's that?" he asked me.

I introduced Claude to him.

"Ah," he said, "so you're the supporter of the fascist Zionists!"

Claude turned pale, took off his glasses, handed them to me, grabbed the young man, lifted him off the ground, and began shaking him.

"You want to see what fascists do with garbage like you?" he shouted.

The young man struggled in vain. Judith Magre and I managed to pull him away from Claude, then we led Claude into the courtyard. He was beside himself with rage.

"I was shooting Nazis when I was only sixteen, and he calls me a fascist! Just because I support Israel! If we're ever unlucky enough to have people like that take power, the first thing they do will be to set up concentration camps for people who don't agree with them."

Judith also had an outburst of feeling.

"That poor guy didn't represent anything," she said to Claude, "but you had to rip into him so you could tell your papa about it later!"

By "papa" she obviously meant Sartre. She and Claude were off to a bad start. I guided them toward Marguerite Duras, in the middle of the crowd. Hundreds of people were talking about Israel, the Arabs, the Jews, and the Palestinians. Discussions were becoming dangerously animated.

"We ought to do something to calm everyone down," said Duras.

"There may be a flare-up any minute," said the film producer Jean-Paul Rappeneau, who had just joined us. "And then they'll say the Sorbonne is closed because of the Jews and the Arabs!"

The next day, we handed out our first leaflet. It urged the Israeli and Arab students to begin a real dialogue, rather than making the Sorbonne an extension of the battlefields in the Middle East. Not that our leaflet was a masterpiece of its kind, but it evidently met a need: we were immediately supported by everyone who had had enough of sterile discussions. I was soon surrounded by a crowd of unknown young people who followed me like shadows, stood guard around our stand, sold *Eléments*, and distributed our leaflets.

It was the Palestinians who had suggested that we set up a stand at the Sorbonne. "Since you're afraid," said Daoud Talhami, president of the Union of Palestinian Students, "that our fight with the Zionists may cause a break in the movement, come and explain your position publicly, instead of asking for our stand to be closed down." So we set up our own. People listened to the propaganda of Al Fatah and the Zionists, but they came to us to discuss it. This was when we invented a slogan that soon spread all over the world: "In the Middle East, only peace is revolutionary."

On one of the few nights during that period when I went home, I was awakened by Moshe Sneh, our friend from the Israeli Communist Party. He had come from Israel by way of Belgium and wanted to know when the symposium on the Middle East was going to be held. Captivated by the movement and spending all my time at the Sorbonne, I had completely forgotten about that symposium, which was scheduled for May 17. Pierre Mendès-France, Simone de Beauvoir, the British playwright Arnold Wesker, Angus Wilson, and Iris Murdoch were to take part in it. It had to be canceled. Sneh was determined to meet Roger Garaudy, then a member of the French Communist Party, now a convert to Islam. We called him at Party headquarters. He was very reluctant at first — Sneh had been excommunicated by the Soviet Union — but finally consented to give him a quarter of an hour in a nearby café.

There were nightmarish traffic jams all over Paris. Sneh and I abandoned the car, got out, and walked, threading our way between mounds of the garbage that was no longer being picked up. We were forty-five minutes late. Garaudy was waiting over a cup of coffee. For more than an hour, Sneh explained his Party's positions and his conviction that one could be a Communist without always being in line with Moscow's policies and even if one joined with other forces in certain cases.

"Isn't that what the French Communists did during the war, and right afterward?" he asked.

Garaudy didn't answer. He hadn't said a word during the whole time when Sneh was talking; he had been taking notes. When Sneh had finished, Garaudy stood up, still without making any comment, told us good-bye, and left.

Clara came back from Israel a few days later, after a roundabout trip that was a result of circumstances as well as her unease about flying. We took her straight to the Sorbonne, where she spent most of her time leading debates on the Middle East.

That was how she discovered one evening that the Israeli students were planning a coup, their own version of the Six-Day War. Everything was ready: six groups of three men each had been formed; one of them would snatch the Palestinian flag away from the Al Fatah stand; while the Palestinians were chasing them, two other groups would destroy the stand and another would hold back the two or three Palestinians left behind to guard it. The last two groups would be on the lookout for outside intervention and, if there wasn't any, they would take up a position at the entrance of the Institut Anglais on the Rue de la Sorbonne, to which the first group was to lead the Palestinians.

"And what will you do to them?" asked Clara.

"We won't hurt them, we just want to scare them."

Clara and I had managed to assemble them in the Place de la Sorbonne, in front of the statue. We had to persuade them to call off their raid: it would be sure to degenerate into something more serious.

We patiently explained how absurd it was. Another stand, even bigger, would replace the one destroyed; it would be guarded by other leftist groups; pro-Palestinian solidarity would be roused to greater intensity, which was just the opposite of what they wanted. It was a strange scene: we were speaking Hebrew, and the statue of Auguste Comte had surely never heard that much of it before. The Israelis gave up their plan.

A few days later, Cohn-Bendit clandestinely returned to France and announced a press conference at the Sorbonne. Thousands of people were packed into the great amphitheater and the courtyard. Amos Elon asked us to help him "get as close as possible." Clara led him through the checkpoints of the security services. At the entrance of the amphitheater, young men wearing red armbands recognized Clara but refused to let Amos pass.

"He's a journalist," she said.

"All the more reason to keep him out."

"But he's from a foreign country," said Clara, not wanting to say which one, considering the anti-Israeli atmosphere in the Sorbonne at that time.

"Let's see his press card."

Amos held out his papers.

"You're from Israel! *Shalom!* Come in, we'll give you a good place."

"You speak Hebrew?" Clara asked in surprise.

"A little. We were on a kibbutz. As a matter of fact, most of the people in the security service have been on kibbutzim. The reactionaries can talk about a Jewish plot if they want to!"

Laughing, the young men took Clara and Amos straight to the rostrum, where William Klein was filming the crowd while everyone waited for Cohn-Bendit.

I remember saying to Cohn-Bendit one day, at the Sorbonne, that the "revolution" was about to end. He seemed surprised.

"Why do you say that?"

"Look at all those posters on the walls."

"What about them?"

"Mao, Stalin, Trotsky, Bakunin, Luxemburg, Marx, Lenin, and even Kropotkin. They've taken their iconography from dusty attics. When people begin searching for answers anywhere but in present reality, it's because they feel lost."

"I hadn't looked at it that way," Cohn-Bendit said thoughtfully, "but you're right."

And in fact the movement was beginning to crumble. It may have been only by chance, but I found the first signs of it in Belleville, in a confrontation between Jews and Arabs. An argument in a café had escalated; first there was a raid against all Jewish shops, then a counterattack against everything Arab. At the Sorbonne, the news came to us in a highly simplified form: the police were attacking Arabs in Belleville. A group of several hundred formed immediately and began marching toward Belleville, led by people carrying flags. Near the Couronne subway station, they learned that it was only a fight between Jews and Arabs. The procession slowed hesitantly, then stopped. What was the "revolution" supposed to do in a case like this? After half an hour of discussion, they all turned back. It didn't concern them.

I had a hollow feeling in the pit of my stomach: this was the end. The marchers hadn't reacted spontaneously; they hadn't gone, as they would have done at the beginning of May, to talk with both sides, in this case the Jews and the Arabs.

People no longer had endless discussions. They only brandished a few simplistic slogans invented by cliques. It was now a time of solitude and dirty dishes after the feast; everything was going to be the same as before, or almost the same. As soon as they were able to get some gasoline, many of the companions of May left the congested city and went to the country for a change of ideas.

We walked along the Boulevard de Belleville with several American journalists. Broken shop windows, burned furniture. Groups — of Jews on one side of the street, of Arabs on the other — were passionately talking over what had happened. But there was no longer the rich disorder of an impromptu celebration, there was only the disheartening continuation of a conflict between two peoples, a conflict whose substance the left was unable to analyze.

Some time later, I was in Tel Aviv for an exhibition of my drawings. The Tzafta Club held a debate on the meaning of the events of May in France. There were many participants. They expressed two opinions, always the same: the "May left" was anti-Israeli, and it hadn't been able to explain what it wanted.

For the Israelis, heirs of Aristotelian rationalism and the great currents of Russian populism, it was inconceivable to want to destroy a system without immediately proposing something to replace it. They continued to see May 1968 as the doings of irresponsible, anarchistic, and anti-Zionist children.

The opinion that prevailed in the Arab countries was that the Jews, and therefore the Zionists, had fomented that disorder as a counterstroke to de Gaulle's pro-Arab policy.

I spent so much time with both sides, trying once again to explain. . . .

10

Aragon and Elsa

Most intellectuals in Western Europe are somewhere to the left of center. Not that they adhere to a single policy, but they support, and sometimes produce, the type of humanitarian ideas that are usually defended by the left.

In the period immediately after World War II, most of them either joined the Communist Party or stood close beside it. Some left it after the invasion of Hungary in 1956; others, more numerous, after the invasion of Czechoslovakia in 1968. And still others, such as Louis Aragon, one of the most famous of them, remained faithful to the end.

To some extent Aragon, who became a surrealist writer in the 1920s, joined the Communist Party out of love for Elsa Triolet, a young woman of Russian origin, friend and translator of the Soviet poet Vladimir Mayakovsky, and herself a writer. With time, they formed the best-known couple in the Communist world. In 1969 they were at the apogee of their lives.

At about that same time, I often had lunch with Jean-

François Revel, author of the worldwide best-seller *Without Marx or Jesus*. During our conversations he developed the ideas he eventually presented in that book.

"If the revolution ever comes," he said to me, "it will be in the United States, because everything is possible there."

"If everything is possible there," I asked, "why make any changes?"

I was delighted with my question, like a child who asks a single "Why?" that blows up the superb, patiently constructed systems of adults. It really seemed to me the best argument that could be opposed to Revel's views.

I had had the same thought in Israel, long before the Six-Day War. No society had ever seemed to me so open as Israeli society at that time. Everyone was interested in everyone else. People talked to each other in buses and cafés. The spirit of the kibbutz reigned over the whole country. All outer manifestations of social hierarchy were despised, and the new president, Yitzhak Ben-Zvi, had to be pulled out of the wooden hut where he would have been content to go on living. Politicization was general, as was respect for the freedom of others. One day a young man took the floor at a public meeting and said, "I'm uneasy because I'm going to try to convince you, and whenever I convince someone I feel as if I'd taken something away from him." The magnificent openness of Israeli society was so great that everything was possible. And the question occurred to me: "Why make any changes?"

One day I received a call from a lady with a marked Russian accent. It was Elsa Triolet. She invited me to take part in a radio broadcast devoted to her.

Slender and delicate, with her hair and the upper part of her face hidden by a veil, she hurried toward me (we had never met before), took my hand between both of hers, and expressed surprise at seeing me younger than she had expected.

"Your last article," she said, "is the best one I've ever read on the subject. I'd like you to give some good opposing answers to Monsieur X, the lawyer, who just came back from

Egypt. He's very biased. I invited him before I read your article. It's a problem that touches me."

She let go of my hand and hurried over to Louis Malle.

"I'm glad to see you," she told him. "We were discussing your film *Calcutta* the other day. It's very strong." And, turning to me: "Have you seen it?" Before I could answer, she went on: "I've forgotten. . . . You two know each other, don't you? Ah, here's Picasso! Dear man! He's made a special trip from Vallauris for my broadcast!"

And while Elsa left us to go and greet the famous actor Jean-Louis Barrault, I shook hands with Picasso and said a little abruptly, "I like you very much."

"I prefer to be respected," he replied in the same tone. Then, smiling: "I'm glad to meet you. The Arab–Israeli conflict interests me. We Catalans all have a little Marrano in us."

Elsa came back and whispered in my ear, "That lawyer is an old friend — a Communist like me, of course — and I had to invite him, but I would rather have had you present your ideas alone."

When the broadcast began, she stated that she had no specific viewpoint on the matter.

"Sometimes," she said, "when I think that the Arabs are a poor people being helped by the Russians, I wonder if someday they'll behave like the Chinese, those vipers, those dragons that the Russians warmed in their bosom. Maybe it will all turn against the Soviets."

Later, Elsa Triolet and Louis Aragon invited me to their home several times. I wanted to organize a trip to the Middle East for them. It seemed to me that Elsa would be delighted to visit Israel. But Aragon said he couldn't travel by air because of his high blood pressure. I suggested that they go by ship. But the truth was that Aragon conformed to the policy of the Communist Party, which took its cue from the Soviet Union, and the Soviet Union was against Israel, so that was that.

Aragon said he was mainly concerned about Czechoslovakia, and Elsa swore she would never set foot in the USSR as long as Soviet soldiers were stationed on Czech soil. In her opinion, it was a remnant of Stalinism. I disagreed.

"I don't believe one man can be responsible for a war like that," I said. "In the same circumstances, Lenin might not have acted very differently."

"What do you mean?" asked Aragon.

"When a minority, no matter how good its intentions, wants to impose its concept of happiness, justice, and freedom on a majority, it can only resort to force. And once the process is set in motion . . ."

Aragon appreciated my reasoning, but he had already made his choice between the everyday repression of our society and the possible violence of revolution. For my part, I rejected that Manichaean dilemma which prohibits trying to find any other course of action and eventually leads to despair.

This reminded me of an extraordinary passage in Kafka's *Report to an Academy*, the story of a wild ape captured by men and locked in a cage. I found the book on one of the shelves and read the passage aloud:

> That progress of mine! How the rays of knowledge penetrated from all sides into my awakening brain! . . . There is an excellent idiom: to fight one's way through the thick of things; that is what I have done, I have fought through the thick of things. There was nothing else for me to do, provided always that freedom was not to be my choice.

Aragon was silent for a few moments, then he asked, "Yet you've taken part in actions with the Communists, haven't you?"

"If the Communists say the sun is shining and it actually is, I'm not going to contradict them just because they're Communists. I've already told you that I don't question their honesty or their ideal. I only wonder if a standard happiness can be imposed on a majority when they evidently don't want it."

Aragon remained smiling, calm, and thoughtful. When he spoke in his soft, deep voice, he never tried to give the impression that he had a monopoly on truth. Yet I couldn't help always being vaguely disappointed. Maybe I expected too much of him, maybe I was too respectful in our discussions, but I wasn't satisfied with hearing from him only a few commonplace remarks about Stalinism. I suppose I resented the fact that he didn't make me be intelligent.

When I left Elsa and Aragon, they usually gave me autographed copies of their books and I gave them my latest prints.

One day they invited me to meet the Soviet poet Yevgeny Yevtushenko. I had read his poem *Babi Yar* and I was glad to become acquainted with him. I spoke Russian with him, as I usually did with Elsa and Aragon also. The conversation turned to the Middle East.

"In the Soviet Union, we're pro-Israeli," said Yevtushenko. "Israel has succeeded where the Soviet Union has failed: in making a marriage between collectivism and freedom."

Aragon protested. It was a strange situation: the French writer seemed closer to the Soviet government than the Soviet writer did, at least when the latter was abroad.

Late that night, when Elsa showed me to the door, she said to me, "I've just realized what the bond between us is, Marek. It's Judaism." And, sadly, "In old age, you begin missing your childhood. I'd like to go to Israel . . . someday."

I was in Geneva — where a printer passionately interested in the Arab–Israeli conflict had agreed to print our magazine *Eléments* free of charge — when I learned of Elsa's death. I went to the post office to send Aragon a telegram. I stared at the blank form a long time without thinking of words to express my sadness. Death, always death. Finally, powerless and disconsolate, I simply wrote, "Heard the news. Marek."

11

Conference
in Paris

Trying to convene an international conference without money, a secretary, or an infrastructure seemed to me uncertain at best, and maybe ludicrous. But it was not for nothing that I had been brought up in the voluntarist tradition that animated the Jews of central Europe.

I had an unexpected stroke of good luck when Sam Lefrak, an American collector passing through Paris with his wife, Ethel, bought several of my paintings, which made it possible for me to reserve my conference room on the Rue de Rennes in Paris.

This was in February 1969, and there was again talk of war in the Middle East. Israel was bombing Palestinian camps in Jordan in retaliation for attacks on El Al planes in Athens and Zurich. Demonstrations were being held here and there to protest public hangings of Jews in Baghdad. The Egyptian newspaper *Al Ahram* wrote that there had been a sharp break in relations between Egypt and the United States. Dr. Gunnar Jarring, the United Nations emissary to the Middle East, was disheartened when he left Cyprus: for weeks he had vainly tried to bring about contacts among Israel, Jordan, and Egypt. In Europe and the United States, supporters and opponents of Israel battled each other with press releases.

In that explosive climate it was important for people like us, who felt that the search for peace was incompatible with anathemas and exclusions, to make themselves heard. The idea for the conference was mine. I felt that the time had come for us to say publicly what we thought, for as the Book of Proverbs (25:11) says, "A word fitly spoken is like apples of gold in a setting of silver."

Yes, I know: at that time it took a good dose of naïveté, madness, or (why hide it?) megalomania to believe that an appeal from a Paris painter would be enough to move the stars.

The day got off to a bad start. Claude Lanzmann woke me up to tell me that Jean-Paul Sartre was dissatisfied with me, but he didn't know why. And what about the others? Would they all come? I was also worried about the press and television. Yet I was sure that we were right, that peace, the only guarantee of Israel's survival, was possible. The idea was simple, but not so easy to disseminate. To disseminate it, we were dependent on the media, and the media would send reporters only to an event. Could an international conference attended by a certain number of intellectuals be regarded as an event? I kept coming up against the same problems.

Finally, the first encouragement: that evening I received word that André Schwarz-Bart, author of *The Last of the Just*, would come. Then I got letters of support from Joan Baez and Italo Calvino. With my heart a little lighter, I began writing my opening speech but fell asleep with all my clothes on, pen in hand.

Morning brought me a new stack of telegrams, from Herbert Marcuse, Günter Grass, Noam Chomsky, Angus Wilson, C. P. Snow, and Julio Cortázar. Old Ernst Bloch, one of the best Marxist philosophers, who had moved to West Germany in 1961 after being dismissed from his university position in Leipzig because of his unorthodoxy, took such a positive view of what we were doing that he gave me permission to use his name in any way I saw fit.

The guests had arrived. Large delegations from all over the world had taken their places. Interpreters in three languages were ready. We had handed out painstakingly prepared dossiers. The conference could begin.

With the authors of the Bible, I have always believed that the right to express opinions and ask questions represents an enormous power. In a democracy, people who question the government are the only real counterpower. As long as the government accepts being questioned, society remains free. When it evades questions, or imprisons those who dare to question it, freedom disappears. The first to understand this was the last of the Judges, Samuel. When the elders of Israel came to him at Ramah to ask him to appoint a king for them, he tried to dissuade them. He described how a king would exploit them, use their men as soldiers and their women as servants, crush them with taxes, and imprison anyone who opposed him. But the people refused to listen to Samuel. They wanted to have a king, like other nations. After consulting the Almighty, Samuel made Saul, a handsome, honest shepherd, the King of Israel.

What matters here is the Hasidic commentary attached to that Biblical story: because Samuel knew that there were no perfect kings and that there was no power without the temptation to seize absolute power, to maintain balance in the kingdom he decided to create a counterpower by founding the first school of prophets.

The word "prophet," *navi* in Hebrew, does not designate a man who foresees, a *roeh*, but a man who speaks, an orator. The prophet sees reality and tells what he sees. He sees the unbreakable connection between spiritual strength and historical destiny. He sees moral reality and possibilities of change. The prophet announces what he sees. As Amos says (Amos 3:8), "The lion has roared; who will not fear? The Lord God has spoken; who can but prophesy?"

Were we prophets that day? Orators? Or simply people who expressed themselves? The fact is that on the day after our conference we received official encouragement from the cabinet of Egyptian President Gamal Abdel Nasser, from the cabinet of Golda Meir, the Israeli prime minister, and from Abu Iyad, Yasir Arafat's second in command. But Naief Hawatmeh, head of the Popular Democratic Front for the Liberation of Palestine,* was the first to invite us to see him.

Clara decided to leave for Beirut as soon as possible. Her trip probably wouldn't be entirely safe: in 1969 there was a certain danger involved in presenting ideas like ours to fedayeen organizations. So I wrote to Maurice Schumann, the French foreign minister at the time, asking him for help and protection from the French embassies in Beirut, Damascus, and Amman, the main stopovers in the trip.

Clara left on a Friday morning, with letters of recommendation, addresses, and secret phone numbers. In Beirut she stayed at the Hotel St. George, as Eric Rouleau, a specialist on the Arab world, had suggested. All journalists stayed there.

*The Popular Democratic Front for the Liberation of Palestine was born of a split in the Popular Front for the Liberation of Palestine, headed by Dr. George Habash, in 1969. Hawatmeh's organization is called the Democratic Front, and Habash's the Popular Front, in the following pages.

12

Clara in Beirut, October 1969

In the hotel, Clara immediately began trying to call her "contacts." But the weekend, along with the curfew ordered the day before as a result of clashes between Palestinians and Lebanese Christians, had nearly emptied the city. On Saturday, however, she arranged to meet with representatives of Dr. Habash, the most intransigent, and the leftist Christians, the most intolerant, one of whose representatives, George Corm, came for Clara and took her to his home. There, with a few friends, they began talking about the conflict. Clara asked if she could record the discussion. Corm consented, but the atmosphere deteriorated as they all revealed their positions. Corm considered that it was unthinkable to accept a State of Israel, no matter what it was like, and that those who defended Israel's right to exist were dangerous fanatics.

He took Clara back to her hotel, but an hour later he called to ask her to lend him the tape she had made because he wanted to listen to it again. The next morning he sent her a little package in which she found a blank tape and a letter saying that he had "confiscated" the other one.

Feeling a bit depressed, Clara went to the offices of *El Hadaf*, the newspaper of the Popular Front, where she was to meet Ghassan Kanafani, a spokesman for the movement. While she was waiting for Kanafani, she had to put up with a Danish leftist's theoretical exposition of the Palestinian struggle. She finally told him she hadn't come to Beirut so that a Dane in search of a revolutionary cause could explain things to her that she already knew, and the conversation then became more and more acrimonious until Kanafani arrived.

He invited Clara into his office, where a portrait of Lenin occupied a place of honor, and readily gave her permission to tape the interview.

"If Israel gave back the territories it conquered in 1967," she asked, "do you think you could accept the principle of its existence as a state?"

Kanafani didn't even accept the existence of an Israeli nationality and, carried away with indignation, compared the Israelis to the Nazis. Clara turned off the tape recorder and told him it did no good to misuse such terms. But he insisted that she leave the comparison in the tape, "because the Israelis, like the Nazis, occupy other people's territory."

"Occupying territory isn't enough to turn someone into a Nazi," said Clara. "And if Israel gave back the territories occupied during the Six-Day War, would you change your attitude?"

"No. All of Palestine belongs to us, and to get it back we're ready to shed the last drop of our blood."

"But you'll have to deal with the Israelis' resistance."

"Do you really think the Israelis are ready to fight to the last drop of their blood?"

"*You* don't think so?"

"It would be very sad . . ."

Clara was also able to meet Rosemary Sayegh, who headed an information and propaganda organization called June Fifth in memory of the 1967 war. She gave her a copy of *Eléments*, and Rosemary Sayegh promised to call her the next day. She didn't. From then on, everyone Clara tried to visit disappeared as soon as she announced her name: So-and-So was in Damascus, So-and-So was sick, So-and-So would call her back. A young man stayed in the lobby of her hotel and kept track of all her movements. She was the object of an organized boycott and strict surveillance.

Through a friend, she became acquainted with an important magnate of the Arab press, a Christian leader named Abu Adal. He received her at home (an immense house, a superb collection of ancient icons), was amused by her misadventures, and asked his son and his collaborator Antoine Chouery to act as her guides in Beirut. That was how she became one of the first journalists to discover the Lebanese Kataeb organization, with its armed militia and training camps. "The Palestinians had better steer clear of us," said Abu Adal's son. "And if they're bothered by us, they can go and live in Israel."

"Big Antoine," as Clara and her friend called him, took his mission very seriously. Clara asked him to find out why she was being boycotted. Since he had easy access to Palestinians, he quickly brought her the answer.

"They're saying in Beirut that you may be a spy. Some people are talking about liquidating you. The official order is not to talk to you."

"Since they'll talk to *you*, tell them that I was invited by the Democratic Front, that I'm not going to leave here, that I'll stay till I meet Hawatmeh, however long it takes."

She tried to call me, but I was in Strasbourg for a meeting with representatives of the European Parliament. I called her as soon as I was back in Paris. She seemed glad to hear my voice.

"How's it going?" I asked.

"Badly."

"Why?"

"I can't tell you, someone's listening."

"Do they want to beat you?"

"It's worse."

"They want to rape you?"

"Worse than that."

"Kill you?"

"Worse."

I was puzzled.

"They won't talk to me," she finally said.

I advised her to stay in the hotel and said I would call her as soon as I had seen Absi, the Algerian who was our contact with Naief Hawatmeh.

Absi came to me the next day, after his work. He seemed annoyed. We tried to call Amman, where Hawatmeh was still staying. We had to wait several hours and got through at about midnight.

After hanging up, Absi told me that Hawatmeh regretted the misunderstanding, but he felt that Clara had made a mistake by not waiting and first meeting people from the Democratic Front. In the atmosphere of suspicion and violence that now surrounded her, and with the mistrust that reigned among the different organizations, we would surely understand that it would be difficult for him to see her. He had done what was necessary to guarantee her safety in Beirut, but he asked her to postpone her trip to Amman.

The next day, Nagi Abu Khalil, one of the editors of *Al Huriah*, the newspaper of the Democratic Front, came to Clara's hotel and, ill at ease, asked her to excuse all the unpleasantness that had occurred during her stay in Beirut. She was not being accused of anything, but, in views of the negative attitude that Al Fatah and the Popular Front had taken toward her, the Democratic Front could not receive her as planned.

Two hours later, George Aissa came to her in the name of Al Fatah and said that certain accusations had been made against her, but that if she wanted to defend herself against them, representatives of the different organizations were willing to listen to her that evening. She accepted the offer.

At six o'clock, Aissa came for her and invited her into a long black car in which two Palestinians were already sitting. The car took the Raouche road, which runs along the sea to the

Mazraa road, where the Palestinian general staffs had their headquarters. Not one word was exchanged during the drive.

The meeting was held at the headquarters of the Popular Front, where about twenty men were waiting for Clara. A chair was brought out for her. Around her, the Palestinians were talking loudly in Arabic and she heard her name spoken several times. Sitting beside a window, Aissa listened to a tape in which the children of the Shatila camp shouted in unison, "Al Fatah, Al Fatah . . ." As though hypnotized, he repeated along with them, "Al Fatah, Al Fatah, Al Fatah . . ." It was an obsessive incantation, and Clara was beginning to be afraid when someone turned off the tape recorder. Everyone sat down. The tribunal was in place.

"Why have you come to Beirut?" asked Kamal Nasser, the spokesman of Al Fatah.

"I've already explained that," Clara replied. "I'm the editor of *Eléments*, an important magazine devoted to the Middle East. We want to publish an issue on the Palestinians. I'm also a member of the International Committee for Peace in the Middle East. You may not agree with some of our ideas, but a large part of world public opinion does agree with them."

"Are they Zionist ideas?" asked Bassam Abu Sharif, one of the leaders of the Popular Front.

"If, for you, being a Zionist means accepting Israel's existence while condemning its Palestinian policy, then most countries, including the Soviet Union, are Zionist."

They all began talking at once. Clara was accused of being a spy.

Exasperated, she reached into her handbag, took out the tape of her conversation with Kanafani, and put it down on the table.

"I came here as a friend," she said, "and I was invited as one. We support your claim to national rights, and you know it. But I've told you about our reservations. We feel that Israel has a right to exist, but that there's room for a Palestinian state beside Israel: on the West Bank, in Jordan, in Gaza. We know that Israel is a democratic country in which there are conservatives, liberals, and a left that's just as revolutionary as yours, and if you're really leftists, it's incomprehensible that you don't hold out your hand to the Israeli left. If saying that makes me your enemy, I'll leave. I'll go back to Paris tomorrow and you can talk with people who agree with you, even though they represent only small groups."

Clara said all this rapidly, without pausing to catch her breath. No one answered. She stood up to leave.

"Please sit down, Lady Clara," Ghassan Kanafani said with a smile, "and take back your tape. I give you permission to reproduce that conversation in *Eléments*. I don't agree with you, but I trust you."

The atmosphere relaxed, the tone changed, and the discussion went on for several hours. When they separated, Kanafani asked Clara not to go to Amman.

"Here," he said, "we control the situation. In Jordan it's different: at any moment you might come across some fanatic who would empty his machine gun into your belly." He added, laughing, "That would be a pity: we might be losing a friend."

Clara followed Kanafani's advice and went back to Paris the next day.

13

East Berlin

The purring of the propeller-driven plane had lulled me to sleep. It was dark and someone was asking me the time. I had to climb up on a stepladder to reach a board, attached to the ceiling, into which the hours had been carved. I took a ruler from my pocket and began measuring time. "Do you know what time it is?" the voice asked me again. I opened my eyes. It took me several seconds to realize that I was in a plane of LOT, the Polish airline. The face smiling at me belonged to Madame Nguyen Thi Binh, foreign minister of the South Vietnamese Provisional Revolutionary Government.

After the reunification of the two Vietnams, she completely disappeared from the political scene. It was even said that she had been imprisoned by her Communist brothers in Hanoi. But at the time of my trip in June 1970, her round, youthful face personified the Vietnamese people struggling against the world's greatest military power. We were on our way together to East Berlin, where a meeting of the World Peace Council was being held. The committee had been invited, and three of us had gone: Fernand Rohman, a professor of philosophy; Bernard Kouchner, founder of Doctors Without Frontiers; and me.

It had been hard for me to leave my studio. I had just published the album of my drawings of May 1968 and finished an exhibition; I had begun another series of drawings on everyday life, and I would have liked to finish it before plunging into the political arena again. I was a little tired of bouncing from airport to airport, following the trail of my hopes or appointments. But my friends had told me that my presence in Berlin could be useful. Even so, I wondered about the importance of that kind of meeting. Would the people who went to it really be able to make themselves understood?

"If you have to shout, you'll shout," the sociologist Edgar Morin had told me. "You're a character out of your drawings: always in motion and always ready to react against violence."

"Why are you always shouting and fighting?" my father often asked me. But it's when I shout that I get a reaction. Everyone who has written about my drawings has commented on their violence, to praise it in some cases, to deplore it in others. "Violence is part of our era, but must art also deal with it?" asked a Belgian critic. "With Halter, the image is only a function of judgment, and ink, charcoal, and brushes are only tools of intelligence," the writer Claude Roy noted with regard to what he called my "drawn newspaper." And the Belgian critic added, "Granted, but all that will not calm the violence now raging all over the world. For artists who love nature in its moments of lyricism, there are certain spectacles that should be allowed to settle before they are painted. They will not be discovered by someone with a pistol in his hand." And in *Le Monde*, its editor, Pierre Viansson-Ponté, said: "Thus militates Halter. Is he an abstract, representational, realistic, classical or revolutionary painter? Who knows? He doesn't care; he talks, explains, strikes, rouses. In short, he militates. And since he is a good militant, he is also a good painter. Or vice versa, as you choose."

"If you have to shout, you'll shout." Did I really have to go on shouting, using up most of my time and the most ardent part of my strength in that endless fight for an understanding between the Arabs and the Israelis, for peace here and peace there, for a better society? Maybe the time had finally come for me to stop running and saying to myself, "Fantastic! Here I am, a little Jew from Warsaw, being accepted by the greatest people everywhere!"

That constant need to be reassured, that search for love and certainty, was what Clara called my "Chagall complex." Once in the days when, as a young student, I used to spend hours copying Michelangelo's frescoes in the Sistine Chapel, I heard a voice behind me saying in French, "He's got talent."

I turned around. A couple. I thought I recognized Chagall.

"Are you Chagall?" I asked.

"A little," he answered disconcertingly.

We talked awhile and he invited me to visit him in Paris. As they were walking away, I heard him say, this time in Russian, "I was recognized here!"

"Even here," said his wife, affectionately patting him on the shoulder.

It was a shock to me. Chagall was at the peak of his glory — what need did he have to be recognized by a young anonymous student? I didn't understand it till later: he, the little Jew from Vitebsk, the uprooted exile, with his accent, wasn't sure of anything, not even of being the Chagall honored by the Metropolitan Museum, the Louvre, the Hermitage. Being recognized by a stranger was reassuring to him. That recognition served as an identity.

I always remember these lines by Swift: "All my endeavours to distinguish myself were only for want of a great title and fortune, that I might be used like a Lord by those who have a high opinion of my parts; whether right or wrong, no matter. And so the reputation of wit and great learning does the office of a blue riband or a coach and six."

Wasn't I, like so many others, buying my coach on the pretext that only people who ride in coaches are listened to? And wasn't I about to forget that the coach was only a means of making myself heard? Painting, selling, living better. However satisfied my vanity may be when I read articles about me, I can't help feeling different from those self-satisfied painters who enjoy telling about their shows, detailing the fluctuations of the art market, and talking about their country houses and their next vacations under sunny and fashionable skies. They, of course, don't ride in a coach to be accepted: they already are accepted. On that level, at least, they aren't in a contradictory situation like mine: I criticize the society to which I address myself, and which feeds me. But on the whole I prefer my contradictions, anxiety, impatience, and problems to their peace of mind and the satisfaction that comes to them when they hear the chatter of society people above the clatter of forks.

So I went to Berlin.

I like airplanes, I dream well in them. . . . I looked at my watch.

"It's two o'clock," I said to Madame Binh. "We ought to be there soon."

The East Berlin airport seemed empty. A fine rain was falling, so dreary that the red brick building looked gray. Bleak silence suddenly enveloped us when the engines stopped. It lasted only a few seconds. Suddenly the runway became extraordinarily animated: hundreds of Vietnamese holding roses were running toward us and calling out greetings to Madame Binh, who waited for them on the steps.

Trip to the Unter den Linden Hotel, wait, distribution of dossiers, welcoming speech, issuing of restaurant tickets. The atmosphere was strange, formal, and constrained; I even heard a woman from Franco–Arab Friendship ask a functionary, as though she were in school, if she could go to the bathroom. Finally we received a questionnaire in which we were to indicate the committees in whose work we wanted to participate. We chose the Middle East, of course, and divided the subcommittees among us: the political subcommittee for Fernand, the information subcommittee for Bernard, and the judicial subcommittee for me.

After settling into the rooms provided for us — we had two for the three of us — we went out to take a walk on Karl Marx Allee, formerly Stalin Allee. I still remembered my first trip to Germany, in 1964, for an exhibition in Cologne. The sound of the language alone had been enough to make me bristle, and I couldn't look at a man older than forty without asking myself, "And what about that one? Where was he?" In the beautiful city of Munich, only a short distance from the Dachau death camp, I had seen the daughter of Carlo Schmid, the old socialist leader, crying. "Must we pay all our lives for what our parents did?" she asked. I told her I didn't want revenge, but I urged her not to forget or forgive.

This time, on that rainy Friday at the end of June, it was Bernard, Fernand, and I who formed the spectacle. We strolled from one display window to the next, among buildings in the bathroom style of the Stalin era, joking and laughing, and people looked at us with a mixture of mistrust and envy.

The next day, we began working. The colorful crowd, from all over the world, filled the impressive meeting room, where, among the flags, the slogans, and the word "peace" written in all languages, the names of Madame Binh and Walter Ulbricht, head of the East German Communist Party, set off tremendous enthusiasm. My two friends were unlucky with their subcommittees, especially Fernand: his contributions were brilliant, but he remained an outsider to the end, as if he were playing a violin in a fanfare. With the help of his temperament, Bernard got along more easily with the members of his subcommittee, but they all clung firmly to their original positions.

There were only a dozen of us in my subcommittee, and I was the only one who wasn't a jurist. First, we had to elect a chairman. The Palestinian Jamal Surani nominated Abib Daoudy, the Syrian ambassador to Belgium. Acting on the principle that, given a choice between two enemies, it is better to choose the one who at least has the power to make decisions, I nominated a Soviet professor, Igor Blishchenko, of the Moscow Institute of International Relations. I had been able to exchange a few words in Russian with him before the start of the session. He was elected.

As soon as the discussion began, I realized that once again it was those outside the Arab–Israeli conflict who were the most intransigent, in this case a Belgian, a Greek, and a Yugoslavian. With spiteful passion they described Israel's violations of international law and even went so far as to oppose the very existence of the Jewish state. When it was my turn to speak, I asked them if they would accept Israel if a revolution should change the regime there.

"Change it into Palestine?" asked Surani.

"No, change it into a socialist regime, but still within Israel."

"For us, accepting that product of American imperialism is out of the question!" said the Yugoslavian.

"Then why go to so much trouble to prove that Israel is guilty, since you reject it no matter what it does?"

I added that I hadn't come to defend Israel's policies, but that I had hoped I could take part in a calm, constructive debate. And with a certain mischievous pleasure I recalled the fact that the Soviet Union had been the first to recognize the State of Israel and had supplied its first weapons.

The Syrian Abib Daoudy attacked me personally; the Austrian Alfons Dur and the Rumanian Emil Furnica supported me. Inevitably, two camps formed, and Blishchenko ably tried to appear neutral. My relations with Daoudy were friendly outside the debates, but the others either stopped greeting me or avoided me altogether, and I sensed in them a feeling of hatred or suspicion that I recognized all too well from having encountered it in my childhood.

In the evening, before going to a performance of *Don Giovanni* being given at the opera house in our honor, I found the two Rumanians, Furnica and Grigorescu (the latter was vice president of his country's television network), waiting at the door of my room like conspirators. They only wanted to assure me of their support, and they shook my hand warmly.

"It's important that someone dares to say what you say."

At the next day's session there was a newcomer, Krishna Menon, Nehru's former defense minister, who attacked me violently: I was a lackey of Israeli imperialism. He raved on and on. Finally I expressed my surprise at what he was saying, since he didn't know me or my views. Although I wasn't a jurist, I reminded him that hearsay wasn't admissible as evidence. Then I referred to the incidents created on the Chinese–Indian border by India's territorial demands, and spoke in favor of China's viewpoint. Krishna Menon became even more overwrought.

"That has nothing to do with the Arab–Israeli conflict!" he cried.

"What happens there," I said, "can serve as an example for the Middle East, assuming that precedents create case law."

He didn't answer and preferred to leave the session.

When Fernand, Bernard, and I went back to the hotel, we saw Yehia Hamuda, of the PLO. We asked him why he hadn't answered the letter that the committee had sent him, but he claimed he hadn't received it. Just then a group of Arabs came toward us, and among them I recognized Mehdi Alaoui, the representative of the Moroccan opposition. They excitedly said something to Hamuda in Arabic, literally pulled him away from us, and hurried off as if the devil were after them.

To change the atmosphere — and the menu — a little, Fernand, Bernard, and I, accompanied by the three hostesses who had been assigned to us, went out to have a good meal at one of the big restaurants in the center of the city. At the Warsaw, we were told that all the tables were reserved. Same thing at the Budapest, even though we saw only three couples dining by candlelight. At the Sofia, same answer. Bernard was beginning to lose patience. He asked for an explanation, and the headwaiter told us that a certain number of tables were always held in reserve for dignitaries of the government or the Communist Party.

In desperation, we went back to the Unter den Linden, where we found our usual places, the glum whispering of the delegates, the standard menu, and the heavy gray curtain drawn between us and the outside world. This time, however, we were entitled to a glass of *Sekt,* the German version of champagne. We were starting to eat our soup when Bernard, still exasperated, stood up with his glass in his hand, proud and erect beneath his shock of blond hair, and offered a toast to Comrade Ulbricht. Fernand and I found him such a fine sight, with his bright eyes defying everyone in the room, that we stood up and clinked our glasses against his. Then the two hundred delegates stood up one by one and waited with calm dignity for the rest of the ceremony. The three of us sat down, laughing: a second earlier, we had been the only ones standing while everyone else sat, and now we were the only ones sitting while everyone else stood. It was like a scene from a Charlie Chaplin film. The silence was overwhelming. The delegates, glasses in hand, looked at each other discreetly, not knowing what to do. Finally they sat down, one after another, resigned to not understanding. Before we had finished the stewed apples, two German functionaries came up to us and asked for our names. They informed us that there were some things one didn't laugh at, and that they hoped they wouldn't have to tell us again.

That same night, after one of our hostesses had taken us to visit her parents and sing old revolutionary songs, we began looking for a restaurant or a café that was still open, because the international-conference-style menu had left us still hungry. We weren't the only ones: we met a group of Arab delegates, including Mehdi Alaoui, who, like us, were in search of something to complement the stewed apples. We combined our efforts and finally found some bread and a few bottles. We shared them and spent the rest of the night telling each other jokes.

"You see how hunger unites people," I said to Mehdi, the man who had pulled Hamuda away from us a few hours earlier.

"It's a friendship of the stomach," he replied.

And we remained friends.

*   *   *

Since the Arab delegations shared the limelight with the Vietnamese, Khaled Mohieddin, leader of the Egyptian delegation and formerly Nasser's companion, was always surrounded by many people. It was only on the last day that I was able to approach him to talk, as usual, about our idea of holding an international conference in which Israelis and Arabs would take part. He told me that he had thought of it himself, but that he was afraid there would be complications if the Europeans and their political parties became too heavily involved in the conference. Then he introduced me to Lotfi El Kholi, editor of the Egyptian magazine *Al Talia,* a man with an engaging smile, shrewd eyes, and ready wit. It was he who, after the formal closing of the meeting, told us that if we wanted to organize a conference on peace in the Middle East, we should begin by going to Egypt and discussing it with the leaders there.

14

Fouad El Shamali

I had committed myself to preparing for an exhibition in Geneva and I wanted to finish my album on everyday life,* so I went to work as soon as I came back from Berlin. I remember that during this time I questioned myself a great deal on the meaning I gave to the album: I couldn't separate what I would have liked to say about it from what my friends actually did say about it. Thus Giacometti explained his sculpture by simply repeating Sartre's analysis of it, as if it had always been his own; thus Baudelaire reproduced whole pages from Poe, without quotation marks, because they corresponded exactly to what he would have liked to write. There always comes a time when the artist's ideas on his work become inextricably mingled with gratifying things that others have said about it. I talked about this with Maurice Clavel and Edgar Morin, whose questions troubled me.

Once again, however, what was happening in the Sinai

---

*Published in 1971, with a preface by Maurice Clavel and Edgar Morin.

turned me away from myself. In the hope of exhausting Israel by keeping its armed forces mobilized at the borders, Nasser had begun his "war of attrition," and the list of casualties lengthened every day — Israel lost as many soldiers as during the Six-Day War. And the air raids that Israel launched deep into their territory led the Egyptians to ask for help from the Soviets, who were delighted at being invited to go exactly where they wanted to be. All our efforts were in vain, and peace seemed more and more remote.

Yet this was the time when some Swiss friends of mine decided to ask me to take charge of organizing a conference that would bring together at least one Israeli and one Palestinian. Letters of invitation, a list of notables — we were beginning to be used to those preparations. The Israeli would be Saul Friedlander, a historian who was always ready for dialogue; the Palestinian would be Fouad El Shamali, a representative of Al Fatah in Geneva, a passionate militant who wrote poetry under the name of Fouad Khaled. His interest in art and literature enabled him to avoid the political dogmatism enthusiastically embraced by less intelligent propagandists. He didn't agree with me, but he realized that a movement like ours could get at least some of the Palestinian demands accepted by that part of the left which wasn't deliberately anti-Israeli. We saw each other often. He consented to participate in that conference, but first he wanted to go to Beirut to consult with Yasir Arafat. He called me a month later to confirm his participation.

"Have you seen Arafat?" I asked.

"Yes. He agrees with your position."

"A Palestinian state beside the State of Israel?"

"Yes."

"Then why doesn't he say so publicly?"

"He can't."

"Why not?"

"Because the extremists would kill him. But he's authorized me to say it."

"In his name?"

"No."

At the conference in Geneva, Fouad El Shamali spoke immediately after Saul Friedlander.

"I'm not here to take up a challenge," he said. "The only challenge that interests me is to be taken at my word, and I ask to be taken at my word. . . . Although I'm speaking only for myself, I believe I reflect the opinion of members of my generation, the generation that has a memory of the land of Palestine. In twenty years, that memory has become a dream. Twenty years of childhood and adolescence, of apprenticeship, learning, militancy in Arab parties, strikes, street demonstrations for Nasser, against Nasser, for Hussein, against Hussein. . . . For that generation of the dream, the dream appeared precisely in 1957, not marked by powerlessness, but closer to reality than the two lips of a wound are close to each other. And now that dream is not only shaping a people, but also revolutionizing the region. . . . The Palestinians demand that land not only because it is their home, they demand it because it is the dimension they need in order to become wholly themselves again, to fulfill and assert themselves. And when they assert themselves, everything will become possible."

In conclusion, he mentioned the plan of a Palestinian state on the West Bank and in Gaza, but immediately added that he foresaw its creation by no other means than armed struggle.

Saul Friedlander asked to answer.

"As an Israeli," he said, "I would simply like to thank Fouad El Shamali for being here as a Palestinian. It's so rare that we take part in a public discussion together that, for my part, I see this one as a reason for hope. I don't, of course, accept the idea that armed struggle by the Palestinian people is the only way to solve the problem of coexistence with Israel. I would like to add, finally, that although our friend may not know it, many people in Israel are aware of Palestinian national existence. Come to the debates that our hosts will organize in the future, and you'll see that, beyond all our differences, many of us think like you to some extent — and then discussion will surely be possible."

The press greeted that encounter as a significant event. Maybe a small stone actually had fallen from the wall that still separated the Israelis from the Arabs, but the main conclusion I drew was that it was easier for them to understand each other in direct talks than in indirect ones, with their respective supporters acting as intermediaries. Fouad El Shamali thought so too, and he told me how one day in New York an American member of the Palestine Committee had reproached him for associating with us.

"What do you do?" Fouad asked him.

"I'm a law student."

"When will you graduate?"

"Next year."

"How are you going to spend your summer vacation?"

"I don't know yet."

"Then come and join the fedayeen in Jordan."

The student walked away without answering.

"Think of it," Fouad said to me indignantly. "I was the Palestinian, I was the one who struggled, suffered, and hoped, and he peacefully lived in New York, yet he thought he had a right to choose my friends for me!"

We saw him each time he came to Paris, where he was taking medical treatment. We shared political interests with him, of course, but I think there was also personal liking between us.

We usually talked about the Arab–Israeli conflict, sometimes at unreasonable length. He repeated his belief in the future coexistence of two states, side by side, but the time for it hadn't come yet, he said, and meanwhile, out of conviction or fear, he defended the PLO's advocacy of a single secular and democratic state.

By way of answering, I quoted Rabbi Enoch: "Israel's real exile was having learned to bear it."

But Fouad didn't want to hear about the good rabbi's pronouncement, or about inflicting or submitting to exile. One day he became angry and I never saw him again.

Three years later I learned of his death in the newspapers.

They presented him as having been the brains of the Black September organization, and said he had been responsible for various operations, such as the sabotage of gasoline storage tanks in Trieste and the taking of Israeli hostages at the Olympic Games in Munich. In Beirut he was given a state funeral.

Was he a terrorist, my friend Fouad? Maybe. He lived and died in the century of Auschwitz and Hiroshima, of the massacre of Biafrans and the reign of the Gulag. No one had taught him that it sometimes takes more courage to speak to an enemy than to kill him.

For my part, I was brought up with a certain idea of good and evil. A wild hope was passed on to me: the forces of light would always triumph over the forces of darkness, the human race would always move forward. Nazism would be defeated and disappear, the Nazism in whose name two soldiers took hold of me one day and said to my mother, "Tell us where your husband is and your son will be given back to you."

At that time I didn't yet know that darkness would always cut off light, that Nazism had rubbed off on each of us, and that life had lost its absolute value and become only a medium of exchange.

That last idea is repugnant to us, and I think that in a way it was repugnant even to the Nazis. How else can we explain their need to hide their crimes, or to justify them by supposedly scientific theories? When political movements or parties state their aims, I always take them very seriously and try to discern what they are hiding or revealing about the forces of darkness.

15

Operation Eliav —
Early 1970

O ne morning I got a call from Guido Fubini, a lawyer, leader of the Jewish community in Turin and representative of our committee in Italy. He was excited.

"Do you know about Goldmann?"

"What about him?"

"Nasser has invited him to Cairo!"

I didn't share his enthusiasm. Meetings like that should be announced only when they have taken place.

"You don't think it will happen?" Guido asked me.

No, I didn't think it would. And Nahum Goldmann never went to Cairo. The episode made quite a stir at the time: it was said that Golda Meir, who had become prime minister after Levi Eshkol's death, refused to give Goldmann her blessing, and this set off a demonstration by leftist Israeli students.

I was surprised; Goldmann was president of the World Jewish Congress and held three passports — did he need permission from the Israeli government to go to Cairo? He would, of course, need it if he intended to pass as an official representative of Israel in his conversations with Gamal Abdel Nasser.

Nahum Goldmann was always greatly disappointed at not occupying the position in the Jewish state to which he considered himself entitled. His collaborators admired him for his culture and his sense of humor, but the Israelis mistrusted him as they did everyone who claimed to speak in their name but hadn't been with them at the crucial time: at the beginning of June 1967, when the vise of the Arab armies seemed to have closed on Israel, Goldmann was shopping in Paris.

What I knew about him made him seem rather likable to me, but when he received Clara and me in his apartment on the Avenue Montaigne I discovered an aging, perfumed dandy in a scarlet silk dressing gown who spoke to us in a condescending tone. There was a wall between us and that old-style man of distinction.

Now and then I saw him again, however; he had promised us financial help in organizing our first international conference for peace in the Middle East. He would ask me to sit down in a massive armchair, then walk around me like an animal circling its prey, extracting information from me which, I later learned, he used as if he had gotten it firsthand. He wanted to know everything about our contacts in Europe, the United States, and the Arab countries; he was especially interested in the opinions of the German intelligentsia, and he asked me to bring him the letters that Ernst Bloch and Günter Grass had sent us.

He gave only evasive answers to my questions. He seemed to feel that our actions didn't concern him. As for ideas, he was satisfied with his own. He charmed people in order to use them, and he always had a glib tongue when it came to promises. He never kept his promise to help us with our conference. I probably should have offered to let him be its chairman.

Our concerns were not the same, and neither were the considerations that drew us toward Israel. For him, Israel's existence seemed to depend exclusively on the fate of Zionism within Jewish communities throughout the world, whereas I thought of Israel mainly in relation to the four million Israelis working, dreaming of the future, and fighting to live in that state whose creation represented both the end and the fulfillment of Zionism.

Only *Realpolitik* dictated Goldmann's conduct and aims: closer relations with Egypt, which he regarded as the only real power in the Arab world; contacts with the Soviet Union, which had been present in the Middle East since 1956; almost total ignorance and disregard of the Palestinians, who didn't yet represent a force worthy of his interest. His criticisms of the Israeli government were primarily tactical.

I much preferred Golda Meir's "flayed alive" style to the calculated maneuvers of that politician without power. I stopped seeing Goldmann.

I wasn't really surprised when I learned about Golda Meir's refusal to give Goldmann official sanction for a trip to Egypt. I discussed it a few days later with two Egyptian diplomats who were friends of mine.

"Goldmann has an engaging personality," I said, "and he represents one of the most important international Jewish organizations, so a meeting between him and Nasser might have been a step in the right direction. But since you Egyptians are making war against the Israelis, not the Jews, it's the Israelis you should talk with."

"Aren't the Israelis Jews?"

"They're Israeli Jews. It's as if you Egyptians agreed to settle the Palestinian problem with Israel because you and the Palestinians are all Arabs. You know Golda Meir's position: Goldmann is free to go to Egypt whenever he likes, but he can't claim to represent Israel there."

"Who do you think we could have invited? And don't talk about someone like Uri Avnery. Someone on the fringes, even if he's an Israeli, wouldn't make much sense either."

At that time, Uri Avnery was a member of the Knesset, the sole representative of his party. He was also a well-known journalist, the editor of a sensationalistic weekly paper, *Hao-*

lam Hazeh, and a veteran campaigner for Arab–Israeli rapprochement.

I told them that even inside the Israeli establishment there were people who were trusted by the population, yet had views close to ours. I was thinking in particular of Lyova Eliav, who was then general secretary of the ruling Labor Party: he had often taken "dovish" positions, notably in an interview that Clara had published in *Eléments.*

"May we see that interview?" asked one of my Egyptian friends.

I brought it to them at their hotel the next morning. They called me that afternoon.

"This interview is very interesting. We've thought about what you said. We're leaving for Cairo this evening. We'll sound out Nasser and call you if he seems at all interested."

A month later, when I had forgotten that promise — I had been given so many of the same kind! — we were awakened by a phone call from Egypt. It was one of the two diplomats.

"We're interested here," he said, "but we don't want any publicity. We want to be sure that the person we talked about won't be disavowed later."

Following his lead in not mentioning the name, I told him I would go to the place in question as soon as possible to get the necessary assurances, and that I would keep him posted.

I was excited when I hung up. That evening I began getting ready for my trip. I then realized that I didn't have enough money to buy my ticket and that the committee's treasury was empty — we had even had to borrow money to bring out the last issue of *Eléments.* It was Jean Daniel, director of the *Nouvel Observateur,* who paid for my trip, in the name of his newspaper.

As soon as I was in Tel Aviv I met Lyova Eliav at the headquarters of the Labor Party. He was in his shirtsleeves, with his eyes as blue and his smile as timid as ever. He introduced me to two of his collaborators, Misha Harish and Yoram Peri. I asked him in Russian if I could talk to him in front of his friends or if I should wait till we were alone.

"You can talk now," he answered.

I told him the story from the beginning: Goldmann's failure to make his trip to Cairo, my conversation with my Egyptian friends. . . .

"Have you talked to Golda yet?" Eliav interrupted.

"No. I wanted to talk to you first, because you're the person we have in mind."

It seemed to me that he turned pale, then he said, this time in Russian, "You were right, we should have talked about this alone. When Golda said no to Goldmann, it was like a bomb in Israel — if the same thing happened to me, it would be like an *atomic* bomb!" He continued in Hebrew: "Do you want me to call Golda?"

I told him that, if he had no objection, I would rather talk to her first. When I had left him, I called Simcha Dinitz, then Golda Meir's principal private secretary and later Israeli ambassador to the United States. Avi Primor, of the Israeli embassy in Paris, had warmly recommended him to me. Probably notified of my arrival by Primor, Dinitz made an appointment with me for the next day in Jerusalem.

"I'll tell Golda Meir that you want to see her," he said.

That evening I told Clara on the phone that Eliav was afraid Golda might refuse, but that I thought I could convince her.

I had dinner with Reni and Hezi Carmel (he later became the Israeli consul in Los Angeles). I felt uneasy at not being able to tell them anything, but I still thought it would be better to avoid publicity. That night the copies of *Eléments* I had brought with me were stolen from my borrowed Ford, which allowed the Israeli press to announce ironically that someone in Israel had stolen "Marek Halter's elements of peace in the Middle East."

The next day I met Simcha Dinitz and repeated my whole story to him. His eyes smiled at me from behind his glasses. He had a sense of humor, and that comforted me; in politics, people who have no sense of humor belong to a dangerous species.

He asked me to wait while he went to ask Golda Meir if she

would see me. I don't know if I waited fifteen minutes or an hour. The room in which I was sitting — a long teak table, a big map of Israel on the wall — was probably the one where the prime minister's advisers gathered. I was vaguely wondering what I, a painter, was doing there when Dinitz came back. Golda, he said, had good memories of our first meeting. She was waiting for me.

Strong and square, she seemed to be part of the big desk at which she sat. She was smiling. She crushed out her cigarette, stood up, and held out her arms to me.

"I'm glad to see you again."

What a change in her! Two years earlier, I had met a sick old woman who had to be supported and treated gently. Now she was solid as a desert rock, and chain-smoking. I told her I found it strange to see how much the exercise of power and responsibilities — she had been prime minister since 1969 — could change people. We philosophized awhile, then she began asking me questions about my work, the left, and what had brought me to Israel. We spoke Yiddish. She listened without interrupting when I gave her an account, beginning with the Goldmann affair, of why I was there. And I added that even if there was only one chance in a thousand of succeeding, it was worth a try.

"Of course," she said, "I can't ask you to give me any guarantees. Eliav isn't Goldmann. He's one of us, he's part of Israel. But I hope you realize how hard it is for me to start us on an adventure like that without knowing where it may take us."

I answered that Israel had nothing to lose, and everything to gain, by proving its willingness to take any chance for a dialogue. She was surely aware that a large part of Israeli public opinion, and world public opinion, held her personally responsible for the failure of the Goldmann plan.

"Were your two Egyptian friends serious when they talked about Eliav going to Cairo?" she asked insistently.

"Perfectly serious."

She was silent for a moment, then said, "Personally, I have

nothing against it. And, as I told you, Eliav isn't Goldmann. Anything that may help to promote peace is important. Believe me, that's constantly been on my mind ever since I became responsible for this country and all the Jews living in it. But I can't make a commitment all by myself. We have a national-unity government.* It will fall if your plan succeeds. I don't mind that, but I wouldn't want it to fall for nothing. I'd like to be sure we have some chance of succeeding. I'll meet with a few friends in the cabinet. Come back and see me at five o'clock tomorrow afternoon, in my Tel Aviv office." She stood up and held out her hand to me. "Good luck."

"Good luck to you too."

Those twenty-four hours went by very slowly for me. Long before five o'clock I was already wandering around the Kirya, where the government buildings are grouped. I kept going in and out of the café at the corner of Ibn Gvirol and Kaplan. I couldn't sit still. Finally, fifteen minutes early, I went to wait at the door of Golda Meir's office. After twenty minutes I saw two men come out: Dayan and Israel Galili, the *éminence grise* of successive Israeli governments, an expert on conciliation and compromise. Five minutes later Golda Meir received me, smiling.

"My friends agree with me," she said. "We trust you. You have a green light. I ask only one thing of you: report to me directly on what happens. I hope you succeed. For us, for the Arabs, for all of us."

When I left her office I felt as if I were floating on air. I wanted to share the news with someone but I had to keep it a secret. I could talk about it only with Eliav and Clara. Eliav already knew I had permission to carry out my plan. As for Clara, she was jubilant.

"We've won!" she said.

I suddenly realized that we were only at the beginning and that nearly everything still remained to be done. It reminded

*Formed shortly before the Six-Day War, this national-unity government disintegrated in 1970, when the right withdrew from it in the course of the "war of attrition" imposed by Nasser on the Suez Canal.

me of a story by Sholem Aleichem, the famous Yiddish humorist. A matchmaker has spent hours and hours trying to convince a poor peasant that he should have his daughter marry Rothschild's son. He has used all his talent, experience, and persuasiveness, so much of it that the peasant finally consents. "Good," says the matchmaker, "now all I have to do is convince Rothschild."

Doubt was seeping into me. By exploiting the privileged position I had acquired, maybe I was doing nothing but giving illusions to governments. Who was I to ask them to commit themselves only on the basis of my goodwill and my faith in humanity and the peace movement? I felt anxiety at the thought of the disproportion between what I was asking and what I could offer in return. And what did I know about the real political facts here and elsewhere, about the plans and ulterior motives of this or that leader? How would my Egyptian friends react to Golda Meir's answer?

I decided to go back to Paris as soon as possible so that I could make contact with Cairo.

From Paris I was able to call one of my two Egyptian diplomats. He seemed surprised and delighted by the Israeli response. He promised to discuss it with Nasser.

"It's only a matter of setting a date," he said.

He called back a week later to suggest that I come to Cairo and present my idea to Nasser in person.

I left a few days later. My two Egyptian friends met me at the airport and pushed aside the young men who swarmed around me in the hope of buying whatever I might have been able to acquire at the Paris airport.

"Nasser is expecting you in two hours at his home in Manshiyyat Al-Bakri," one of my friends said when we were in the car. "Would you like to stop by the hotel?"

They had reserved a room for me at the Sheraton on the Nile.

"Will I have time?"

"It depends on the traffic."

Meanwhile I was completely captivated by Cairo, which I had never seen before. First of all the light, ocher from having gone through the impalpable dust from the desert; the buildings, heavy as the Pyramids; the numberless crowd, in which the faded blue of djellabas predominated; the clusters of people clinging to the packed streetcars; the immense portrait of Nasser at Midhan El Tahrir Square. We followed the stream of honking cars moving toward the Kasr an-Nil bridge, ran a red light in front of a smiling policeman, and reached the Sheraton on El Giza Street.

In the lobby were German and British businessmen, French tourists, Italian journalists, and sheikhs from the Persian Gulf, wrapped in white silk, who had come for a meeting of the Arab League. Under the windows, the river. I could have spent hours looking at the old boats with heavy white sails that had been hastily tied up, the bales of white cotton piled on the bridges, the ballet of men in white caftans and white turbans balancing themselves at the ends of their long oars. All those whites, each different from the others, were reflected in the oily gray water of the broad, powerful river flowing northward.

I couldn't believe I was there. In my memories from my Polish Jewish childhood, Egypt was the country where the Hebrews had lived in slavery, as described in the Passover story. It was where they had built pyramids, and here, on the banks of the Nile, they had freed themselves and left for the Promised Land. Now there were pyramids at the end of the street.

Except for his broad shoulders, Nasser reminded me of a pyramid: his head narrowed at the top and he stood with his feet wide apart. He shook hands with me warmly but I thought I saw a glint of mistrust in his eyes.

I don't know if he could speak English or even understand it. He spoke to me in Arabic and a young man translated.

"Why are you doing this?" he asked.

"What do you mean by 'this'?"

"Trying to promote peace in the Middle East. You live in Paris, you're a painter, you write — so why? Have you ever had a show of your paintings in Cairo?"

"No, never."

"You must have one. Come back."

"Later."

"Do you seriously believe it's possible to talk about peace with Israel?"

I tried to explain about Israel and the different forces at work inside it. The desire for peace . . .

"What about the Palestinians?" he interrupted.

After half an hour his smile became more natural.

"You're an artist," he said, and stood up. "I'm glad to have met you. Come back to Cairo."

That evening, while we stood on the balcony of my hotel room to avoid indiscreet ears, my friends, obviously excited, told me that Nasser had consented to Operation Eliav.

I slept very little that night, and in the morning I took a plane to Paris. I was eager to announce the news to Golda.

A week later I got a phone call asking me to bring Lyova Eliav to Cairo on the seventh of August.

At last something had "clicked" and the plan was really working. Even Jean Daniel, usually so hard to rouse to enthusiasm, seemed deeply moved.

But early in August another call from Cairo asked me to postpone the meeting. Then there was silence. Out of patience, I asked Jean Daniel to intervene by going to see Esmat Abdel Meguid, the Egyptian ambassador to France. Meguid knew about our negotiations; he felt that Eliav was the person best qualified to carry out the mission and that it would eventually be successful, but that we had to be patient: Egypt still had many internal problems to solve. A new date was set, early in September.

Once again a call from Cairo asked me to postpone the meeting: Nasser was going to the Soviet Union — a trip that remained secret a long time.

In September 1970, King Hussein of Jordan decided to suppress the Palestinian organizations that exercised dictatorial power in his kingdom. The resulting civil war lasted several weeks and the number of Palestinian deaths was somewhere between fifty thousand and two hundred thousand (estimates vary with sources). These events, called Black September by the PLO, delayed us again. This time Nasser was occupied with reconciling Hussein and Arafat in the name of Arab unity. A visit to Egypt by an Israeli had become hard to imagine in such an atmosphere. Wait. I stayed in constant contact with Cairo, but the limits of our plan were cruelly marked by the need to wait for events beyond our control to turn in our favor.

Finally Jean Lacouture called me.

"Nasser is dead. I'm going to Cairo."

"Nasser is dead?"

I wanted to ask him when and how, but he had already hung up.

We had to start over again from zero.

16

"Where will you ride to, sir?"

"You mustn't give up," Jean Daniel told me.

We were in his office at the *Nouvel Observateur*. With his hand in front of his mouth, his feet on the desk, a faraway look in his eyes, his voice soft and his tone neutral, he had, as usual, put between us that barrier which had to be broken through each time. I asked him leading questions that gradually made him come out from behind his reserve and take a position. He finally took his hand away from his mouth and his feet off the desk; his voice became animated, his eyes began to shine. It's always the same with him: at first he irritates me, then I like him.

"I can understand why you're discouraged," he went on. "You thought you were just about to succeed, and then you failed."

He had once had personal experience of an attempt to bring Castro and Kennedy closer together — and its failure. In 1963 he was in Havana with Castro, who was ready to meet with Kennedy, when they learned that the American president had been assassinated. Another time, King Hassan II of Morocco, during a visit to Paris, sent word to him that he had worked out a peace plan for the Middle East and would like to discuss it with him and me: he thought that an independent group like the one that published *Eléments* might take it over and promote it. The king, staying at the Hôtel Crillon, offered to make an appointment with us. He did, but Jean Daniel was unable to get in touch with me, so he went to the appointment alone and some time later I learned, like everyone else, that he had gone to Morocco with Nahum Goldmann.

That enterprise — which I hardly believed in, since Hassan II was only on the fringes of inter-Arab politics at that time, and Goldmann was only on the fringes of Israeli politics — left me upset for a long time. I was, after all, Jean Daniel's friend and kept no secrets from him. In his book *Le Temps qui reste*, he explained his trip by the possibility that Arafat, who had told King Hassan he was willing to have an ultrasecret meeting with Goldmann in Rabat, might be present in Algiers. But Arafat wasn't there.

"I'm not discouraged," I told Jean Daniel, "but one of the basic principles of my upbringing has been placed in question: the power of the will, the power of ideas."

Jean smiled. I went on:

"If people who have the same concept of the world, or claim they do, even if they're citizens of two countries in conflict — if people like that can't meet and talk with each other, it implies the collapse of everything I believe in. We've been unable to bring the Israeli left and the Arab left together, and usually we haven't even tried. That's where we, the left, have failed."

That left exasperated me. It wallowed in its revolutionary logorrhea instead of thinking about assuming its responsibilities, and, before the indulgent eyes of the media, we served as its alibi. Wouldn't it be better to refuse to play the game, to reject meaningless words and concepts without reality?

And on top of everything else, I had my own personal problem. Being a painter gave me my social identity. I was born in Poland, I had lived in the Soviet Union and Argentina, I was French, I spoke Uzbek and Yiddish — in short, I was exotic enough for society to see me as an artist in accordance with its imagery. But had anyone ever seen a painter get involved in politics?

I was bitter and disappointed. I wanted to go away, like the hero of a Kafka story who says, more or less, "I ordered that my horse be brought to me. The servant didn't understand me, so I went to the stable alone and saddled and mounted my horse. I heard a trumpet call in the distance. I asked the servant what it meant. He didn't know, he had heard nothing. In front of the door he stopped me and asked, 'Where will you ride to, sir?' 'I don't know,' I said. 'I only want to leave here, go away from here. That's the only way I can reach my goal.' 'Do you know your goal?' he asked. 'Yes,' I answered, 'I've already told you. Going away from here, that's my goal.' "

I had discovered that passage, which I have quoted here from memory, in Argentina, when I had left Paris and the Ecole des Beaux-Arts and gone off to find out what the world was all about. I was eighteen. The pampas were bigger than the Kazakh steppes and the Andes were higher than the Pamirs. I learned Spanish, found friends, and began showing my art. I quickly became fascinated by that new country whose problems were close to me. Fascist repression was then beginning in some Latin American countries, and some of us proposed creating a battalion of solidarity, a kind of intervention force that could always be mobilized.

In 1954 the American Marines landed in Guatemala to prevent the liberal President Arbenz from nationalizing enterprises belonging to large American corporations. Our plan then began to be taken seriously. Luis Franco, an Argentine writer who had been a friend of Trotsky, invited us to Belen, in the northern part of the country, to discuss it. We spent a week with him, but we were separated from him by personal differences and factional quarrels, and we had to give up the idea of our battalion. I realized how naive our plan was, and what a frightening gap there was between the power of the American Marines and that of our argumentative little group, but, to me, ideas were stronger than anything else, provided you tried to materialize them. I was revolted — and I still am — by leftist intellectuals' inability to go beyond abstractions and confront reality. They seem to feel that all they have to do is avoid recognizing that gap between powers.

Be that as it may, I left Luis Franco's big estate, our vehement discussions, and the nostalgic songs of the gauchos. I boarded a bus, intending to go to Tucumán, and from there to Buenos Aires. As the dilapidated old bus rattled across the pampa, it raised a cloud of sand and cactus thorns and left behind a long trail of dust that briefly relieved the emptiness of the landscape. I felt tired and a little dead, as I always do after the failure of a project close to my heart. I would have liked to share my disappointment and sadness, but the two Indians in front of me seemed to have been looking at the horizon since the beginning of time and I didn't dare to disturb them.

That night I found myself in Catamarca. In my haste to leave Belen, I had taken the wrong bus. Catamarca is a ghost town at the end of the pampa: drab houses and windowless facades, lonely streets in which sandy whirlwinds chase the few people who walk along them. I was gripped by a murky, painful anxiety that I can still feel now, as strongly as ever.

In the darkness, a man offered to take me to a hotel. I went with him. He led me to a room filled with iron beds, pointed one of them out to me, asked me for a peso, and disappeared. Everyone was asleep. Faceless shapes, unequivocally foreign. No one knew I was there, except for a man in one of the beds next to mine, who interrupted his snoring long enough to tell me to wake him at seven-thirty, then immediately went back to sleep.

I lay down fully dressed on a colorless blanket. I was alone. No one wanted my love, my friendship, my hope. I felt like shouting, "Wake up, all of you! How can you sleep when people are killing people all over the world? We're all survivors! Wake up!" I didn't do it, of course. Desperate as a child in the dark, I cried a long time.

In the morning, sunlight gave faces to the shadows. I recognized one of the Indians from the bus. He introduced me to a truck driver from Tucumán. I reached Buenos Aires.

A week later, a freighter named the *Lamartine* took me back to France.

"Where will you ride to?"

I don't know. I only want to get away from here.

This time, as when I was eighteen, I had only one idea in mind: to leave, to get away from there. Jean Daniel didn't find the words that might have warded off my disenchantment. So I left.

I found myself in the United States. But wherever I went, I couldn't help wondering if I shouldn't stick to my painting. Art for artists, politics for politicians. Society celebrates our dreams, visions, and obsessions on the walls of its museums and in the catalogues of its exhibitions, provided we stay where we belong and don't try to disrupt the order of things.

17

The Artist
and Politics

Art and politics. Having learned English at Harvard, where
I was a guest, I was sometimes asked to conduct debates on that theme. I like American students' unending curiosity, which Europeans regard as incurable naïveté, though
it is actually a sign of great open-mindedness. How, the students asked me, can the artist be satisfied with bearing wit-
ness to his time? Doesn't looking at society in a certain way
necessarily lead to political action? Even though we raised more
questions than we answered, I valued those discussions, and
the students' tirelessly repeated "Why?" finally made me try
to situate myself in the world I lived in.

"Why," they asked me, for example, "did you take up political action?"

The reason, I answered, might lie in my past, but, aside
from that, political action was part of my idea of the artist's
role in society.

"Aren't your drawings enough for you?"

No, my drawings weren't enough for me. If art alone couldn't change the world, maybe it could contribute to changing the consciousness and impulses of people who could change the world. That was why I went on painting and writing.

In May 1968 there had been much talk of Marcuse. He was one of the philosophers of the "Frankfurt School." Soon after the Nazis came to power, he emigrated to the United States. Analyzing the economic and technological development of industrial societies in the light of Marxism, he was led to advocate replacing the proletariat with "explosive antisocial elements" (with whom students liked to identify themselves) in a new, nonrepressive society. I remembered being struck by one of his sentences: "The truth of art lies in its power to break the monopoly of established reality." As soon as I could, I went to see him at the university where he taught, in La Jolla, California.

Chekhov tells somewhere how he had long dreamed of meeting an extraordinary uncle he had heard about since childhood. When he had become a village schoolteacher he learned that his uncle was coming to visit him. He was feverishly excited in the days that separated him from that visit. Finally his uncle was there. A handsome man in spite of his advanced age, he made a strong impression on Chekhov. But something bothered him: his uncle wore a pearl attached to the silk scarf around his neck. That pearl obsessed him all through their conversation and he couldn't take his eyes off it; he felt that somehow it must play a part in his uncle's life. The discussion turned to the abolition of serfdom: Chekhov was for it, his uncle was against it. And that evening Chekhov didn't even ask his extraordinary uncle to stay for dinner.

Like Chekhov's uncle, Marcuse was finally in front of me. He spoke to me in French. He tilted his gray-haired head and emphasized his words with gestures. When a question made him uncomfortable, he would take a blunt pencil in his freckled hands and nervously toy with it, clutching it as if it were saving him from drowning. That pencil fascinated me as the pearl had fascinated Chekhov. And in fact it is the main thing I remember about my meeting with Marcuse.

The French student movement of May 1968, which claimed him as one of its inspirations, had taken him by surprise but reinforced his idea of the philosopher's role in society: to conceptualize reality and avoid action. To him, action was suspect, even impure. He was irritated by the way Sartre took sides. He distrusted intellectuals who were always ready to go out into the streets. He preferred the force of ideas to human commitment.

He had been invited to Jerusalem by the Van Leer Institute and was tempted to accept, because the Arab–Israeli conflict interested him greatly — to the point of causing friction between him and his wife, who was resolutely anti-Israeli — but he was upset at being invited by the establishment. I suggested that he get himself invited by Siah, the new Israeli left.

"But then shouldn't I also go to the Arab countries?" he asked.

I promised to see to it that the magazine *Al Talia* would ask him to come to Egypt. He was delighted. "Although," he said with a timid smile, "that probably won't resolve the Arab–Israeli conflict."

"If you can make both sides take an interest in the same problems, it may contribute to bringing them closer together."

"Have you ever shown your paintings in both Israel and an Arab country?"

"Yes, in Tel Aviv and Beirut."

"Were you criticized for it?"

I was embarrassed to realize that Marcuse was a soft, comfort-loving old man afraid to leave his library: going out meant running the risk of bumping against the sharp corners of everyday people and things.

The artist's involvement was what interested me. It was precisely what didn't interest him. It seemed sinful to him. He didn't want to talk about it. But while there is little I can do simply as an artist, as an artist recognized here and there I have a certain power of action. My concierge and I have the same political ideas; no newspaper will publish her letters, but when I write one it is printed. That makes me my concierge's spokesman. Society grants me privileges of that kind and I can, of course, exploit them to become rich and famous, buy myself a second car or a house in the country. Can I put them into the service of a political cause? If so, how?

At the inauguration of the House of Culture in Amiens — the city of Jules Verne, where one of the most beautiful of all Gothic cathedrals stands — I told André Malraux, the minister of culture, who had come to see my exhibition, that I was sorry that recognized artists felt they had to give the government their unconditional support, which probably made them lose the influence they had acquired in society. The complex mechanism of his tics suddenly accelerated, deforming his face. He answered that when the government took some of an artist's ideas as its own, he should be neither afraid nor ashamed to support it, and that it was too easy to keep one's hands clean and expound abstract theories without doing anything to put them into practice. As for the influence we might have on events, he added, it was stronger when it could be exerted through the government.

Noam Chomsky thought exactly the opposite. We discussed it one day at Chez Dreyfus, the French restaurant in Cambridge where we sometimes went for lunch. Those who didn't know him often took him for a student, with his shy look, the youthfulness of his smile, and his habit of always carrying around a stack of books and papers.

In his view, intellectuals and artists should take advantage of their privileged situation to defend the ideals they valued, even if it seemed that they couldn't be realized in the near future. To him, that was realism.

"But," I objected, "that's just another way of not facing reality, of ignoring urgent everyday problems for the sake of a faraway goal."

He saw no contradiction. He told me that socialist binationalism was the ideal solution he proposed for the Middle East. It was a faraway goal, of course, but that didn't stop him from taking part in the everyday struggle.

"Besides," he said, "for a long time I've been supporting what you're doing as well as I can."

I was still amazed by Noam's extraordinary accumulation of knowledge. He had an answer to everything. His reasoning was logical and awesomely coherent, as if he had a key that could open all doors. Yet something bothered me: to make his key work, he had to reduce all types of societies — capitalist, socialist, fascist — to a single mechanism. Unlike me, he didn't make allowance for chance, the accidental, the personal.

Art and politics. . . . After all my questions, I, the artist, found only my old feeling of solitude and powerlessness. Should I resign myself to it?

That day, when I had left Chomsky and was walking across Harvard Square, a woman student came up to me.

"What are you doing now?" she asked.

"I'm going home."

"Would you like to take me to a movie? This is my birthday."

"How old are you today?"

"Twenty-two."

I wished her a happy birthday and added, "But I have to go home."

She looked at me with her blue eyes, disappointed and amused.

"Too bad. . . . So long."

I couldn't help watching her disappear into the crowd of students going into the movie theater on the square. Why had I turned down her invitation, when ordinarily I liked to see where chance would take me? Because I had to go and see Rashid Hussein in New York, to discuss an Israeli–Palestinian meeting that wouldn't come off. One more. And what about my painting? Wouldn't I have been better off in my studio? It would feel so good to smell my paints, dive into ink, and forget time. . . .

But an hour later I was on a plane to New York.

18

Does Peace Come
by Way of Rome?

All action is made of hope and despair. For some, the two
counterbalance each other, which enables them to trot
placidly through life. As for me, I am like those beasts of Hi-
eronymus Bosch that, having been plunged into a pit full of
phantasms and temptations, keep climbing toward the light,
clutching at all branches of hope. So a few weeks later, in
Israel, I began believing again, thanks to the enthusiasm of
two young kibbutzniks: Ran Cohen, of Kibbutz Gan Shmuel,
now a member of the Knesset, and Yossi Amitai, of Kibbutz
Gvulot, now a professor of history at Tel Aviv University.

The torrid south wind known as the khamsin overwhelmed
the landscape, and the fan in Ran's room made a lot of noise
for nothing.

"You have to keep trying," Yossi told me. "You're lucky
enough to have all those contacts. We have to meet with the
Palestinians. There's no other way to settle our differences."

"Maybe they'd rather talk to Dayan," Ran said with one of
his bright smiles.

He was probably right. Moshe Dayan represented power; we represented only ideas and, at most, part of public opinion. But, little by little, we finally convinced each other of a need to organize an Arab–Israeli conference. So that the Arab intellectuals could avoid being alone with the Israelis, we would also invite about a hundred eminent people from all over the world, who would provide reassurance and serve as a buffer. We were thinking of people like Sartre, Günter Grass, Heinrich Böll, Noam Chomsky, Norman Mailer. Ran's and Yossi's enthusiasm was so contagious that by the end of the day we had practically eliminated all problems.

The next day I went to Yitzhak Ben-Aharon at Histadrut and presented our conference to him as an obvious solution whose success could almost be taken for granted.

I flew back to Paris with the plan we had prepared and the list of eminent people we intended to invite.

"Are you sure they'll all come?" my Arab friends asked me.

I ventured to answer yes. They also asked me if I had notified Lotfi El Kholi; I had. Now all we had to do was wait for things to come back to the surface after their usual slow underground movement.

"A moment given by chance," say the Chinese, "is better than a chosen moment." Maybe so; in any case, at that moment I got a call from the Egyptian embassy: "Will you receive a delegation led by Khaled Mohieddin, one of Nasser's companions?"

The discussion was perfectly friendly. Mohieddin knew about our plan, and the Egyptian Peace Movement had a similar one; why shouldn't we work together in organizing a great international conference for peace and justice in the Middle East?

Mohieddin had a round head and a jovial face. He seemed glad to be with us. He kept eating grapes, carefully removing their seeds, and rubbed his hands together after each of his sentences. He accepted all our conditions: participation of an Israeli delegation and a Palestinian delegation, democratic rules, shared responsibility for organizing the conference. I had the impression that he had expected us to be more difficult.

I immediately sent all our friends a detailed account of that meeting and published an article in *Le Monde* (April 2, 1971) urging support for the idea of a Middle East peace conference in which Israelis and Arabs would take part. Then we learned that a preparatory meeting had been scheduled for a month later, in Rome. Mohieddin had sent out the invitations without even consulting us about the date.

Rome really isn't a good city for organizing political meetings. It was a beautiful day, and the Piazza Minerva, where my hotel was located, was all colors and movement. The newspaper seller opposite the hotel also sold flowers. A dark-haired young woman was buying roses and I felt like asking her to go with me to the Piazza Navona. The Arab–Israeli conflict seemed remote.

No one from Paris had been able to come with me. Guido Fubini was to join me in Turin and I had an appointment in the Hotel Minerva with Aldo Zargani, a high official in Italian national television, whom I didn't yet know. I had come two days early to make contact with various political leaders.

"*C'è un signore che la cerca*," the doorman told me.

It was Aldo Zargani, a thin, exuberant man with a little goatee and big, lively dark eyes. He hugged me and said he was at my disposal. He began by summing up the situation. Several delegates had already arrived, most of them either Communists or affiliated with organizations close to the Communist Party. The socialist far left was also very active. Its representative, Luzzatto, was always at the Casa della Cultura, where the meeting was to be held.

"He doesn't like you at all!" Aldo warned me.

"But he doesn't know me."

"There's a rumor in Rome that you'll try to sabotage the conference."

I was dumbfounded at the idea that anyone could think *I* might sabotage that conference. But maybe some of the delegates had decided to turn it into nothing but an outlet for their propaganda — if so, they surely considered me a first-class

nuisance. We would see. . . . Meanwhile I had to meet Riccardo Lombardi, formerly head of the anti-Mussolini resistance and an outstanding leader of the Socialist Party. While
Aldo was making the appointment, I called the film director
Bernardo Bertolucci: I had promised a group of Africans to
bring them one of my paintings for an auction; the money
from the sale was to be used for buying food. The writer Carlo
Levi had organized the auction.

Unable to get either Bertolucci or Levi on the phone, I left
the painting at the hotel when Aldo and I set off for the headquarters of the Socialist Party, where Lombardi was waiting
for us.

"Long ago, in the second century A.D., there were about
fifteen thousand Jews in Rome," Aldo told me on the way.
"They were organized into congregations, each with its own
school, synagogue, and community services. Two of those
synagogues were in the Trastevere, which used to be a vacant
piece of land on the right bank of the Tiber. Two centuries
earlier, Emperor Augustus had cleared out its prostitutes and
robbers and made it the fourteenth district of Rome." He
laughed. "Have you seen Titus's triumphal arch? No? You
should see it, because it's encouraging: the world's greatest
empire took pride in having put down the revolt of the little
Jewish people, and to commemorate that victory it built a
monument covered with all the conquered enemy's symbols,
including the seven-branched candlestick! It's not always necessary to win battles. . . ."

Walking along the streets of Rome with Aldo Zargani was
an adventure. He knew everything, down to the smallest story
of the smallest stone in the smallest street, and he liked to tell
about it. His anecdotes were often bloody, and punctuated
with laughter. As seen by Aldo, history was only a series of
jokes. Now and then it occurs to me that he might be right. If
you look at events from a distance . . .

On the Via del Corso, Lombardi, a tall, thin aristocratic-
looking baronet, was waiting for us in front of the building in
which the Socialist Party had its headquarters. He received us

under its red flags as if he were on the steps of his ancestral castle. We went up to his office, making our way through a crowd of militants who kept stopping him.

"Do you know that you're greatly feared here?" he asked me.

"Aldo told me that, but I don't understand why."

"Some people think you're a leftist, others think you're a Zionist."

"What about you?"

"I'm walking with you," he said, laughing.

In one day, Aldo took me to the offices of all the political parties and introduced me to the editorial staffs of their newspapers. I was reassured: when I faced the intransigent Communists and Arabs the next day, I wouldn't be alone!

In the meantime, Aldo and I decided to stop by the Casa della Cultura and see which way the wind was blowing. So many people were there, and they were having such passionate discussions, that it was as if the meeting had already begun. Romeh Chandra, the Indian minister, passed by us without greeting us; the Italian Luzzatto ducked into an adjoining room as soon as he saw me; Khaled Mohieddin, unable to avoid me, threw his arms around me, greeting me in the Arab manner.

"The meeting doesn't begin till tomorrow," he said.

"I know. I just wanted to know if things were going well."

"They're going very well," he told me, showing me a list. "Most of the delegates have already arrived."

I asked him who those people were; their names meant nothing to me.

"They represent organizations in touch with the Peace Movement."

I felt relieved when I was back in the crowd on the Via del Corso. Aldo walked beside me in silence. The balmy Roman evening was alive with overheard laughter and snatches of conversation. It was hard for me to accept all the clearly shown hostility I had just experienced. With my great need to feel liked, would I be able to bear that climate? Would I succeed in getting our ideas across?

At that same time, my friends Ran Cohen, of Kibbutz Gan Shmuel, and Amos Oz, of Hulda, had been pressed into service again; in Beirut, maybe Ghassan Kanafani and Bassam Abu Sharif were sitting under the portrait of Lenin and planning another terrorist action. And here in Rome, I would soon be trying to affect their future by working with people whose concerns were foreign to me. Wasn't it all absurd and useless?

It took Aldo's good humor to revive my fighting spirit. If we were able to bring Israelis and Palestinians together, which I couldn't resign myself to regarding as impossible, wouldn't we be saving human lives? Wouldn't we be speeding up history a little? After all, it was the Mediterranean Conference in Florence, organized by Giorgio La Pira, that had brought about the first contacts between the French and the Algerian National Liberation Front, which led to peace in Algeria a year later.

I made a few more phone calls, including one to Umberto Terracini, one of the outstanding leaders of the Communist Party and a descendant of an old Italian Jewish family, who promised to support us. Then Aldo and I went to the Piperno, the restaurant I liked so much in the old Jewish quarter, in the shadow of the Colosseum. The stones were softly illuminated by light from the old streetlamps and the high sculpted windows. There was no noise, no cars. For a time I forgot the conference, Mohieddin, Luzzatto, and the Casa della Cultura.

Not for long. Soon after I returned to the hotel — it was past midnight — a call from Uri Avnery, in Tel Aviv, plunged me back into reality. He wanted to know how the conference was shaping up. He firmly believed in it and, with unabashed optimism, already saw himself having discussions with the Arab delegates. I told him bluntly that nothing was sure, that most of the delegates saw the conference only as another way of showing support for the Arab nations, that they didn't regard a meeting between Arabs and Israelis as indispensable, and that we couldn't even be certain of having an Israeli delegate at the second preparatory meeting. Poor Uri. . . . Maybe I was wrong to be so pessimistic. The first meeting, after all, wouldn't begin till the next day.

I got up early. At the Casa della Cultura dozens and dozens of delegates, in groups and ragged clusters, filled the rooms and halls with their gesticulations and polyglot conversations.

"The whole Italian Parliament is here!" Aldo said to me. "And look who else is here," he added, pointing toward the ceiling.

I looked up. There were Stars of David all over the ceiling! Although the Casa della Cultura was an institution with strong Communist leanings, it had been set up in a former Jewish community house.

Finally Khaled Mohieddin presented the agenda of the meeting. I spoke immediately after him and tried to be as clear as possible. I told about our initial plan, my discussion with Mohieddin, and our decision to organize the conference together. I said that our main objective was to make possible a meeting among representatives of Israel, Arab countries, and Palestinian organizations. I also said that we would have no chance of succeeding unless we limited the conference to political, intellectual, and trade-union groups in favor of that objective.

Giancarlo Pajetta, secretary of the Central Committee of the Italian Communist Party, was the first to attack me. He maintained that even people who didn't favor Arab–Israeli dialogue should be able to take part in the conference if they wanted to.

"When I take a train to Naples," he said, "I don't demand that the other passengers all go there too; they're free to get off at whatever stations they want, but we'll at least have traveled awhile together."

He seemed delighted with his image. I had to answer that the conference was not a train on which anyone was entitled to go anywhere as long as he paid for his ticket. We had to decide on our destination, our goal, before convening the conference, if we didn't want to fall into disorder and failure once again. For us, who represented no government, the goal could only be a meeting between progressive Israeli and Arab forces.

I immediately felt the atmosphere become heavier.

"We must first make sure of Palestinian participation," said Maxime Rodinson, "because the Israelis will come in any case."

"I agree: Palestinian participation is essential," I answered. "But we still mustn't neglect the Israelis. The Palestinians will have to carry on a dialogue with them, not with us."

"We can't force Palestinians to sit down with Israelis, even progressive ones," Chandra said brusquely. "The conference must begin by demanding that Israel give back the occupied Arab territories. That's the first condition for any solution of the conflict."

A Soviet delegate spoke in favor of what Chandra had said, stigmatizing those — he gestured in my direction — who tried to turn the conference away from its proper goal. He launched into a long speech, but I had stopped listening.

The air in the room was blue with cigarette smoke. To my right, the stiffly dignified Syrians showed nothing of their feelings. The thin-faced Yugoslavian delegate nodded his little head. The two Lebanese Communists were hurriedly looking through a copy of *Eléments* that I had given them before the meeting began. I was so far away. . . .

That night I dreamed, which I seldom do, and for once I remembered my dream exactly. I was alone on a yellow Middle Eastern beach. On the translucent blue water of the bay, dozens of galleys, each rowed by a hundred men, were towing tugboats with smoke rising from their stacks. I wanted to leave the beach, but it was enclosed by an unbroken chain of steep mountains. As I vainly looked for a way out, I was seized with panic. I then noticed a wooden house perched at the top of a cliff. Behind one of its closed windows were two women whose faces I could hardly make out. They were pointing to something and gesticulating. I looked in the direction they were indicating and saw a big green rope. I was about to climb up it when I saw a door. I opened it and found myself in a tower, at the foot of a spiral staircase. I sang and danced as I went up it. The walls and steps were white, and the steps were decorated with flowers painted in delicate colors. I passed an Arab wearing a djellaba and a turban. He was painting the flowers; above him, the cement walls and steps were gray and bare. The staircase ended at a door, behind which was a long, gloomy hall lined with wooden doors. I opened some of them and found only empty rooms. Fear began rising inside me. I was about to open another door when I woke up.

I felt a hard knot in my stomach, and I was under the influence of that dream for a long time. I had to call Paris, call Khaled, find out about my return flight, stop by the offices of *Il Manifesto* (the newspaper of the dissident Communists), and call Lombardi. It seemed impossible for me to do all that. I was too weary. I clearly remember the anguish of that morning, when it seemed to me that I could feel time flowing drop by drop and swelling the ball in my chest that made it hard for me to breathe.

It was a beautiful day. American tourists, with their cameras, were already invading the Piazza della Minerva. I stood looking out a window, watching the shadows of buildings slowly moving on the pavement of the square. Even though the two big bay windows were wide open, the room smelled musty. I thought of Venice. A sentence from André Malraux's *Man's Fate* came into my mind: "He had become used to the idea of death, but he could not bear its smell." Was it still the idea of death that kept me always on the go? I had to make those phone calls. Shadows in the square. Why was I involved in politics? Ambition? A woman once came up to me at a party and asked me with a venomous smile if my political activism helped me to sell my paintings — it happened that an Antwerp diamond merchant had just changed his mind when he was about to buy two large paintings from me, because he had read an interview of me and didn't want his money to be used for stirring up revolutions. At most, it is acceptable for an artist to sign a press release or an appeal to be published in the *New York Review of Books* and sanctioned by Nobel Prize laureates. The rest of the time he is expected to float above reality and wait in solitude for a visit from his muse. After all, maybe I was on the wrong track; maybe painting, in which I at least felt at home, would better enable me to influence events. I didn't know. And I felt paralyzed as time kept passing without bringing me any understanding. Of course I had to call Khaled. I had to shake off my lethargy. But what an effort it took to pick up the receiver and dial the number! And what a relief when a voice told me that Mr. Mohieddin wasn't there!

I hung up, packed my suitcase, and took the next flight to Paris.

Resuming my work habits made me feel more like myself again. I wrote an account of the meeting in Rome for our friends everywhere. I began painting again. Ten days later, on May 7, I read a brief article in *Le Monde* and realized that it would set off disagreeable reactions. Under the headline "Arab and Israeli Delegations at a Peace Conference?" it described the preparatory meeting in Rome and, referring to my article of April 2, in which I proposed such a peace conference, it said that "the participants accepted the proposal of the International Committee for Peace in the Middle East to invite to the conference a large Israeli delegation and representatives of the Palestinian organizations."

It was an accurate report. But two days later its accuracy was denied by an official statement from the Peace Movement. The meeting, the statement said, was convened by Khaled Mohieddin, and its goal was to bring peace and justice to the Middle East by having the Israelis withdraw from the occupied territories and recognize the legitimate rights of the Palestinians.

So the dark predictions that had been made to me seemed to be coming true: political forces were hijacking our conference. I was no match for them.

And my exhibition didn't seem to be going much better. Meanwhile our account of the meeting in Rome had been sent out and our friends were getting in touch with us. I was unable to concentrate on my painting. I had to answer the phone and give endless explanations. Among all those calls there was one from Pierre Mendès-France. That man who kept power in France for only seven months, 1954–55, was a prime example of a politician who did not compromise with morality. It was he who negotiated the independence of Tunisia and put an end to the French military presence in Vietnam — where it was replaced by the Americans. In 1969 his prestige was still intact. He wanted to see me.

19

Mendès-France's "Little Plot"

I saw Pierre Mendès-France for the first time in 1969, on the evening of the presidential election in which he had campaigned. I was visiting friends, and he came in just as the results of the voting were being given on television. He forced himself to smile, a little awkwardly, as though to say he was sorry for having caused all that hullabaloo. He reminded me of a photograph my mother had cut out of a newspaper, showing him in Parliament after being defeated in a vote of confidence: he was sitting down, with that same surprised look and apologetic smile, while people standing behind him and above him were bustling and gesticulating. He really looked as if he were from another world. My mother saw the whole Jewish tragedy in his face; I saw the tragedy of solitude, without being sure it wasn't the same thing.

I saw him again at the cocktail party given for the publication of Jean Lacouture's book on Nasser. Jean introduced me to him as someone who had friends on both sides and could therefore organize a trip to both Israel and the Arab countries. That was the beginning of what he called "our little plot."

Actually, the idea was only to take advantage of the respect that both sides had for him and make a tour of the battlefield countries with him — we were still in search of an opportunity or a pretext for bringing Israelis and Arabs to talk to each other, and we hoped that discussions carried on by Mendès-France with the leaders of both sides would make a common denominator appear.

We notified Israelis and Arabs, beginning with the Israeli and Egyptian ambassadors in France, then I described our plan to Adel Amer, head of the French office of the Arab League, an intelligent, courteous diplomat, level-headed and open-minded in spite of his startling statements. He said he would inform Mahmud Riad, head of the Arab League in Cairo. While we waited for answers, we carefully made preparations for the trip. Lacouture, Mendès-France, and I met nearly every week.

In Mendès-France's book-lined office on the Rue du Conseiller-Collingnon, I enjoyed following conversations between him and Lacouture, a tireless perennial adolescent, always ready to become enthusiastic over an idea and make vast plans. Mendès-France, calm and thoughtful, always gathered information before making suggestions. He was still recovering from an illness and seemed very weak, but his listeners forgot his pallor and drawn features as soon as he began talking; they were captivated by the charm of his voice as much as by the intelligence of his words.

We received answers form Israel and Egypt on the same day and couldn't help regarding it as a favorable sign. The Arabs and Israelis were willing to receive Mendès-France. He was to go to Cairo, Beirut, Damascus, and Amman, and then to Jerusalem. If necessary, he would go back to Cairo after his stay in Israel. Lacouture and I would travel with him.

He met with Golda Meir, who had come to Paris for a meeting of the Socialist International, and with Adel Amer the next day. A time was set: June (1971). I don't know who talked about our plan, but a newspaper learned of it and said ironically in a headline, "Mendès-France becomes the Cairo courier."

Things had evidently gotten off to too good a start, because Mendès-France soon became sick again. We put off the trip till autumn, but at the end of the summer he was still in bed and the doctors said he should not travel.

Yet it was during this time that he began to take a passionate interest in the Arab–Israeli conflict, sincerely believing that he could succeed where everyone else had failed: in bringing the Israelis and Palestinians together.

I later introduced him to some of them: Azedin Kalak, head of the PLO in France; Issam Sartawi, Yasir Arafat's adviser and roving ambassador; and many others.

Pierre Mendès-France — his certainties irritated me, his determination to give everyone lessons tried my patience, and his pride tempered by aggressive humility exasperated me, but I liked that man who reverently kept family documents in a chest; his family had come to Bordeaux in 1492, when the Jews were expelled from Spain and Portugal.

We saw him often, at first in our apartment, then in his, when the state of his health no longer allowed him to climb our five flights of stairs.

Airplanes, exhibitions, hotels, conference rooms, streets, taxis, phones. . . . So many names, so many cities, so many faces. . . . With my drawing, my painting, and one meeting after another, my life became so hectic that I began dreaming of time again, dreaming, for example, that I measured it with my footsteps, alone in a landscape that seemed to be a desert.

I have to refer to my notes to reconstruct the organization and logic of those tumultuous days, but the memories of them that still remain, like the sedate pictures in a family album, revive in me the smells and colors of moments that I lived through without knowing where they would take me.

Amsterdam, The Hague, Cologne, Frankfurt, where I saw Daniel Cohn-Bendit again, and Budapest, where we were again invited to the assembly of the World Peace Council. Committees, debates, resolutions, amendments. I was glad to see Mehdi

Alaoui and Lotfi El Kholi again. Lotfi wanted to know how preparations for the Bologna conference* were progressing. I had to tell him that there were still differences between us and the Peace Movement, and that we were thinking less of propaganda than of having Arabs and Israelis meet with each other. Lotfi, who seemed to approve of what we were doing, invited me to Egypt in the name of the Arab Socialist Union.

Red carpets, Viennese waltzes, sumptuous buffets — things in Budapest were much less regimented than in East Berlin, and the civil-servant musicians in the tourist restaurants sometimes became caught up in their own music. But I still remember the three religious Jews — beards, earlocks, skullcaps — I saw at an official reception where they represented the Jewish community. When I went up to them and asked them in Yiddish how they were doing, they looked at me mistrustfully and gave me only a laconic answer.

"If it bothers you to talk to me, you can at least tell me so," I said.

This time they gave me no answer at all. Silence fell between us while they furtively looked around as if they were afraid of being caught in the act of plotting. I walked away from them.

I also remember the taxi driver who told me in heavily accented English, "Communism no good." There was no place in Budapest, he told me, where he and his girlfriend could make love. The housing shortage made it impossible for them to marry, and they couldn't stay in a hotel together because they weren't married. Like so many other couples, they had no choice but to meet at night on the banks of the tender Danube.

Almost as soon as I was back in Paris, I went off to Italy after a call from Aldo Zargani telling me that our friend Riccardo Lombardi was going to meet Farouk Kaddoumi, the PLO's foreign minister, in Venice. Aldo felt it was important

*That conference, scheduled to be held in May 1972 in Bologna, Italy, was intended to bring Israelis and Arabs together for the first time. It finally took place in May 1973.

for me to take part in the discussion. When I arrived in Venice, he told me that a PLO member named Abdallah very much wanted to meet me and would get in touch with us at the Chichi boardinghouse, near the Cà d'Oro, where we were staying.

For me, Venice is Tintoretto, the one-eyed cats of the Piazza del Ghetto Vecchio, and Thomas Mann. But it is especially a smell, that insidious, bluish-green smell that overwhelms me, no matter where I am, whenever I think of Venice.

We strolled along the narrow streets of the Giudecca, we sat in cafés near the Accademia, but we didn't have enough money to take one of the gondolas floating on the murky water of the Grand Canal. For once, we gave ourselves the luxury of letting time pass without us.

Not for long: the man from the PLO came to the Chichi two days later. He was young and spoke English well. He wanted to know if we could sway Israeli public opinion, if we knew any Israeli leaders who would be willing to meet with Arafat, and if we thought that the peace conferences organized in Italy were at all useful.

I answered that Israel was a democratic society and that some of its most important newspapers were open to us. As for the Israeli leaders, some of them would be willing to meet with Arafat, provided he publicly started along the road to mutual recognition. Dayan, for example. I said that instead of conferences in Italy I would rather have a direct encounter between Israelis and Palestinians: I mistrusted intermediaries. An Arab proverb says, "The horse and the mule kick, and between them the donkey dies."

Abdallah liked the idea of bringing Arafat and Dayan together. He promised to get in touch with me soon, in Paris.

In the dark it is good to believe in light. To celebrate that hope, Aldo took me at nightfall to a little bar in the Ghetto Nuovo, near the San Girolamo parish where four centuries ago the Venetian Senate regrouped the Jews of the city "to protect them."

It was a strange trip, and it now seems to me that I experienced it in another life. I don't know why, but it is linked in my memory with a story told by Orson Welles. In the cemetery of an Armenian village, he noticed that the dates on the gravestones always showed an interval of only two, three, or five years. He thought that children died young there, and he expected to find only a few old people in the village. To his surprise, he saw a normal village with a normally constituted population (all ages, from children to old people) engaged in normal occupations. He asked a villager sitting on the front steps of his house to explain the inscriptions in the cemetery. "It's simple," said the villager: "with us, a human life is measured by the time of a friendship."

In Paris, I found a letter from Lotfi El Kholi. We had to continue our efforts to bring about a meeting between Israelis and Arabs, he said; and, stressing the importance of our coming to Cairo, he repeated the invitation of the Arab Socialist Union.

20

Hope in Cairo

Clara and I decided to begin with Beirut. We arrived there a month later. Beyond the overwrought customs officers, the travelers in djellabas and turbans waiting for the flight to Kuwait, the crying children, and the cages packed with terrified chickens, I noticed a man gesturing to us. I didn't know him. Outside, he made his way to us and asked, "Are you Marek? I'm your friend André's father. He told me you were coming, so here I am."

He had reserved a room for us at the Hotel Alcazar: "It's next to the Hotel St. George, and less expensive." He took us there in a taxi, accompanied us to our room, tipped the bellhop, locked the door, stood listening for a few moments, then stepped closer to us and asked in a conspiratorial undertone, "How are things there?"

"There? Where?"

He seemed surprised by my surprise.

"In our country!" he said.

I finally realized he was talking about Israel. We sat down

on the bed and tried to answer his many questions. When he left, he promised to call us. He never did; the interview we gave the next day to *L'Orient–Le Jour*, a Lebanese French-language daily, must not have seemed pro-Israeli enough to him.

After my friend's father had left, Clara and I were standing on the balcony of our room, looking at the serene magic of the sea with sailboats gliding across it, when a man named Jean-Pierre Sara called us, having been told about us by an American journalist. He wanted to give a little party for us in his summer house at Sofar, on the road to Damascus. He told us how to get there and said he would be waiting for us near the gas pump at the edge of the village.

We left. People are my drug. I can't resist an invitation from a stranger. Only living people give meaning to space; without them, it is only dead space. For me, events are abstract when the human actors in them are abstract, and they don't take on their real dimensions unless the humans are materialized. In my painting, landscapes come to life only when there are people in them. There have been so many people in my life!

Jean-Pierre Sara was waiting for us near the gas pump, just as he had said. He took us to his house. It was one of those mountainside villas around Beirut, in which well-to-do families take refuge during the summer months. We spent the evening there, discussing peace in the Middle East with about fifteen people. They had been reading *Eléments* since it became available at the Antoine bookstore, and they wondered what the outcome of our efforts would be. Jean-Pierre Sara was writing a book.

"I've changed a lot recently," he said, "like many Arab intellectuals. At first I wrote like Shukeiry, thinking I could wipe Israel out of existence with my pen. Then I read, I gathered information, I thought things over. . . ."

He intended to describe this process of development in his book, and present a plan that was close to his heart: a federation that would include Israel, Palestine, Jordan, and Lebanon. He had even used a computer to demonstrate the economic viability of such a federation. The distant lights of Beirut were reflected by the sea, and once again we were remaking the world. . . .

The next day, I had to deal with bureaucratic complications caused by my having forgotten to get a visa — I was regarded as a suspect for half a day. Then Clara recorded an interview for *Eléments* with Jad Tabet, an architect and president of the Union of Democratic Youth, and Amin Maalouf, a writer and a journalist for *Al Nahar*. We had lunch with Fuad Zehil, of the newspaper *Al Nida*, who told us that in his opinion the Arab masses were beginning to turn away from the Palestinian Resistance "because of its official character, its lack of any sense of democracy, its wildly exaggerated claims of victory, and its way of behaving as if Lebanon were a conquered territory."

Back at the hotel, I tried to call Lotfi in Cairo to confirm that we would soon be there.

"You'll have to wait," the operator told me.

I had expected that, of course, so I hadn't made any plans for the afternoon.

"How long?" I asked.

The operator made inquiries and finally said in a perfectly natural tone, "Six days, if there are no problems."

In Beirut, we still had to meet Yasir Arafat. I went to see Marwan Dajani, a prosperous Palestinian businessman who owned the Strand Building in the elegant Hamraa quarter. I knew he was closely connected with Al Fatah, and that Arafat and his friends stayed at his hotel. The receptionist told me to go "in back," where armed fedayeen screened visitors. Marwan was waiting for me in his office on the fifth floor. Modern furniture, telephones, secretaries: he seemed to be a model of the efficient, dynamic businessman. He asked me what he could do for me. I told him.

"Arafat and Abu Iyad will be here tomorrow," he said. "Call me in the morning and I'll tell you when you can come to see them."

As for George Habash, he called him immediately. They talked for a few minutes, then Marwan said to me without hanging up, "He's leaving for Baghdad in an hour. He suggests that, while he's away, you see Ghassan Kanafani."

"No," I said, "not Kanafani."

"Why not?" Marwan asked in surprise.

"Because he behaved badly with Clara."

I briefly told him how in 1969 she had had to appear before the "tribunal" convened in the headquarters of the Popular Front. Marwan translated for Habash and relayed his answer to me:

"Habash is very sorry about what happened and he'll ask Bassam Abu Sharif to see you in Beirut."

And Bassam Abu Sharif called a few minutes later to invite Clara and me to have coffee with him. We met him at Popular Front headquarters on the Mazraa road, in a building that reminded me of those in Tel Aviv. Two fedayeen showed us inside. Bassam shook hands with us.

"So you're the famous Lady Clara," he said.

We had coffee in his big office. On its walls were pictures of Che Guevara and Lenin, and a map of Palestine on which Israel didn't exist.

He was a likable man. We talked about our disagreements, and he told us the fantastic stories being circulated in Beirut about Clara. The door opened halfway and I saw a pale, handsome man with a mustache. He said something in Arabic, then left.

"That was Kanafani," Clara told me.

We were served more coffee and the door opened again. Kanafani, looking embarrassed, came in, said hello without looking at Clara, and sat down. He was sulking.

"I've heard a lot about you," I said to him.

He muttered something or other. I decided to take a light-hearted approach.

"Look, you can't go on sulking for the rest of your life!" I said. "There was a misunderstanding between you and Clara, so why don't the two of you talk it over?"

He pushed an ashtray in front of Clara. Then all at once he went to the desk, struggled for a time with a lock and a key, finally took a thick folder from a drawer, and tossed it onto the table.

"That's what she's done!" he said.

The folder was overflowing with letters and newspaper clippings. The situation amused me enormously.

"You're not trying to tell me she wrote all that, are you?" I asked jokingly.

He laughed and began explaining.

"Clara published an interview with me in *Eléments*. That interview was picked up all over the world. A group of American professors took enough material from it to organize an anti-Palestinian campaign."

"And the material they used," said Clara, "was from the passage I advised you to take out."

"That's true," Kanafani admitted. After a silence he added, "She's the most intelligent of all the people whose ideas I don't accept."

Then he abandoned the third person, spoke to Clara directly, and held out his hand to her. The incident was closed.

We talked for a long time. Clara and I were opposed to the goals of their struggle and the means they used to pursue them. Finally Kanafani asked me if I would like to illustrate a collection of short stories set in Palestine that he was writing. I agreed to do it and told him that the Israeli writer Benyamin Tammuz, a friend of mine, had expressed admiration for his stories, some of which had been translated into Hebrew. Kanafani had read Tammuz's stories and been greatly interested by them.

"But it's odd," he said, "that Tammuz begins each story like a leftist and ends it like a rightist."

He also liked the books of the Israeli writer Amos Oz, which he read in English. Hearing that, Clara proposed a meeting between Palestinian and Israeli writers.

"Maybe someday," Kanafani answered, "in liberated Palestine."

He and Bassam took us back to the hotel in the car he had just bought with the money from a literary prize. He had patched it up himself.

"I'm very satisfied with it," he said as he drove down the Raouche road at breakneck speed. "It's in good shape now. Except for the brakes."

The breeze blowing in through the windows put him and Bassam into a good mood, and they began singing an Arab song that reminded us of a song we had sung in Ran Cohen's home at Kibbutz Gan Shmuel. Clara mentioned the similarity to Kanafani. He asked us to send him the documents we had on Siah. We all took up the song again together.

The next day, while we were waiting to call Marwan Dajani to ask when we could meet Arafat and Abu Iyad, we went to the French embassy, where Renard, the chargé d'affaires, had invited us to breakfast. A drawing room in Middle Eastern style, with ottomans and low tables — this was where the French foreign minister, Jean-Victor Sauvagnargues, would officially meet Arafat a few years later. Renard was very well informed on Arab politics and maintained good relations with the Palestinians. We talked awhile, then he offered to call the Egyptian embassy so that we could get, without too much delay, the visas we had neglected to get in Paris.

"They're expecting you," he said when he had hung up. "You'd better go there now."

I called Marwan Dajani from a phone booth near the Egyptian embassy.

"Arafat and Abu Iyad are here," he said. "Finish your business as quickly as you can and then come."

Gamal Abderahman Ibrahim, the Egyptian chargé d'affaires, received us in his office overlooking the sea and told us how honored he was by our visit. He wanted to give us our visas immediately, he said, but unfortunately the man in charge of the official stamps had gone out for coffee. We waited a long time. While the chargé d'affaires talked to us about Egypt and obligingly drew up a list of places for us to visit there, I wondered anxiously if we would arrive in time to meet Arafat. Gamal Abderahman Ibrahim, whose nerves were becoming frayed in spite of all his patience and courtesy, was describing the colors of sunset on the Nile when the man in charge of the stamps finally came back. With the self-important air of someone who knows he is indispensable, he pasted two stamps on each passport and we jumped into a taxi. I asked the driver to hurry. At first he overdid it by nearly hitting an old woman, but then he took time out for a long argument with some other taxi drivers over a traffic light that may or may not have been red. We finally got to the Strand Hotel an hour and a half after my phone call to Marwan.

"Abu Iyad has already left for Damascus," he told me, "and Arafat is about to leave."

Arafat looked taller than in photographs or on television, and his whiskers seemed to have been trimmed. He wore his usual kaffiyeh on his head.

"Welcome to Beirut," he said to us in English, then he continued in Arabic while Marwan Dajani translated: "So you want to arrange meetings between us and the Israelis? But we meet Israelis every day."

"To kill them?"

Arafat's face darkened and his eyes became moister.

"It's not our fault. It's self-defense. Israel doesn't recognize our rights or even our existence."

"Are you fighting to destroy Israel, or to have a state like all the other peoples in the region?"

"We've accepted all the UN resolutions recognizing Israel's existence — "

"You've never said that in public," I interjected.

" — but Israel exists and we still don't have a state."

"Where would you locate that state?"

His lips parted in a crafty smile.

"Is that question a trap?"

"No, it's a key question."

"Let's suppose we wanted to build a state next to Israel, where part of our people live . . ."

"If that's your goal, why not say so?"

"Would it change anything in Israel's attitude?"

"It certainly would! A statement like that might make it possible to begin peace talks."

"But the Israeli government — "

"Israel is a democratic country: its government has to take public opinion into account. Do you think Jewish mothers like having their sons die on battlefields?"

"Palestinian mothers don't like it either."

"Then make a public statement to that effect and things will start to move."

"A public statement?" Arafat laughed. "It's up to the Israeli government to make public statements, not me!"

The audience nodded agreement. In the Middle East, every private conversation is followed by at least a dozen people. So, to survive, every politician must have at least a dozen friends.

I was about to answer Arafat when we were interrupted by a tall, thin Palestinian armed with a submachine gun. Arafat smiled and excused himself.

"My car is waiting for me. I have to leave for Damascus. Come to see me tomorrow and we'll go on with our conversation."

He told the tall, thin Palestinian to make arrangements for our trip to Damascus and our stay there. We went with him to Al Fatah headquarters. He gave us a rubber-stamped sheet of paper on which only my name was written in Latin letters. I later had it translated: it recommended "Brother Marek Halter, accompanied by his wife" to the Al Fatah leaders in Damascus and asked them to arrange a meeting with Arafat and Abu Iyad as soon as possible.

But we didn't go to Damascus. That evening we received a telegram from Lotfi: we were expected in Cairo the next day.

Our taxi, whose brakes were as weak as those of the other cars that raced along the roads of Lebanon, ran into a cart drawn by a broken-down horse and we reached the Khalde airport too late to take the plane on which our seats were reserved. I sent Lotfi a telegram telling him we would be late, but I had no illusions about its chances of getting to him. When we arrived in Cairo in the afternoon, there was no one waiting for us.

I called Lotfi at his home. He hadn't received my telegram, of course, and had been wondering what had happened to us. He was heartbroken.

"We waited for you," he said, "with flowers and an official car."

He had reserved a room for us in the Sheraton on the Nile, where I had stayed before. On the way there in a taxi, I saw a sign: "Suez, 120 km," which meant that a hundred and twenty kilometers from where we were, the armies of Egypt and Israel were face-to-face. Here, it was considered improper to mention Israel without immediately expressing a wish for its annihilation. Were we, who defended the Jewish state's right to exist, going to be regarded as Zionist agents? My stomach tightened. Would anyone at least listen to what we had come to say?

That evening Lotfi and his wife came by for us and took us to eat fish on the bank of the Nile. He seemed to know everyone; he told jokes and people laughed heartily. With Yusef Shahin, he had just finished a film, *The Sparrow,* which was still being held by the censors because it contained criticism of Nasser. The process of "de-Nasserization" was just beginning, and the Egyptians' sharp humor didn't spare their former ruler.

"Did you know," Lotfi asked me, for example, "that a telephone monitoring center was found in Nasser's own house?" He paused, then added, "It seems he preferred to listen to himself."

The Egyptian left, he told us, was sometimes allowed to run loose, to attract the Soviets, and sometimes kept on a leash, to put pressure on them.

"We've had as many as seventeen Communist parties with different leanings. Now we have only two: one is banned and the other is in prison."

Khaled Mohieddin was under house arrest, and Lotfi asked us to mention our interest in him, if the occasion arose: "It might help him."

He asked us about the Bologna conference: how its prospects looked, how far preparations for it had gone, and what we thought of it. He finally told us something about our schedule. It was heavily loaded; many people had said they wanted to meet us.

"Here," said Lotfi, "we know nothing. Tell us about what's happening in Israel."

The next day, however, when we visited the newspaper *Al Ahram* we saw a center for Israeli studies, the only one in the Arab world where magazines, newspapers, and books in Hebrew could be found. Some important articles were translated into Arabic as soon as they appeared. But access to that center was highly restricted. The time hadn't yet come to give Egyptian citizens information about the people they were fighting and would have to make peace with someday.

Al Ahram, the great Cairo daily, was a state within a state, installed in a big modern building where the editor, Hassanein Heykal, a former close associate of Nasser, exercised his power. It was said that *Al Ahram* had the world's only two computers that worked in Arabic. One thing was sure: its big, well-lighted, comfortable offices contained the best brains in Egypt. Whether they belonged to the left or the right, Heykal preferred to have them with him. There were paintings everywhere, because Heykal wanted to help Egyptian painters. It seemed that nothing happened in Egypt without him, and we naturally wanted to meet him, but he was then on vacation in Alexandria and no one knew when he would be back.

We were given a complete tour of the newspaper's facilities. In the printing plant, the typesetters offered to compose our names in Arabic letters. I knew what they were up to. In Warsaw, my father had often done the same thing. Holding it with his toughened fingers, he would give a visitor the line of hot lead in which the letters of his name appeared in reverse. The visitor, pleased by that favor, would unsuspectingly take the lead, then feel its heat and drop it with mingled surprise and pain while the printers laughed. "A printer's joke," my mother used to say. Now I was going to see it played in Cairo. A typesetter composed my name and handed me the line, closely watching my reactions. He was disappointed. I took the hot lead, pretended to be interested in the style of the letters, acted as if I felt no heat at all, and thanked him. I left them to their astonishment for a few moments, then explained that I had worked for several years as a linotypist before I began selling my paintings. They all began laughing and talking at the same time. Lotfi couldn't go on interpreting because he couldn't follow what they were all saying. An old worker came over to me and, in a tone that touched me, said in halting English, "Worker French, Jew, Arab, the same."

I wondered if the charm of those hours came from mutual understanding among people who knew the same trade, or if it was a tentative sign that we could agree on the same ideas. I probably could have found out by asking direct questions but, to tell the truth, I was afraid to resolve the ambiguity that for the moment was my only ally.

Later, Ismail Sabri Abdallah, the minister of planning, a brilliant man who was introduced to us as the Marxist in the government, received us at the ministry. With him, we went straight to the heart of our subject. He maintained that Israel could not go on existing. He quickly added, "But I want to be clear on this point: it's out of the question to eliminate the Israelis and throw them into the sea."

"How will you go about explaining to them that they have to give up their state?" I asked.

"I see the future in the form of a great Arab federation that will include national minorities."

"Then you approve of the Palestinian plan to destroy Israel's governmental structure and create a single state?"

"I've often had differences of opinion with our Palestinian brothers. They're the ones who have been harmed the most, of course, the ones most directly concerned by the conflict, but they have too strong a tendency to think in terms of all or nothing. Personally, I'm convinced that the conflict will be settled only by taking long-range developments into account, proceeding by stages, allowing for delays . . ."

Instead of bluntly telling him our ideas at the risk of causing a break between us, I preferred to lead him to contradict himself. I said I agreed with him, but that the first stage had to be proposed.

"The UN resolution is a basis for that stage," he answered, "and we've accepted it."

"What if the Arabs and Israelis carried it out and then decided not to go any further? Nothing basic would be settled."

"That's a possibility," he acknowledged.

That first step no longer seemed to be very important to him. In his view, the future could only be socialist. I pointed out that in Israel there were many people ready to fight side by side with him to bring about a socialist society.

"But," I added, "first you'd have to agree to meet them. Maybe you'd then find the path to peace."

"You're an idealist. That's not how things are done in politics."

All this was taking us nowhere. At that time, as Clara and I realized all during our stay, the conflict with Israel was not the Egyptians' main concern: they had stopped talking about the 1967 war, they weren't yet talking about the next one, the Sinai was an empty desert that interested no one, and the Palestinians were making a nuisance of themselves. The bourgeoisie expected Sadat to restore their old privileges and create an American-style consumer society, the intelligentsia were preoccupied with the economic future of the country, and the people were beginning to stir, as they had recently done at Helwan. Ali Shalakani, one of those who had been fired from the great industrial complex for having supported the strike, told us how the workers had occupied the factories and sequestered the representatives of the Arab Socialist Union, demanding a pay raise and better management. To show that it was possible, they started the machines and produced more in a few days than was usually produced in a few weeks. When they were accused of "playing into the hands of the Israeli enemy," they answered that Israel had strikes too, and that it didn't prevent them from winning wars.

Pierre Butros Ghali, a professor of political science, felt that Egypt's economic backwardness was so great that it jeopardized the solution of the Arab–Israeli conflict that he envisaged: a federation of independent states forming a kind of Middle Eastern Common Market.

"I'd be curious to know," he said to us, "if among all the people you've seen here, you've met anyone as pessimistic as I am. And if I'm the only one who believes as I do, it's even worse than I thought. I often tell myself that things aren't so bad for me, that a professorship is waiting for me at Princeton, that I could become an associate professor in Nice or Paris. I'd be paid five times as much as I am here, I'd do what I enjoy doing, I'd write. . . . In the streets of Cairo, poverty weighs down on me, intellectual as well as physical poverty. Reality never lets you forget it; it's always there, oppressing you."

And, after two hours of discussion: "I like your enthusiasm and faith. With my pessimism and your optimism, maybe we can accomplish something for peace in the Middle East."

That day, we were invited to visit Abdel Salem El Zayat, general secretary of the Arab Socialist Union and an adviser to President Sadat — we were officially his guests. When evening had come, we went to the enormous building that housed the single Egyptian party. It seemed deserted. In the antechamber of Zayat's office, there was only a guard sitting under the portraits of Nasser and Sadat.

Clara noticed the contrast between Nasser's bright smile and Sadat's constrained expression. To fill in the time, she asked Lotfi, who had come with us, "Why is one smiling and the other isn't?"

Lotfi, amused, translated the question for the guard.

"It's because President Sadat is smiling inwardly," the guard answered imperturbably.

Zayat gave us the traditional embrace. Short, with his head

sunk down between his shoulders and a modest, thoughtful look in his eyes, he physically reminded me of an old friend of my father, Zvi Assaf, general secretary of the Israeli printers' union. I was soon led to talk once more about how important a meeting with the Arabs would be to Israeli public opinion. I felt it was the only way to make a breach in the wall of mistrust that separated the two sides. I told about our efforts to bring an Israeli, Lyova Eliav, to Nasser, and I asked Zayat to talk to Sadat about taking up that idea again.

"Eliav is an interesting man," he said, "but he's no longer general secretary of the Labor Party. Sadat would probably prefer someone closer to the government."

I answered that once there was an agreement on principle, I could suggest to Sadat several people acceptable to the Israeli government, and he could choose one of them.

"Unfortunately we haven't yet reached that point," said Zayat. And, as though to comfort me, he added with a smile, "I hope we'll get there someday."

That may not have been a definite promise but, coming from him, it gave us hope.

We were to see him again in two days, when he was going to give an evening party in our honor.

During those two days, we kept going from one appointment to another. Our discussions were always centered on our main project: an Arab–Israeli meeting. The people we encountered were eager to hear us talk about Israel, but our stories and analyses disturbed the superficial ideas they had formed on the subject. We realized that our insistence annoyed them, and that what we said was considered suspicious.

Most members of the Egyptian left came from the same great families that rule the country. In a country where three quarters of the people are illiterate, the leftist cousin benefits from the same countless privileges as the rightist cousin: they belong to the same class. Since the notion of socialism is also exploited by the government, the left tries to define itself on the basis of the Arab–Israeli conflict; and since the right, turned toward the United States, accepts the principle of a settlement with Israel, it can only refuse all compromise.

We met with three specialists on Israeli matters for an "exchange of views," and they expressed the harshest judgments we had heard in Cairo. They listened to us, doing a bad job of hiding their irritation, only because we were official guests. All three had written books on Israel, about which they knew practically nothing. We also had to make an effort to stay calm, confronted with all that ignorance, misunderstanding, and hatred.

At Zayat's reception, Lotfi happily told us that he had a surprise for us: he had invited Abu Iyad, second in command of Al Fatah, and Abu Khol, the organization's representative in Cairo. Abu Iyad was sorry, he said, that he had missed us in Beirut.

With his pack of cigarettes in the pocket of his white open-necked shirt, what differentiated him from a Meir Pail, the Israeli "red colonel"? And what differentiated that simple apartment, with its terrace facing the garden, prints on the walls, and sandwiches on the tables, from the apartment of any member of the Knesset? I almost pointed out that they were probably much closer to each other than they thought, but I decided against it because I didn't want to seem, once again, to be living in the clouds.

"You favor the existence of two states, an Israeli and a Palestinian one," Abu Iyad said to me, with Lotfi's wife, Liliane, acting as interpreter, "but, as a leftist, don't you think our proposal is more progressive?"

"You mean a single state?"

"Yes."

"In itself, having a single state is neither progressive nor reactionary. It all depends on what the political and economic structures are. And you're very discreet on that subject."

"For the time being, there's no point in giving precise details and definitions," replied Abu Iyad, "since the basic idea of a single state is rejected by the Israelis."

"All the more reason to meet with them and work together

to find a way of coexisting. You might be able to persuade them."

"Meeting with them would mean recognizing them."

"The fact that you fight them implies that you admit they exist."

"Maybe, but you don't expect the Palestinians to recognize the State of Israel, do you?"

"Why not?"

"Because the Israelis created the Palestinian problem, and they now occupy territory inhabited by a million of our brothers and sisters. It's up to them, first, to recognize our rights."

"Sometimes you talk about the State of Israel, sometimes about its government, and sometimes about the Israelis, the people formed by the Israelis. I'm not asking you to agree with their government's policies — we don't always agree with them either. But you should talk with those Israelis who have already recognized you and never miss a chance to show that they support the Palestinians' national rights."

"Who are they?" asked Abu Iyad.

Clara briefly described Israeli society, explained the positions taken by the different political groups and tendencies, and demonstrated that contact between Israeli "doves" and the PLO might set off a movement of public opinion that would not regard an understanding with the Palestinians and restitution of the occupied territories as one more trap that history had set for the Jews.

"I've heard that in Bologna you're going to have a conference for peace and justice in the Middle East," said Abu Iyad. "Have you invited those Israelis you're talking about?"

"We're not the only ones who are organizing that conference," I said, "and we're not always in agreement with our partners on that subject."

"Why?"

"Because, unlike them, we want to create the basis of a dialogue."

"Why don't you go to the conference too," Lotfi asked Abu Iyad, "and explain your idea of a single state to the Israelis?"

Knowing that he was supporting my argument, he winked at me, then added, "And if you succeed in convincing them, it will be the sensation of the conference."

"If *you* want to go there, we certainly won't object," Abu Iyad replied, laughing. "Furthermore, we're not opposed to a peaceful settlement between Egypt and Israel. We feel that, provided the Arab countries don't make any concessions in things that concern us, it would strengthen the Resistance."

It was hot; Zayat suggested that we go out onto the terrace. Abu Iyad and Abu Khol sat down beside us. The former spoke a little English, the latter a little German; it was enough to enable us to reach agreement on Black September and the mistakes made by the Palestinian Resistance in Jordan. Clara said she had been wondering since 1969 why the Palestinians didn't take power in Amman. Abu Iyad said she was right and told us that Al Fatah was forming a Jordanian–Palestinian front to overthrow King Hussein.

"The population of Jordan is seventy percent Palestinian," he added, "and I think that once the Hashemite regime has been overthrown, it will be possible to create a democratic state."

We talked for a long time. Clara and I were sorry we hadn't brought our tape recorder. Abu Iyad told us that our analysis was correct, and that the two-state stage was necessary, but that the Israelis would accept it only if the Resistance was strong and recognized by the world's other nations. We repeated to him that if they held out their hands to at least some of them, the Israelis would accept it much more quickly than he thought.

"According to you, where is Palestine?" asked Abu Iyad.

"Today, taking realities into account," I said, "it's where Palestinians are in the majority: the West Bank, Jordan, Gaza."

Abu Iyad said nothing. Clara asked him if she could publish in *Eléments* the conversation we had just had with him.

"Of course," he answered.

"But we haven't recorded anything. I'd like to have you put your ideas on tape, so we won't risk distorting them."

"I trust you," he said with a smile.

When Clara insisted, he made an appointment with us for the next day in Lotfi's office. There he more or less repeated what he had said to us on Zayat's terrace. Ali Shalakani translated and a young journalist from *Al Talia* took notes; these proved to be wise precautions, because publication of the interview was to set off violent polemics a few weeks later.

That same day, Heykal called Lotfi from Alexandria: he wanted to see us when he returned, in a week. We decided to go to Beirut and interview the leaders of the various factions of the Palestinian Resistance, then go to Cairo to meet with Heykal. We were very hopeful about a conversation with him, since he was one of the most influential people in Egypt.

At the Hotel Alcazar in Beirut, we were greeted as habitual guests and a bellhop went to get flowers for Clara. Amin Maalouf had left a message for us: Ghassan Kanafani and Naief Hawatmeh were expecting us.

We worked a few days but were unable to meet with Hawatmeh: he had to go to Damascus in the constant round of travel that kept the Palestinian leaders moving from one Arab capital to another. Instead of him, we saw Abu Leila, the ideologist of the Democratic Front, a blond-haired young man who told us how the left wing of the Resistance, after a dark period, would come to take leadership of the Palestinian struggle, and how that purely national struggle would become a struggle for the transformation of the whole region.

We also met with Kanafani, the spokesman for the Popular Front. He gave us a brilliant impromptu exposition of the strategy and goals of the Popular Front, and its relations with Israel and the Arab countries. I didn't understand why Clara hadn't turned on her tape recorder.

"Were you afraid to record me?" Kanafani asked her, smiling.

"After the scene you made last time — "

"You were wrong," said Kanafani. "This time it was Habash who asked me to talk with you."

He made it clear that he didn't want to repeat his little speech for the tape recorder. He asked Clara to put her questions in writing and said he would send his answers to us in Paris.

When we had gone back to Cairo, I made a detour along the road that runs past the "City of the Dead," a vast cemetery where peasants from the upper Nile had settled after coming to Cairo to look for work. In the evening, smoke from cooking fires rose into the calm air while smaller flames flickered all over the strange necropolis and the shadowy population moved busily among the graves.

The day before we arrived, Egyptian and Israeli planes had fought above the Suez Canal. The Cairo newspapers announced it in big headlines: for public opinion, the fact that Egyptian pilots had been willing to engage in combat against the "invincible enemy" was in itself a significant victory. At the same time, the trial (instituted by Sadat) of Ali Sabri, regarded as the "eye of Moscow" and accused of plotting against the state, took place in the midst of general indifference. Finally, the United Arab Republic, a federation of Egypt and Syria, was dissolved, and the Egyptians were delighted to have their country regain its name. Not much of Nasser's dream was left now. As someone pointed out to us, the Arab world had been pursuing three objectives for the last twenty-five years: unity, socialism, and freedom; and when two of them were achieved, it was always at the expense of the third one. There was now a great deal of talk about a new federation, this time among Egypt, Syria, and Libya. A referendum had even ratified the idea of such a federation — yet no one believed in it.

We had an appointment with Heykal for the next day. Meanwhile I went to a meeting with some students, among whom was Ala' Hamrush, son of the editor of the weekly newspaper *Rose Al Yussef* and president of the Egyptian Students' Union. As soon as I asked my first question, they pretended to look for hidden microphones under the tables and chairs and in the corners of the windows, then one of them concluded, "Now we can tell you what we really think."

"But not everything," said Ala' Hamrush. "Maybe our search wasn't good enough."

Actually, however, they disguised their thoughts so little that I didn't have to ask any more questions: they spent the evening arguing with each other. For some, the conflict with Israel was the cause of Egypt's deplorable economic situation; for others, the conflict made it possible to camouflage the real reasons for the deterioration of living conditions; for still others, including Ala' Hamrush, the real reasons lay in the rise of the middle class, the profits it wanted to make for itself, lack of planning, and bad management. At midnight, we were still carrying on our discussion in the street.

Hassanein Heykal's office met my expectations: big windows, dark wooden furniture, intercom, a battery of telephones, closed-circuit television. His head firmly planted between his broad shoulders, his dazzling smile, and his square jaw reminded me of Nasser. When he stood up to greet me, I was surprised to see that he was less tall than I had thought.

"So it seems you intellectuals want to make peace between Israel and us," he attacked.

"That's not a good idea?"

"The idea may be good, but it needs means of carrying it out."

"What are they?"

"Economic and political means."

"Then it concerns only the great powers?"

He went over to the window and made a gesture asking us to join him.

"Come here, look. . . . Investments can be made at every street corner. You see all those people hanging on to the streetcars? They're labor in search of work. Our problem isn't only war or peace with Israel, but also industrial development, and therefore investment of capital."

Heykal was imposing. Because of the self-assurance his power gave him, and the casual attitude he seemed to have toward it, he reminded me of Dayan. His hard, massive appearance made me think of the Pyramids.

"But we're a five-thousand-year-old country," he went on, "and we have plenty of time ahead of us."

He smiled. In a flash, I saw the nervous, anxious Israelis hurrying along the streets of Tel Aviv, arguing over peace plans, writing public statements, devouring newspapers, organizing symposiums — and I was afraid for them.

"As long as the war lasts," I said, "capitalists won't invest in Cairo. An in the meantime you're becoming more and more dependent on the great powers."

"I know you're a painter," said Heykal, "and I liked your album on May 1968. I know you're an idealist, and that's good. But politics is neither painting nor idealism. Politics is the exercise of power."

"You don't think we can play a part in it?"

Heykal gripped his cigar more tightly between his teeth. "How?"

"We'll bring you an alternative, and contacts, and the support of the media, and we won't ask anything in exchange."

I couldn't think of any other arguments to justify our visit to him. He laughed.

"My dear Marek, I've had several proposals like that in the last few months."

"For example?" asked Clara, obviously irritated.

"For example, a message that Dayan had a British diplomat bring me. He proposed a meeting with me. For example, a message from Shimon Peres. . . . Less than two weeks ago the papal nuncio — wearing his ceremonial costume, probably to impress me — told me in great secrecy that Abba Eban wanted to see me."

"And what did you answer?" asked Clara.

"I read Dayan's and Peres's statements, and I don't really see what we could talk about. What they say is unacceptable to us."

He lit another cigar.

"Don't you think that when they read your statements, the Israelis might have the same reaction as you?"

"First of all, I'm not asking to see them. But when they say they won't give back Sharm al-Sheikh, and when getting back Sharm al-Sheikh is exactly what I want, it means that we can't even begin a discussion."

"But if Dayan asks you to see him, it must be because he has something to tell you that's different from what you can read in the papers. It's the same as in poker: you don't announce your hand before you bet."

"In poker, you have to pay to see, but if the price is too high, you drop out."

"If you drop out too often, you lose everything."

"In that case, you draw your pistol and take back your money!"

"You see: you're still talking the language of force!"

Phones began ringing, and on the television screen we saw other visitors arriving. But Heÿkal still took time to talk about the peace conference with us. He told us he didn't believe in the importance we attributed to "a meeting among intellectuals." I had to remind him that the Arabs' refusal to talk with the Israelis was seen in Israel not only as a refusal to recognize their state, but also as a pure and simple denial of them as individuals; any beginning of dialogue — and intellectuals seemed to be in the best position for taking the first step toward it — would be better than that silence and mistrust.

"What do they represent," he asked, "those people you think you can bring to such a conference?"

"Public opinion."

"Is that important?"

"In Israel it is."

He showed all his teeth in a smile, then said, "All that won't be enough to settle the conflict."

"What *will* settle it? War?"

"Maybe. . . . Our army isn't the same as it was in 1967, you know."

"You'll win the next war?"

Heÿkal's face became serious and he pointed his cigar at me.

"We're not thinking of winning the war. We'd only have to provoke a clash on the canal that would be violent enough to frighten everyone. The Israelis would realize that they're not invincible and the great powers would realize that they might be dragged into a world war. Then other countries would flutter around us again, and both sides would be made to compromise."

The new visitors were now lined up, waiting. Heykal stood up. He looked like the pharaohs in the wall paintings at Saqqara. Slowly, as though regretfully, he accompanied us to the door. We were about to cross the threshold when he took hold of us and drew us back into his office.

"After all," he said, "if you have some plot to offer me, I'm your man. . . ."

We were to leave Cairo the next morning. At nightfall we went to spend our last Egyptian evening with Hussein Fahmi, a former confidant of the Egyptian president, who had built himself a little house near the pyramids. With us were Lotfi, Mourad Ghaleb, and their wives. Ghaleb, the Egyptian ambassador to Moscow, was on vacation. We had met him in the hotel bar as we watched the waiters pretending not to understand that a group of Russian technicians were asking for watermelon.

That evening, Hussein Fahmi told us about the time when he had been Nasser's official confidant. He punctuated his anecdotes with hoarse laughter that broke over us and made us laugh too. We were all a bit drunk by midnight, when an official car came for Mourad Ghaleb: the president wanted to see him without delay. We didn't know what that meant, and it sobered us a little.

The next morning, we found out what had happened. As I was about to leave the hotel for the airport, I met Mourad in the lobby.

"Congratulate me," he said, "I've become the foreign minister!"

* * *

When we were back in Paris, the press questioned us at length about our trip, and a weekly published our story under the title "Two Jewish Pilgrims in Egypt." Clara began transcribing all the tapes we had recorded; we wanted to bring out the issue of *Eléments* devoted to "the new Arab thought" as soon as possible. All we lacked was Kanafani's article, which we hadn't yet received. Clara tried to call him in Beirut; he wasn't at home, but she was given another phone number. She called it and was able to talk with him after saying who she was.

"Do you know where I am now?" he asked. "In jail. I was given a two-week sentence because I attacked King Faisal in *El Hadaf*."

"In that case," said Clara, "you've had time to write that article for *Eléments*."

"I'll send it to you, I promise," Kanafani was able to say before he was cut off.

We received the article a few days later, accompanied by a letter in English in which he asked Clara to write to him. "Everything is boring here," he added. "I read a lot and try to work. Seven days more and I will be free."

The Arab press reported extensively on that issue of *Eléments* and commented particularly on Abu Iyad's statements, wondering if they indicated a change in the goals and strategy of the Palestinian Resistance. A statement from Al Fatah, published in Beirut, put an end to those hopes: "The office of Al Fatah has declared that Mr. Abu Iyad, its second in command, has not given an interview to the French magazine *Eléments*. . . . According to *Eléments*, Abu Iyad said that the Resistance was no longer opposed to a peaceful settlement of the conflict in the Middle East and was trying to take power in Jordan to establish a democratic regime there. Al Fatah states that the words attributed to Abu Iyad are imaginary, and reiterates that the total liberation of Palestine is a clear objective which will not be reconsidered."

We responded with a statement of our own, issued to the news agencies. In it we reaffirmed the content of our interview with Abu Iyad, pointing out that it had taken place in the presence of several eminent people and had been tape-recorded in Cairo in September 1971. It was lucky that Clara had insisted on recording Abu Iyad!

But the affair was only beginning. Mahmoud Hamshari, representative of the PLO in France, Adel Amer, of the Arab League, and the Egyptian writer Lotfallah Soliman, among others, besieged us to get that tape. We naturally refused to let it leave our apartment. We didn't know the details of the PLO's internal quarrels and we didn't want to harm Abu Iyad, who, we were sure, hadn't amused himself by telling us a lot of wild stories.

Finally Lotfallah came to listen to the tape, with Ali Shalakani's French translation. All at once, happy as a gold miner who had just found the vein of his dreams, he turned his bony face to me and exclaimed, "I've got it!"

"You've got what?"

"Shalakani mistranslated! Where, according to you, Abu Iyad said he didn't object to the Arab countries' settling their differences with Israel peacefully, provided they regained their territory and didn't harm the interests of the Palestinian people, what he actually said was 'We don't object to the Arab countries' recovering their territory in whatever way they feel is best, provided they don't harm the interests of the Palestinian people and the revolution.' "

I felt as if I had been plunged into a Talmudic argument. It reminded me of a Sholem Aleichem story. A housewife borrows a saucepan from her neighbor and doesn't bring it back to her. A few days later the neighbor loses patience and comes to get her saucepan.

"What saucepan?" asks the housewife. "I never borrowed any saucepan from you. Besides, it was very little, and it leaked. It's nothing to get upset over."

On February 26, 1972, *Le Monde* published a statement by Mahmoud Hamshari in which he maintained that "Mrs. Halter has admitted having misinterpreted Abu Iyad's words," and so on. It wasn't a very elegant procedure. We wrote another answering statement. If we hadn't been sure of what we had heard on Zayat's terrace, and then again the next day in the offices of *Al Ahram*, we might eventually have begun to doubt our own sanity. I wrote a long letter to Abu Iyad.

A few days later I had a phone call from Mahmoud Hamshari. He apologized for the misunderstanding and said, "I had to publish that statement."

And on the occasion of a press conference given by Sadat, Lotfi El Kholi confirmed our version in front of several international journalists.

Shimon Peres talked with me during a brief stay in Paris, and didn't hide his satisfaction.

"Your Arab friends haven't abandoned you," he said.

It was during this time that we learned of Ghassan Kanafani's death. He had been killed by a bomb placed in the brakeless car he was so proud of. The Palestinians accused the Israelis and the Israelis accused the Jordanians. We wept.

21

The Half-Victory

Strengthened by Heykal's half-proposal, we were eager to go back to Israel and foment some new "plot." But first we had to deal with the Bologna conference: the second preparatory meeting was to be held in Rome in March.

There was no shortage of complications. For Khaled Mohieddin, who was now back in favor, inviting the Israelis was out of the question. "The purpose of the conference," he wrote to Guido Fanti, the mayor of Bologna, who was to preside over it, "is not to bring about a meeting between the adversaries. . . . The purpose of the conference is to mobilize support for a just and peaceful settlement of the conflict, based on Security Council Resolution 242." As for us, we again laid down our conditions: Israelis and Palestinians would attend the second preparatory meeting and it would be limited to those who sought peace between the belligerents.

Many people were beginning to wonder about the advisability of taking part in such a conference. Noam Chomsky wrote to tell me how he had been manipulated at a conference against the Vietnam war, in Stockholm. François Mitterrand, who was to become President of France nine years later, told me that we would be turned into figureheads at that conference, whose course and conclusions had been decided in advance. André Schwarz-Bart sent me a blunt telegram: "I will not take part in the Egyptian conference."

But I stubbornly persisted. I knew that in Israel my friends were excitedly preparing for their trip to Rome. I didn't want to abandon them, or leave the conference in the hands of professional propagandists without at least making our voices heard. It must have seemed to our opponents that our naïveté made us all the more dangerous. In any case, since they hadn't succeeded in maneuvering us, they decided to get rid of us. Hostility against the committee was concentrated on me. There were all sorts of attacks and accusations. Finally, in accordance with a time-tested procedure, the Italian Communists requested that Clara and I be excluded from the meeting, their goal being nothing less than "to save the conference from dangerous elements."

Aldo Zargani was so outraged that he sent Guido Fanti a registered letter in which he said, notably, that the initiative for the peace conference had been "taken *jointly* by Marek Halter and Khaled Mohieddin and was to be carried out *jointly* by the Committee of the Left and the Arab Socialist Union. . . . That exclusion, which has no political justification, reveals a decidedly inadmissible personal animosity, and this in itself is a very serious fact capable of giving rise to extreme consequences." He said we hadn't yet received our invitation, and that if we didn't receive it in time, "that might cause a scandal which would make the preparatory meeting fail."

As soon as he received this letter, the mayor called him to say that he agreed with him entirely and that he would talk to Mohieddin. Two days later we received a telegram inviting us to the meeting at the Casa della Cultura in Rome on March 1–2, 1972. The fact that the committee had been invited meant that our conditions had been accepted: the PLO and several prominent Israelis also received invitations.

But nothing had been resolved when Clara, Bernard Kouchner, and I arrived in Rome the day before the start of the meeting. We went to see Zargani. He wasn't in a good mood, and this time his laugh sounded mournful.

"You'll see," he said, "the Israelis won't be allowed into the meeting. The Arabs and the Communists will never accept it."

"We have to fight," I said.

"And we'll lose! People like us are always crushed by political machinery. In other places we'd be liquidated, here we'll be shut out."

Just then Uri Avnery called from the Fiumicino airport: the Israeli delegation had just arrived and wanted to stay at the same hotel as the Arab delegations.

"It will make discussion easier," said Uri, invincibly optimistic.

The Israeli press had given a great amount of space to the meeting in Rome, and Uri felt that an Arab–Israeli parley would be sure to make public opinion regard the Israeli "doves" as capable of doing something the government had failed to do: start along the path to peace. I told Uri that the Arabs usually stayed at the Hotel Pace Helvetia, but that I wasn't sure they would be glad to see the Israelis come there. He quickly understood; the Israelis, he said, would stay at the Hotel Santa Chiara, and he would join us as soon as possible in Zargani's apartment.

When he arrived, Zargani shared his pessimism with him.

"Are you sure they won't let us into the meeting?" asked Uri, still unable to believe it. "Let's not say anything to my friends yet. First we'll try to get some more information."

I made an appointment with Bettino Craxi (who was not yet president of the Socialist Party), and in the meantime we decided to stop by the Casa della Cultura, where Uri would bring his friends a little later.

"We won't take it lying down," said Aldo. "If they give us a hard time we'll walk out on the conference, and I'm sure the Italian Socialist Party will follow our lead."

I had never before seen him in such a state.

At the Casa della Cultura, there was an atmosphere of crisis. Groups were conspiring in the halls and everyone seemed agitated. We found Khaled Mohieddin in an office, vainly trying to put through a phone call to Cairo. As soon as he saw me, he put down the receiver and hurried toward me.

"It's a tragedy!" he exclaimed.

"What's a tragedy?" I asked, pretending surprise.

"The Israelis are in Rome!"

"Well, what of it?"

"If we want to make the conference a success, we can't give weapons to our adversaries by sitting down with the Israelis at this preparatory meeting!"

He was called to the phone. Chandra, the Indian, and Lord Montagu, the Englishman, brushed against us without giving us a look. Giulio Andreotti, the Social Democrat, ran past and went into a room behind them. The Syrian Varouj Salatian stopped in front of us.

"Who are the damned idiots who invited the Israelis?" he thundered.

"The organization committee," I answered.

"It's not their business to invite people!"

"Whose business is it?"

He made a vague gesture and hurried off to join Majid Abu Shazah, head of the pro-Soviet faction of the PLO, the man who had asked that Clara and I be excluded. We made a tour of the meeting rooms: hubbub, agitation, and smoke. Finally we met the mayor of Bologna.

"The Arab delegates absolutely refuse to be in the same room with the Israelis," he said with a helpless gesture.

Just then there was sudden silence in the hall. I looked around: the Israelis were coming in. No one went to welcome them or even greet them. Only Emile Habibi and Uzi Burstein, the two delegates of Rakah, the Israeli Communist Party, found someone to say hello to them: the Communist deputy Umberto Cardia, who hurriedly led them away.

"They don't seem overjoyed to see us here," remarked the Israeli writer Amos Oz.

Uri hadn't told Oz and the others anything about the difficulties that awaited them. I invited them to a nearby café, and there I quickly described the situation to them.

"I have an invitation to the meeting, and I'm going to it!" said the journalist Amos Kenan.

He held up his telegram from Guido Fanti.

"Not going to the meeting would be a disaster for us," said Amos Elon, another journalist. "For years we've been struggling for recognition of the Palestinians and withdrawal from the occupied territories. If the Arabs won't talk to us, who *will* they talk to?"

"Golda will have a good laugh at this!" said Amos Kenan.

Since I was the one who had dragged them into that adventure, they expected me to find a solution, but I had nothing to suggest. They had believed in my dreams, because they had the same ones, and now . . . I wasn't very proud of myself. The indifference of the crowd that surrounded us on the Via del Corso made us feel our distress and isolation even more keenly.

Aldo proposed that we withdraw from the conference. To Bettino Craxi, who was used to political games, that was not what he called a solution. To him, a solution was a compromise. The one he suggested to us was a model of its kind.

"The Arabs," he said, summing up the situation, "don't want to talk with the Israelis, and the Israelis don't want to be thrown out of a meeting they were invited to attend. All that needs to be done is for the Arabs to accept the Israelis' presence in the room, and for the Israelis to agree not to say anything. Then afterward the Israelis can say they took part in the preparatory meeting and the Arabs can say they didn't talk with them."

In other circumstances, that sleight-of-hand performance would probably have amused me, but, aside from the fact that I didn't believe it would be accepted, I saw that it amounted to a humiliating slap in the face for the Israelis.

"You should talk about it with Mohieddin," Craxi told us.

"And you should call Arafat," replied Amos Kenan.

In the Casa della Cultura, Mohieddin gave audiences as if he were a government minister: there were people waiting their turn in his anteroom.

It was hot in his office and he kept mopping his forehead.

"I'm in favor of a meeting with the Israelis," he said, "but this isn't the right time."

"In the Middle East," I answered, "it's never the right time, for the good reason that when people aren't fighting one war, they're getting ready for the next. The Israelis took a risk by coming here, and it's time you took one too — if you really want peace!"

Two men came in. Mohieddin made no reply but he seemed regretful. He continued mopping his forehead.

I went back to the Hotel Santa Chiara to rejoin the Israelis. It was now clear that the Arabs would not accept the compromise of the Italian Socialist Party. But since no one had informed the Israelis of that, they decided to go to the opening of the meeting the next morning.

According to the invitation, the meeting was to begin at ten o'clock. At eleven o'clock the delegates were still bustling in the halls, clustering here and there for conversation or scheming. The Israelis had arrived, but since no one paid any attention to them, they stood off by themselves. Unfortunate pilgrims for peace! The Arab delegates had been closeted with the leaders of the Peace Movement for a long time.

Finally the mayor of Bologna arrived.

"What are you going to do?" he asked me.

I told him we would have to hold a press conference to announce our departure and the reasons for it. He walked away without answering.

The Casa della Cultura took on the aspect of a law court. On one side, the jurors were deliberating. In the hall, groups of delegates were having whispered discussions and giving us furtive looks. The Israelis stood behind us in silence. We claimed to be their defenders. . . . It was all so disheartening!

The door finally opened. A cloud of smoke and an indescribable sound of commotion came out. Fanti walked toward us with an embarrassed smile.

"I'm sorry — " He coughed and went on: "We've found a solution. In Italy, a solution is always found." He coughed again and said almost in a whisper, "The meeting won't take place." And, after a second of silence: "Officially."

The "solution" was as follows: it would be announced to the press that the organization committee had held a series of meetings and consultations with eminent figures and leaders of organizations from various countries; the Israelis would be received by the organization committee on the same basis as the Algerians, who, like them, had not attended the first preparatory meeting. As for the others, they would gather the next morning for only half a day to decide on what course to follow.

The Israelis listened to Fanti without showing any reaction.

"But it's not with the Algerians that we're at war," Amos finally said.

"Yes, I know," replied Fanti, "but we were able to work out the compromise because they weren't at the first meeting either. The main thing is to save the conference."

Andreotti then came up to us, looking perfectly relaxed, and patted Uri on the shoulder, as if he were patting someone who had just been sentenced to two years in prison, to make him realize that it was still better than a death sentence.

The Israelis went back to their hotel to think over what their response would be. With Guido, we went to have a cup of coffee at an outside table of a café on the Piazza del Popolo. The situation had gone completely beyond us. We had overestimated our importance. The Communists needed us in order to give the image of a democratic conference and make it credible, but we had been wrong to think they would give up their usual propaganda.

"We'll have to pull out," said Kouchner.

It was hard for me to resign myself to that. The situation was untenable for us, but I had invested so much hope, time, and energy in it that I couldn't easily accept that failure. Before anything else, we had to find out what the Israelis had decided. We went to rejoin them.

By the time we arrived, they had decided to hold a press conference to explain their departure. The affront was so painfully felt, and the political damage to the Israeli left was so great, that even the two Communists were in agreement with the other members of the delegation.

"But how are we going to present this failure at home?" asked Uri.

For years they had been preaching the urgent need for dialogue with the Arabs, and now they were about to go back to Israel after being rebuffed as if they were criminals, without even having exchanged a greeting or a handshake with those of their adversaries who claimed to want peace.

"I don't care," said Amos Kenan, brandishing his telegram. "Since I have an invitation, I'm going."

"They'll throw you out," said Clara. "I think that first you should all come to a decision on Fanti's proposal. Either you accept it, and then you have to think of the explanation you'll give in Israel, or else you reject it, and then you have to find the most spectacular way to keep the conference from getting off the ground."

"What do you think?" Uri asked Bernard Kouchner.

"One thing I learned in the Communist Youth, before I was expelled for deviation," Bernard answered, "is that you can always turn a defeat into a half-victory."

A half-victory! The Israelis clutched at that idea and decided to accept Fanti's proposal. They met with the organizing committee for an hour, just before the Algerians, and then spent the rest of their stay in Italy with the correspondents of Israeli newspapers, working out descriptions of their "half-victory" for the press of their country.

22

A Missed Appointment
in London

In May 1972 we were again in Israel. The whole world was wondering about the meaning of President Sadat's amazing decision: he had just expelled the Soviet advisers. In Israel, where everyone closely follows the slightest troop movements in neighboring countries, where each minor news item gives rise to several theories, and where everyone eagerly tries to find an overall explanation for each particular happening, we were greeted, having just been in Egypt, as people who were "in the know."

"I'm probably not the first to ask you this question," Yitzhak Ben-Aharon, general secretary of Histadrut, said to us one day when we were having lunch with him in Tel Aviv, "but what do you think of the situation in Egypt?"

I tried to explain how power was exercised there, the rise of the middle class that had supported Sadat, its demands, and its hope of attracting American capital. I reported our conversation with Heykal and added that the time had probably come for Israel to make a gesture.

"What kind of gesture?" asked Ben-Aharon.

"Offering to give the Suez Canal back to Egypt, for example."

"Letting the Egyptians set up their forces on the east bank?"

"Of course. Sadat could present the Israeli withdrawal as a victory, and consolidate his position."

"Is that in our interest?"

"You can say it's a first step and offer to begin negotiations on the terms of a larger withdrawal. If the Egyptians agree to such negotiations, it will be an implicit recognition of Israel, and then anything may become possible. If Sadat really needs Israeli concessions to keep himself in power, he'll have to pay the price for them."

"Have you talked to any members of the Israeli government?"

"Not yet."

"You should talk to Dayan. I think he might be more receptive than Golda on that subject."

"I don't know him personally," I said.

"But Clara has met him, hasn't she?"

"Yes," said Clara, "but I'd rather have you talk to him about it first."

With the forceful expression of an old fighter, as always, Ben-Aharon said he would do it that afternoon in the Knesset. Then he asked Clara what she thought of Dayan.

"I think he's capable of the best and the worst, and knows it," she answered. "With his political sense, his pragmatism, and his charismatic power, he could probably unblock the situation, the way de Gaulle did with the war in Algeria."

"Do you think he'd go so far as to talk to Arafat?"

"Yes, I do, although he seemed rather pessimistic the last time I saw him. He was expecting another war to break out in late 1973."

"That's all the more reason for trying to do something before then," Ben-Aharon concluded, laughing.

He called us the next morning to tell us that Dayan would call us during the day. It was Friday, the day before the Sabbath. We went to Jacki's, the restaurant on the Square of the Kings of Israel where Israeli writers, artists, and even politicians were in the habit of meeting for lunch every Friday.

"Here comes peace!" the writer Amos Kenan exclaimed when he saw us.

They were all there. We had to push tables together and tell once again about our trip to Cairo and Beirut. Then they made friendly fun of my "mania for conferences"; the failure of the meeting in Rome had left its mark on them.

The phone was ringing just as we came back to our room. It was Dayan. He said he would be very glad to see us. Since we were going to have dinner with Shimon Peres* that evening, Dayan invited us to stop by the defense ministry that afternoon. We barely had time to take a shower and change out of the clothes that were clinging to our skin. But I like that thick, heavy Middle Eastern heat; it is a kind of soft yet solid matter that you cut with your body.

The way Dayan received us was as simple as the buildings of his ministry. I sensed that he was sizing me up. He attacked in a casual tone:

"How does a leftist painter feel when he faces General Dayan?"

"And how does General Dayan feel when he faces a leftist painter?" I asked.

"Oh, you know," he said with a vague gesture, "in politics you meet all kinds of people."

"In painting too."

This little skirmish seemed to please him. He introduced us to his adviser Naftali Lavi, then asked us if we wanted tea or Turkish coffee.

"Tea," I said.

"In Egypt," Clara remarked, "it's called Arab coffee."

"Do you want it *mazbut?*" asked Dayan, using an Arabic word that means "moderatly sweetened."

---

*Shimon Peres was at that time minister of transport and telecommunications.

Out of politeness, he questioned me a little about my painting, but I could see that he was eager to hear about our trip to Egypt. The conversation quickly turned to that subject. He interrupted me often to ask for details. Finally he said, "Yitzhak [Ben-Aharon] has told me about a proposal that, according to you, Israel ought to make to Egypt."

"Yes, I think it's time for Israel to make a gesture of goodwill toward Sadat."

"For example?"

I told him my views on the possibility of an Israeli withdrawal from the Suez Canal.

"But that's my plan!" exclaimed Dayan, and he called on Naftali Lavi for confirmation.

I said I knew his plan, but didn't think it went far enough.

"For Sadat, having the Israeli army pull back fifteen kilometers from the canal is all to the good, but what he really needs is to be able to have his soldiers, or at least some of them, cross the canal," said Dayan.

"You know better than I do that a limited, monitored force, without heavy weapons, wouldn't be a danger to Israel. For its prestige and its economy, Egypt needs to reopen the canal. After throwing out the Soviets, Sadat now has to prove that his policy is paying off, and a concession like that from the Israelis — which he would quickly transform into a personal victory — would probably make it possible for him to win his internal battle. And Israel has everything to gain from it. The canal has no security value from a military viewpoint: you can swim across it as easily as the Seine. Reopening it under those conditions would be a signal for normalizing relations between the two countries, and keeping it functioning would require some agreements and mutual commitments."

Dayan had listened to me with a certain amusement.

"You have a better strategic sense than some of our politicians," he said, pivoting his chair so that Clara was in the field of his good eye. "And you, what do you think about it?"

On that point, Clara answered, she agreed with me.

"Then you don't always agree with each other?" Dayan asked.

"If we did," she said, "there wouldn't have been any need for us both to come."

Dayan turned back to me.

"Personally, I also think we should give Sadat something so that he can stay in power without problems for two or three years. By then he'll be so strong that he can safely negotiate with us. But," he added rather ironically, "I'm not the prime minister and it's not up to me to decide. Have you talked to Golda? You're lucky: she likes you."

"I think she likes you too," I said.

"With me, it's a marriage of self-interest; with you, it's a marriage of love. Talk to her, tell her I agree, and call me."

When we were about to leave, he asked, "Would you be willing to go back to Cairo for that affair?"

"Of course."

"Then we'll have to see each other again before you go. Keep me posted."

We arrived in Jerusalem at night. On dimly lighted Jaffa Street, religious Jews were coming out of synagogues. At the King David Hotel, where we had agreed to meet him, we found Shimon Peres's chauffeur; he was to take us to Cohen's, a little restaurant that had only a few tables but served the best food in the city. As we were leaving the hotel, the switchboard operator gave Clara, whom she knew from her previous stays there, a note asking her to call Dayan immediately. He had already left his office at the ministry, but his secretary gave us his message: he thought it would be best, in our conversations with the Egyptians, not to mention that he agreed with our plan, and to limit ourselves to whatever Golda Meir might tell us. He also asked us to keep in touch with him.

"It sounds to me," said Clara, "as if he's already talked to Golda and they disagree."

Dinner with Shimon Peres and his daughter was pleasant, as it always was with him, in spite of our political differences.

He told us about the books he had recently read, and the exhibitions he had seen. He had often told me that he liked my
pictures, especially those with a silver background, so much
that he even tried to analyze that period of my painting in an
article published in the daily newspaper *Yediot Aharanot*. At
the time, many people saw him only as Dayan's shadow. Clara
and I were among the few who knew him well enough to be
sure he would go beyond that phase.

"It seems you've also tried to meet with Heykal," Clara said
to him teasingly.

"Do you know anyone here who wouldn't like to meet with
an Arab leader? Heykal is one of the most intelligent, and that's
why I got in touch with him. Did he tell you why he didn't
answer my offer?"

"He says he's read your statements and Dayan's and that
he doesn't see what he has to discuss with you."

"The Arabs know very well that some statements are meant
for internal use only. If I took literally everything he's written,
I wouldn't see what I had to discuss with him, either."

"You read Heykal's articles?" I asked.

"He's one of the most popular Israeli journalists," Peres answered jokingly. "Complete translations of all his articles are
published in the Israeli press. If he moved to Israel, he could
live on his royalties."

The next morning I called Golda. She was ill and asked me
to see Simcha Dinitz, her principal private secretary. We had
lunch with him in Tel Aviv. He felt that Israel couldn't risk
unblocking the canal without having some serious guarantees.
I told him that guarantees and the terms of withdrawal were
precisely what ought to be discussed between the Israelis and
the Egyptians.

"And who would represent Israel in those negotiations?"

"That's for you and other Israelis to decide," I answered.
"It could be Eban or another minister. Or you. Why not?"

From his smile, I saw that the idea didn't displease him. He
promised he would talk about it with Golda and asked us to
call him.

I tried to call him the next day. He wasn't in, but he had left a message asking us to get in touch with Lou Kadar, Golda's old friend and secretary. She was of French origin, so we spoke French, but we understood each other no better than usual. In her weak, expressionless voice she told me that Golda was feeling better and would see us in two days, in Jerusalem.

I went there alone, since Clara claimed it would make it easier for me to persuade Golda. I found her sitting, solidly anchored at her desk, with a cigarette smoldering in the ashtray; I felt as if she hadn't moved since the last time I saw her. The look in her eyes was both stern and friendly.

Golda often irritated me, and sometimes she even made me indignant, but I could never hold a grudge against her very long. I had for her the kind of affection one feels for one's mother or grandmother. I understood her way of thinking and reacting: it was that of the Jews I had known in my family. And in spite of all our differences, I often felt closer to her than to some of my friends whose political opinions I shared.

After having repeated publicly that Israel had to become a "normal" country, accepted by its neighbors, I had often wondered if there was any real necessity to win acceptance from others by becoming like them. Was becoming normal worth all that struggling and suffering? I think that the friendship Golda felt for me came from the same preoccupation: continuity. She saw me as a younger version of Jews she had known, who were close to her not so much because they spoke Yiddish as because they thought in Yiddish.

"Welcome," she said to me. "Simcha has told me about your conversation. I'm in favor of withdrawing a few kilometers to let the Egyptians reopen the canal. And it wasn't so long ago that Moshe [Dayan] proposed the same thing to Dr. Jarring."

I was about to say something, but she stopped me with a gesture, took another cigarette, and continued: "Letting the Egyptian army cross the canal is unthinkable. The canal is a physical barrier between us and the Egyptians. It's important to our security."

I tried to reassure her by telling her that, in my plan, only a symbolic military force would be installed on the east bank, and that in a modern war, with long-range artillery, rockets, and missiles, the Suez Canal was not a major obstacle.

"As long as a man like Sadat says he's ready to sacrifice a million human lives," she replied, "I can't trust him. Can anyone who doesn't respect human life really want peace?"

"Now you have a chance to put him to the test."

"What guarantees would we have?" she asked curtly.

More accustomed, as Elie Wiesel has said, to believing threats than promises, the Israelis are very mistrustful about guarantees, and always end up asking what guarantees will guarantee the guarantees.

"Golda," I said, smiling, "I'm not the one who's going to give you guarantees. You'll have to ask the Egyptians about them, during those negotiations."

"If they agree to negotiate — which is what we've always asked them to do — we'll discuss it with them then. But we don't have to state our intentions beforehand."

"If you want them to agree to that meeting at last, they'll have to have something to gain from it."

"They have everything to gain from it!"

"Israel has even more. For the Arabs, what's at stake is the territories they lost in 1967. For Israel, it's peace."

"The Arabs don't need peace? The difference between the Arab leaders and us is that we mean what we say."

"In politics, no one asks you to say what you really mean." Golda smiled.

"I agree to a withdrawal from the canal. I also agree to letting in as many Egyptian civilians as it will take to clear the canal. But when it comes to the army, even just a symbolic force, I'm on my guard. But if the Egyptians were to accept direct contacts, then —"

"Then it would be worthwhile for me to try to get the lay of the land. Or should I go back to my painting?"

"You should go on painting in any case," Golda said seriously. "As for what we've been talking about, Simcha will call you in a few days."

As promised, three days later Simcha Dinitz made an appointment with me in Jerusalem. Golda, he told me, was ill again, but she had thought over our conversation; she gave us permission to sound out the Egyptians but she still had misgivings about letting their army cross to the "Israeli" side of the canal.

"I don't think she's formed a definite opinion yet," said Dinitz. "It will all depend on whatever contacts you may be able to establish between the Egyptians and us."

"Then I have a green light?"

"Let's say you have a fairly free hand."

As usual, I had to hurry back to Paris to get in touch with the Egyptians. Clara decided to stay in Israel a month longer to gather material for another issue of *Eléments* on the Palestinians in the occupied territories. (She later used the research for that issue as the basis of a book: *Les Palestiniens du silence*.) Before leaving, I went with her to Nablus, in the occupied West Bank territory, where Raymonda Tawill had gathered a number of Arab intellectuals to talk with us.

Outwardly, at least, things had changed since our last visit: we saw a freshly tarred road, a forest of television antennas over the Ramallah refugee camps, Israeli products in all the shops. But Yusra Salah, a schoolteacher we met on the outskirts of Nablus, got into our car with great reluctance because it was registered and rented in Israel: she had promised herself, she told us, that she would not use any Israeli products.

"The friends of the Palestinians are here!" Raymonda exclaimed when she introduced us.

She had prepared a big meal in our honor, and the little tables in the living room were completely covered with all sorts of dishes. Our discussion began quickly and lasted a long time, but we had to interrupt it for the arrival of Aziz Zouabi and, a few minutes later, of the American consul in Jerusalem. Aziz Zouabi, an Arab, was at that time deputy minister of health in the Israeli government. Happy to see us there, he addressed us in Hebrew, *"Ma shlomhem?"* ("How are you?"), and hurried to Clara to kiss her. She answered him in English. He quickly understood and switched from Hebrew to English.

What an absurd situation! But in that world where judgments were made according to appearances, it was important to know whether a Jew knew Hebrew. In the eyes of the Palestinians in the occupied territories, speaking Hebrew would have transformed us into Israelis, and therefore into enemies. In spite of his belonging to the Israeli government, the Palestinians regarded Zouabi, an Arab from Nazareth, as one of them, and they often went to him when they had administrative problems. He was a broad-shouldered, intelligent, lively man; I liked him very much and I was ashamed to see that he had fewer inhibitions in resolving his contradictions than I had in resolving mine.

We often had to hold ourselves back from telling our Palestinian friends that we had relatives in Israel, because, as far as they were concerned, that fact alone would have deprived us of all impartiality. Being leftist Jews, we had to match a certain image. As for the American consul, the Palestinians welcomed him with pleasure — even though they considered him to be an agent of the CIA.

As soon as I was back in Paris I met with Adel Amer. I told him that in Cairo I intended to speak to either Heykal or the new foreign minister, Mourad Ghaleb. In his opinion, my chances of rapidly getting in touch with Sadat would be better if I went through Heykal. After several unsuccessful attempts to call Heykal, I was finally able to talk to his secretary. She told me that he had gone to Austria in a private capacity, and would go from there to Germany. She didn't know his address. I asked Amer to get it from the Egyptian embassy in Austria, but the embassy didn't even know that Heykal had come there. Jean Lacouture, who was about to go to Germany on a reporting assignment, promised me that he would try to pick up Heykal's trail. Meanwhile I tried to call Mourad Ghaleb in Cairo. I learned that he was at the United Nations, and I was given the phone number of the Egyptian delegation. Finally I was able to call him at the Hotel Pierre, in New York, where he was staying.

"What's new, Halter?" he asked me.

I told him I wanted to see him as soon as possible. He asked if it was important and I answered that it might be. After thinking for a moment he suggested that we meet in Geneva a few days later, when he would be on his way back to Egypt.

I went to Geneva and met him there just after he had seen Dr. Jarring. He was sitting at the edge of the swimming pool of the Hotel La Réserve, with a glass of whiskey in his hand and, beside him, another glass for me. We were alone. That August afternoon was rather cool, but Mourad was in swimming trunks. I told him about seeing Ben-Aharon, Dayan, Dinitz, and Golda Meir. He listened to me attentively, and when I had finished he asked me what I thought of all that. I answered that in my opinion it was a good chance to begin a dialogue.

"According to what you've told me," he said, "there are differences between Golda Meir and Dayan."

"Yes, there are differences of opinion within the Israeli government but I think that, in the course of negotiations, Dayan's pragmatism would win out."

"How would the practical details of a withdrawal from the canal be decided?"

"There would have to be meetings between Israelis and Egyptians."

"It would be difficult for our president to consider such meetings at this time."

I told him that I believed the meetings should be kept secret. He seemed skeptical. I gave him as an example the dozens of meetings between Chinese and Americans that didn't become known till years afterward, when they had resulted in official contacts.

"And what would the Israelis ask in exchange for withdrawing their forces?"

"Remember, Mourad, what we talked about in Cairo: the main obstacle in the search for a solution may be lack of trust, constant mutual suspicion. If we succeed in arranging those few technical meetings, even if they're kept secret, the Israelis will see it as an excellent guarantee, and proof that in Egypt there's a real desire to make peace."

"All right, but who will guarantee secrecy?"

"If I told you that I would, it would seem funny to you. . . . I'd like to propose something that I haven't yet discussed with the Israelis."

He seemed interested.

"During those meetings with the Israelis," I went on, "you would decide on mutual concessions and how they would be carried out, and also on how they would be presented to public opinion. Because the pressure of public opinion is felt in Israel as well as in Egypt, and Egypt also has to deal with pressure from the Arab world, the public version of an event is as important as the event itself."

"For some philosophers," said Mourad, "only that version matters, because the act doesn't exist without it."

As I looked at Mourad looking at me, I wondered what he thought of me. I have often asked myself that question during my talks with Israelis and Arabs. Do they believe in my good faith? Do they take me seriously? A journalist once accused me of being a double agent working for both Dayan and Arafat. I realize that the complexity of my situation can give rise to different interpretations. I have made sincere friendships on both sides; I feel real affection for some of the politicians I have been led to meet, and it is unchanged by any differences of opinion that may come up between us. I remember the night when Lotfi, Mourad, and I got drunk at the foot of the Pyramids, an improbable escapade that undoubtedly brought us closer together.

The waiter brought olives and two more drinks. Mourad got dressed.

"Your idea seems interesting to me," he said. "Maybe we could hold those meetings in London. It would give me a chance to see my children, since they're students there."

He asked who would represent Israel. I answered that it

might be the foreign minister or anyone else designated by the government.

"It's not impossible that it would be Dayan," I said. "He'd certainly be a candidate, but I'm sure there would be personal conflicts and disagreements over different viewpoints."

Mourad stressed the importance of sending someone responsible, empowered to make decisions. Then, as if everything were settled, we began talking about our mutual friends and the time he had spent in Moscow as an ambassador. To amuse ourselves, we even tried to converse in Russian. Under the beach umbrellas of Geneva, everything seemed so simple, between people of goodwill. . . .

When I returned to Paris I wrote, in Yiddish, for Golda Meir's benefit, an account of my conversation with Mourad Ghaleb. I took my "report" to the Israeli embassy, where Avi Primor promised to send it in the diplomatic pouch.

Mourad called me a few days later: the plan had been well received by Sadat, who wanted to know what the Israelis thought of it. I told him I had written to Jerusalem and was waiting for an answer.

It came to the embassy, signed by Simcha Dinitz: Golda agreed in principle to all the proposals in my letter. I immediately wrote to Mourad. Then Jean Lacouture called me: he hadn't found any trace of Heykal in Germany, but he might have a chance to meet him at the Olympic Games in Munich. I told him that Adel Amer had advised me to leave everything in Mourad Ghaleb's hands, to avoid confusion — after all, Ghaleb was the Egyptian foreign minister. Jean asked me if I had seen Mendès-France again. We decided to make an appointment with him for the following week. Jean thought that the three of us might go to the Middle East after the Olympic Games.

About two weeks later, I received a note from Cairo asking that the meeting — "my" meeting — be held in mid-September in London. I immediately notified Jerusalem.

I restrained myself from being jubilant, but this time everything seemed to be settled. From Israel, Clara told me that

Dayan was carefully keeping himself informed. The Israelis and the Egyptians were finally going to meet. I didn't care that it was going to be done in secret; to me, the main thing was for them to talk to each other without constraint. In a way, talking to each other meant recognizing each other.

I was at home, alone, when Günter Grass called me from Germany. He seemed greatly agitated.

"Have you heard?" he asked.

"About what?"

He told me that Palestinian commandos from the Black September group had taken hostages from among the Israeli athletes in Munich, and that two of them had already been killed.

On the radio, there was a steady stream of news bulletins. The phone rang constantly. I was devastated. I knew that Israel wouldn't accept the Palestinians' demands and that the Palestinians would be led to execute their hostages. Tension would increase in the Middle East, and one more possibility of a meeting between Arabs and Israelis would be lost.

The massacre of the hostages taken in Munich* made positions harden on both sides. Mourad Ghaleb either resigned or was dismissed, and he was replaced by Mohammed Zayat. I was trying to decide what to do when I received a letter from a friend in Beirut, telling me that Black September had issued a communiqué saying that the purpose of their action in Munich had been to ward off the danger of an agreement about to be concluded between Egypt and Israel, to the detriment of the Palestinian people.

As I read and reread that letter, my head, arms, and legs became horribly heavy; I felt as if I were going insane. I tried

---

*One of the fedayeen killed was George Aissa, the man who had taken Clara before the "tribunal" in Beirut where she first met Kanafani. The press also spoke of Fouad El Shamali as one of the organizers of Black September in Europe, accusing him of having set up the terrorist attack in Munich and saying that his wife made sure it was carried out after his death. Serge Groussard developed that idea in his book *La Médaille de sang*. The Arab press strongly opposed it, pointing out, notably, that Fouad El Shamali had taken part, with the Israeli Saul Friedlander, in a symposium on the main problems in the Middle East.

to call several friends; no answer. I went to the Place des Vosges and began walking along the metal fence. If what that communiqué said was true, and if it referred to our plan, was I partly responsible for the deaths in Munich? I was like a child who had started a toy train, then watched helplessly as it derailed and killed several people in the next room.

I went back home to call Clara in Tel Aviv. But just as I opened the door, she called me. She told me that the Munich massacre had plunged Israel into mourning; that during the victims' funeral Uri Avnery had been slapped by the father of one of the dead athletes; that threatening letters were being received by everyone who, like Amos Kenan, defended the rights of the Palestinians. The anger was general.

I didn't tell Clara about the letter from Beirut, or how I was feeling. I had to deal with my doubts and fears on my own. I thought of going back to my painting and doing nothing else. Abandoning politics. Sartre wrote that a work of art is nothing, compared with a child dying of hunger. At least my paintings didn't kill. And I would rather be wholly responsible for a mediocre work of art than partly responsible for a successful massacre. I felt myself sinking into despair when it was quite possible, and no doubt even probable, that there was no connection between our plan and the massacre. I angrily plunged back into my drawing. It was a refuge, of course, but what would a professional politician have done in my place? The fact is that he probably wouldn't have asked himself any questions.

23

From Harvard
to Cairo

The *Harvard Independent* of February 1973 devoted its cover to me. It was flattering and I was flattered. "The Art of Marek Halter: A Fusion with Politics" was the headline in that prestigious student publication. As I read the article, however, I had a feeling of embarrassment and bitterness. I wasn't satisfied with my painting or my writing, and my "battle" for peace in the Middle East had so far produced very few results. Operation Eliav had failed, our meeting in London had been called off, and the Bologna conference had been stolen from us.

Where had all my efforts taken me? I had never had so many doubts before, about everything, including myself. As I try to reconstruct that period of my life, I now realize how much it was marked by anxiety. A succession of faces, images, and moments, confusedly bound together in my memory by the futility of an agitation that was leading me nowhere.

New York. I had just had a discussion with some students on the question of what had enabled the Jewish people to survive through the centuries: memory of persecutions, or hope for a life without persecution.

Soon after the Bible opens, there is a transgression followed by a fratricide. But there is also this: "I have set before you life and death, blessing and curse; therefore choose life, that you and your descendants may live" (Deuteronomy 30:19). And so, I told the students, Jewish history is shaped by a constant conflict between the forces of life and the forces of death, between tendencies to grow and tendencies to decay, and especially between good and evil.

If history is the main force in the teaching of the Law, the study and transmission of it are essential to the perpetuation and identity of a people.

Rites and stories were the main vehicles of Jewish memory. A memory of slavery and liberation. "Remember that you were once slaves in Egypt," Jews repeat every year at Passover. Whereas rites show a preference for liberating events, such as the revolt of the Maccabees against the Syrian troops of Antiochus Epiphanes in 167 B.C. (Chanukah), or the victory over the wicked Haman in the time of the Persian King Ahasuerus (Purim), stories are devoted almost exclusively to lamentation and tragedies related to persecutions. And popular memory gives more prominence to the spirit of Baruch's *Apocalypse*, written soon after the destruction of the Temple in A.D. 70, the stories of Solomon ibn Varga, written after the expulsion of the Jews from Spain in 1492, and Emmanuel Ringelblum's chronicles of the Warsaw Ghetto, than to the happier stories of the Carolingian period in France, the Golden Age in Spain, or the Renaissance in Italy. This is probably because suffering is timeless, and Usque's cry in 1553, "Europe, O Europe, my hell on earth!" would not have been alien to a prisoner in Auschwitz.

It seems excessive to me, however, to try to reduce Jewish memory to a martyrology. Jeremiah prophesied the destruction of the First Temple, followed by the Babylonian exile, in 587 B.C., yet in the midst of his famous lamentations he states this surprising vision: "For thus says the Lord of hosts, the

God of Israel: Houses and fields and vineyards shall again be bought in this land" (Jeremiah 32:15). For in order to persevere in the struggle against the evil that both threatens and tempts him, man must have hope. Hope more than justice, more than brotherhood, more than freedom. The hope of someday seeing the world embodied in the Law.

Hope. Those students steeped in the literature of affliction were a little surprised by my optimism, which nothing seemed to justify. Nothing except our discussion itself, in that university, on the meaning of Jewish history. For the Jews, to endure is to conquer.

That evening Lotfi El Kholi called me from Paris to tell me that Sayyid Marei, who was then general secretary of the Arab Socialist Union, had invited me to Cairo for a symposium on French–Egyptian relations.

On the plane, words from a Yiddish song came back to me:

What matters is not to arrive,
But to walk along the sunny road.

As I crossed the Kasr an-Nil bridge, heading for my hotel on El Tahrier Square, I felt that this time I really was walking along that sunny road.

The lobby was swarming with people. The representative of the Arab Socialist Union who was accompanying me had to elbow his way through them to get me to the reception desk. There was a sudden movement in the crowd. I saw a dozen policemen and, behind them, a group of men in which I recognized Pierre Butros Ghali.

"What are you doing in Cairo?" Butros the pessimist asked me in surprise. Behind him was Anwar Sadat. "I'm going to introduce you to President Sadat."

He said a few words to Nasser's successor, who then looked at me with more interest.

"You've come from Israel?" he asked in English.

"No, this time I've come from the United States. I took part in a debate at Harvard."

"Did you talk about the Middle East?"

"No, I talked about peace in the Middle East."

"You think it's possible?"

"Do you, Mr. President?"

Sadat smiled.

"What are you doing in Cairo?"

"I've been invited here by the Arab Socialist Union."

"Would you like to have coffee with us?"

And so, entirely by chance, I found myself with Sadat in the hotel bar, facing the Nile, where the Cairo aristocracy came for five o'clock tea in the English manner.

The first thing we said to each other, he the Arab and I the Jew, was that we both spoke English with the same accent. I told him about our battles for peace and he questioned me about Israel. His speech was vivid, full of unexpected expressions. Of the Jordan he said, "that stream in which more history flows than water."

"Do you really think the Israelis want peace?" he asked me abruptly.

"If you doubt it, put them to the test."

Sadat smiled again, with his whole face.

"How?"

"Talk to them. Jews believe in the power of words."

He laughed.

"You want me to go to Jerusalem and talk with Golda Meir?"

"Why not?"

"To have a real conversation, the two parties must be on an equal footing and, rightly or wrongly, the Arab world feels humiliated."

"But the Arab world is immense and Israel is very small."

"Precisely." Sadat wiped his mustache and stood up. "If you ever come back to Egypt, let me know and I'll be glad to see you again." Then, stepping toward the door, "Go on talking about peace in the Middle East. We Arabs also believe in the power of words."

Paris. As soon as I returned, I was again plunged into the problems of the Bologna conference. The Communists and the Syrians were trying to keep us out of it by any means. After my trip to Cairo, that wrangling seemed ludicrous to me. We decided not to go to Bologna.*

Israel. This time Clara and I went there with the Greek composer Mikis Theodorakis. Everyone wanted to know what Sadat had said to me. Golda Meir questioned me a long time, making me repeat the Egyptian president's every word and gesture. But she remained skeptical. Even so, she called me at dawn the next morning to ask for more details.

As for Theodorakis, he was given an exuberant welcome. Almost the whole government attended the concert he gave in Jerusalem. I remember an evening on the roof of Amos Kenan's house in Tel Aviv. A big puppet with curly hair, a mixture of light and shadow, Theodorakis told us about Greece, making broad gestures as if he were still conducting his orchestra. He also told how Dayan, in Athens to visit his daughter Yael, had come to see him and offered Israeli aid to the resistance against the colonels; the newspapers picked up the story and a spokesman for the defense ministry immediately denied it.

Paris again, where Marcuse was staying. Clara and I went to his hotel to have breakfast with him and his wife. His pale, nervous hands hadn't changed, and their freckles hypnotized

---

*The Bologna conference took place in May 1973. It aroused little interest and the press practically passed over it in silence. The Israelis took part in it in spite of everything. They called us several times to ask that Clara join them, at least in her capacity as editor of *Eléments*. The members of the committee were consulted. They opposed the idea: *Eléments* was the organ of the committee, and Clara's participation would have been interpreted as a surrender on our part. So she didn't go to Bologna. The Israelis, who spoke of the "spirit of Bologna" — this was their "half-victory" — had to sign a resolution in which Israel's name didn't appear. This affair was probably at least a partial cause of Uri Avnery's loss of his seat in the Knesset.

me as they had done the first time I met him. He had finally
visited Israel. He was delighted with his trip and kept talking
about it, pretending not to hear his wife's ironic or caustic
remarks. When he explained the Israelis' morbid preoccupation with security by the memory of Nazi massacres, she said
that that wasn't the Palestinians' fault. We, of course, agreed
with her.

"In that case," she said, "the Jewish state should have been
created in Bavaria!"

The discussion between Mrs. Marcuse and Clara became acrimonious. I did my best to ward off what threatened to be a
quarrel that would lead to a permanent severing of relations.
Marcuse's hands toyed busily with his little spoon.

On October 6, 1973, I was in New York when I learned the
news: war had broken out in the Middle East.

Is it possible to keep the moon in a bucket of water? The
Jews of Chelm, cleverer than the others, thought they could
do it. Every night they waited till they saw the moon in the
water of their bucket, and then they carefully closed the bucket.
The next morning, the moon was always gone.

It was morning and once again my bucket was empty. Was
I going to keep trying endlessly, like those clever Jews of
Chelm?

24

Yom Kippur

I clearly remembered what Heykal had said about a clash on the canal; I knew that the great powers were monitoring the situation — I even had the impression that events hadn't surprised them and that they would let the war go on until the most advantageous time for them to intervene. I then recalled what Sadat had told me about equality as a precondition for dialogue with Israel. But because of the memory that is part of me, and the symbols of the community to which I belong through my history, I was afraid.

I had already known Yom Kippur in wartime. It was in 1939 in Warsaw, a city with a Jewish population of nearly half a million. For Yom Kippur, the Day of Atonement, life stopped. That year, Hitler decided to "light a candle for the Jews" there. For hours, hundreds of Messerschmitts dive-bombed the city. Houses burned, synagogues burned. Pious Jews in their prayer clothes ran through shattered streets filled with the cries of the wounded; they were looking for their wives, their children, their friends. Explosions, fear, tears, shouts — Yiddish.

On October 6, 1973, Egyptian forces crossed the canal while the Jews were in synagogues. There was probably no connection between those two moments of history, but we can't control our memories; while I listened to news bulletins on American radio stations, I inwardly heard the howls of diving Messerschmitts.

In New York, the United Nations Security Council held an emergency meeting. Mohammed Zayat, the new Egyptian foreign minister, was at the Hotel Pierre. Abba Eban, the Israeli foreign minister, was at the Plaza. They would only have had to cross Fifth Avenue to meet. I called them both. They kept putting me off. I didn't give up. I spent two weeks going back and forth between Harvard and New York, where I vainly tried to establish contact between Arabs and Israelis. On the evening of October 18 I met Marguerite Duras.

"Do you think they'll hold out?" she asked me.

"Who?"

"The Israelis."

"I think so, but this time they'll have to pay a high price."

"Won't the Jews ever be left alone?" She leaned her strong-featured face toward me. "You know, I can't talk about all that with my comrades — they're so anti-Israeli! They know what I think, they say I'm a Jew by adoption. When they start talking bullshit about Israel, imperialism and all that stuff, I put my hands over my ears. I tell them I do it out of Jewish solidarity." She began pounding the table with her fists and repeating, "Jewish solidarity! Jewish solidarity! Jewish solidarity!"

On October 7, the day after the war started, the *New York Times* said in a front-page headline, "Arabs and Israelis Battle on Two Fronts."

I bought *Le Monde:* in France, public opinion was hurriedly mobilizing to support one side against the other with a clear conscience. I was beside myself with anger and bitterness.

Finally, on October 20, I called Pierre Viansson-Ponté, the editor of *Le Monde*, to tell him that I wanted to write an article.

"Do it, but hurry!" he said with the friendliness and open-mindedness that characterize the great American journalists.

I dictated the article over the phone. But on October 21 the Arabs and Israelis accepted a cease-fire. I got a call from Paris asking me to make some changes in the article. I made them and phoned them to Pierre Viansson-Ponté in the middle of the night — I had forgotten the time difference between New York and Paris. On the battlefield, the situation was rapidly evolving: fighting had resumed. Outrun by events, I called *Le Monde;* again I had to make changes in my article. But the second cease-fire went into effect before *Le Monde* could publish the article. I had it published in the United States, in *Liberation* magazine, and it stirred up vehement controversy. I entitled it "For Ala' Hamrush and Ran Cohen":

There was a lot to like about them. Ala' Hamrush majored in political science. President of the Egyptian Students' Union, he was removed from that office because he criticized the regime and organized demonstrations against the economic policy of Anwar Sadat's government. A Sephardi of Iraqi origin, Ran Cohen is the general secretary of Kibbutz Gan Shmuel. In his articles, he criticizes the policies of the Israeli government. He has organized demonstrations in the occupied territories, in favor of the Palestinian people's rights.

There was a lot to like about my friends. We made plans for the future, we talked about struggles to change political and social structures in the Middle East. A few days ago, Ala' Hamrush and Ran Cohen may have been shooting at each other. If, by tragic misfortune, something had happened to them, it would have been much more than a victory or a setback for a general staff: it would have been a terrible defeat for all those who claim they want to improve the world, to make it more just and fraternal.

Carried away by its condemnations, manifestos and demonstrations, they identify themselves with one or the other of the two warring sides, forgetting appeals to nations beyond governments and appeals to the individuals of the countries at war. As good pupils of Joseph Stalin, they no longer consider people, but choose their bloc. I asked a friend what he thought of that war. He answered simply, "America is behind Israel and the Soviet Union is behind the Arabs: my choice is clear."

But what about the inhabitants of Ashdod and those of Helwan, and my friends Ran Cohen and Ala' Hamrush?

Right-thinking people condemn them and forget them in the name of a great Whole and its hasty identifications. It was explained to me here that the Arabs needed a little victory to wash away their humiliation. I was told elsewhere that the Israelis could not allow such a victory because, in their eyes, it would be the first step toward realization of the Palestinians' dream: "destruction of Israel's governmental structures." Since then, the cease-fire has gone into effect and we do not yet know the number and names of the victims.

Where are our humanists? Have they nothing to tell us except their regrets?

When war broke out, with its deaths and its passion, the stream of articles and published statements began flowing again — always the same signatures, always the same vocabulary, always beside the historical point. Ever since Hegel, there have been those who try to convince us that an individual's life is nothing, compared with the interests of a state. If that is the theory, where is the difference between respect and contempt for humanity. Members of the inter-

national left have become tacticians and opportun-
ists. They have never tried to bring the Arabs and the
Israelis together, or take an active part in the search
for a solution to the Arab–Israeli conflict. Within that
left, for years, we were unfortunately the only ones
to say that war in the Middle East serves only the
various imperialisms, and to suggest that there could
be another solution: a peace through which all mobi-
lizations would become possible. We repeated that the
Palestinians' national demands — which we support — do not necessarily conflict with those of the
Israelis. We published an appeal to the Arabs, the
Israelis and the Palestinians. Its content is still timely.
For some, that appeal was related to the propaganda
of Al Fatah; for others, it was related to Zionist propaganda. This is one more proof, if any more were
needed, that the left can no longer conceive of taking
a position independently.

My leftist friends debate and make emphatic pro-
nouncements in Paris, Rome, Amsterdam and New
York. Their friends and mine were dying in the Sinai
and the Golan Heights — is there no one who ac-
knowledges responsibility for it? How can you once
again, in good conscience, hand out your good and
bad grades, as though correcting a classroom assignment written in human blood?

What if, in the old universalist tradition, we all issued an appeal to the Israeli, Arab and Palestinian
peoples; what if we now decided to hold a conference and invite Arabs, Israelis and Palestinians to it;
what if we tried to show that peace is possible — away
from the generals and their alliances?

But no, I see you imprisoned in ideology and ab-
straction. Some of you call for a final struggle and
reject the cease-fire, as if you wanted people in the
Middle East to die for your ideas. Others of you are
glad that the great powers have agreed and inter-

vened, as if you always left the decision to them, once the excitement of propaganda has passed. As you elaborate your grand theories, you will helplessly look on while the Palestinian problem and the possibility of real peace between Israel and the Arab countries are shoved aside. Whether you advocate *Realpolitik* or war to the bitter end, it will always have to be others who feed your excitement or your relief. When you read this article, you will talk of idealism. You are already shrugging your shoulders, and that enrages me. And if the rage I feel could only be communicated to hundreds and thousands of people, then maybe it would become obvious that if an Ala' Hamrush killed a Ran Cohen, or if a Ran Cohen killed an Ala' Hamrush, it would not be an exploit for the Egyptian army or the Israeli army, but the failure — everywhere — of the whole left.

An agreement was made between the Egyptians and the Israelis at Kilometer 101; it saved the encircled Egyptian Third Army. Another agreement was negotiated by Henry Kissinger on the withdrawal of forces from the approaches to the Suez Canal. In the Sinai, opposing generals shook hands and ordinary soldiers exchanged photographs of their children. And in the streets of Cairo and Tel Aviv there were newly widowed young women and newly crippled young men. How many lives could have been saved? The agreement on the canal was the very one we had talked about a year and a half earlier. "That's politics!" Heykal and Dayan had told me. They both had to leave power.

25

An Egyptian Woman
in Israel

She was Egyptian, her name was Sana Hasan, she talked
fast and abundantly, she had a round head on the round
body of a Russian doll. She introduced herself as the daughter
of a former Egyptian ambassador to Washington and the wife
of Tahsin Bashir, a spokesman for the foreign ministry. She
was likable. We hadn't been able to see each other in Paris,
when she called me on the recommendation of Ismail Sabri
Abdallah, but we met at Harvard, where she was working
toward a doctorate in political science.

She had been, she said, an enthusiastic reader of *Eléments*,
and she showed me an article she had just written. It was an
interesting article, but too superficial for my taste. I asked her
what she intended to do.

"What do you mean?"

"If you want to please the media, you can have your hour
of glory at a cheap price. But if you want to try to accomplish
something in the Middle East, you'll have to go about it dif-

ferently. If you publish your article the way it is, you'll lose all credibility."

I suggested that she tighten up the article, have it published in the *New York Times,* and then go to Israel.

"The Israelis will never let me into the country," she said. "I've already tried to get a visa at the Israeli consulate in Boston, and I was turned down."

She must have come across one of those unbearable civil servants whom Israel sends to posts in foreign countries as though to get rid of them. Actually, if Arabs wanted to visit Israel, they would get as many visas as they asked for.

I offered to go to Israel with Sana Hasan and put her in contact with political leaders and intellectuals. Then we would go to Egypt, creating a precedent and, I hoped, opening the way for people who would want to follow in our footsteps.

"But what if the Egyptians confiscate my passport when I come back from Israel?" she asked.

"We'll let the press in on our trip, of course, and it will be hard for Sadat to contradict all his statements about his desire for peace."

I finally convinced her and we decided to see each other again. Almost as soon as she had left my room, she came back: she had forgotten her scarf. Then she came back a second time: she had forgotten a book. Then a third time, I don't remember why. I was intrigued by all those comings and goings.

"I hope," I said, half serious and half amused, "that you won't forget our trip to Israel!"

We decided to leave in summer. Sana was intelligent and ambitious; I hoped she would have enough courage to carry out our plan. Her article was published in the United States and, as I had told her, it made her famous for a time: American Jews were delighted at having finally found a "good Arab." Then she met Amos Elon; she had read and liked his book *The Israelis.* They jointly published a dialogue, *Between Enemies.* We agreed to meet at Amos Elon's home in Italy in July. From there we would go to Israel.

Clara didn't expect much from that trip. The Yom Kippur War had made her skeptical about the effectiveness of what we had the means to do. And she saw no point in going to Israel with an Egyptian woman who was better known in the United States than in Egypt. To make things more complicated, when Sana arrived she quickly developed a passion for Clara. She persisted in praising the qualities of intelligence, sensitivity, and intransigence that she found in her and admired in the Jewish people as a whole; she even went so far as to make those qualities a justification for the existence of Israel. This simply exasperated Clara.

The three of us finally left, however, with Sana worried and Clara furious. The El Al plane was late: war had just broken out in Cyprus, and flying over the island was forbidden. Sana didn't fail to see that as a warning against her trip into an enemy country. We arrived at Lod early in the morning.

Sana was surprised to see how modest the airport was: she had expected Israel to be an expression of American imperialism; that is, a smaller version of the United States. But Tel Aviv reminded her of Alexandria rather than Manhattan. As soon as we arrived there, we were assailed by journalists who had been told about us by the customs officials at Lod — an Egyptian passport! They began following us everywhere. Luckily, during our wait in Rome I had taken the precaution of asking the journalist Hezi Carmel to "organize the press a little." I knew how obsessed the Israelis would be when they learned that an Arab woman, with an Arab passport, had come to their country as a friend, and I was afraid the newspapers might turn her visit into a sensationalistic story, whereas I saw it as a political act.

Hezi had done his work well: Sana Hasan, gathering material for a sociological study to be published in the United States, had become Sana Hasan, the Egyptian woman on a peace mission. I didn't feel I was cheating too much by giving that twist to the story; the goal we had set for ourselves — peace — could easily justify more deception than that. Obviously I didn't think that our trip would magically take away all the obstacles that had accumulated between Arabs and Israelis over the past twenty-five years, but I was convinced that it might help to overcome them.

Israel was having a hard time recovering from the Yom Kippur War. Golda Meir, Moshe Dayan, and Abba Eban, held responsible for the "negligence" of October 1973, had had to turn over power to a younger team from the Labor coalition: Yitzhak Rabin was the new prime minister, Shimon Peres was the defense minister, and Yigal Allon the foreign minister.

A friend lent us his house in Jaffa, and Teddy Kollek, the mayor of Jerusalem, lodged us in the Mishkenot Sheananim, a kind of house for artists, facing the Old City. We visited towns and kibbutzim, met government ministers and private citizens, questioned and were questioned wherever we went. Everyone in Israel already knew about Sana Hasan.

We even took her to attend a parliamentary session — an Egyptian in the Knesset! We introduced her to Dayan; he was now only an ordinary member of the Knesset, but to Sana, and many others, he still had his mystical aura. After Dayan's speech on the Palestinians (an ambiguous speech, as usual: he lashed out left and right and reserved the future for himself), Menachem Begin, the opposition leader at that time, came to greet us.

"So the left has managed to bring us an Egyptian!" he said to Clara.

"You're not afraid to talk to the left?"

"We all have our heart on the left!"

After being a little intimidated at first, Sana now accepted with perfect naturalness, and even a touch of coquettishness, the great commotion that the Israelis stirred up in her honor. Only Yigal Allon refused to become involved in it.

"I don't like that circus," he said.

We saw all our friends, and Sana promised them all that they would be her guests in Egypt before long. Her list lengthened with each encounter.

One day, near the Sea of Galilee, we took part in a seminar for high school students. A group of about fifteen of them was formed to have a discussion with us. Each of them in turn told what he thought of his country and its relations with the Arab countries. In a calm, serious tone, a thoughtful-looking boy with blond hair described his childhood in Petach Tikva, near Tel Aviv. His father had been a sports instructor, a man with liberal views who taught his children that the country belonged to the Palestinians as well as the Israelis. After work he coached athletes in nearby Arab villages; he participated in pro-Palestinian demonstrations and always took his children to them. In 1972 he was one of the coaches who went to Munich with the Israeli Olympic team. He was among the victims of the Palestinian commandos.

The boy paused for a moment, then asked Sana in his tranquil voice, "Why?"

No one said anything. The students were weeping. Overcome with emotion, Sana also wept. What impressed us most was that the boy had no hatred, that he was trying his best to understand the incomprehensible, and that no one could help him. Politics has no answer to a child's "Why?"

The end of that day was difficult. When we came back to Jerusalem at nightfall, one song seemed to follow us from window to window, without a break, as it came from a series of radios in different apartments; it was one of the popular songs of the time:

> I promise you, my granddaughter, my child,
> This war will be the last . . .

How insignificant our efforts seemed! Yet something inside me wouldn't let me lose hope. Someone had to keep trying. The temptation to give up and turn inward served only dubious pride or the interests of those who found that constant state of war to their advantage.

Golda Meir had no desire to see Sana. She told me she was tired and that all those discussions with Arabs who had no official position never led to anything. I answered that it was important to show the Arab world that she never missed a chance for dialogue.

"But I'm not in power anymore," she said.

"But you're still Golda Meir."

That reply — we had resumed our old complicity in Yiddish — satisfied her; she invited us, but "only for an hour." She received us in her little house, full of books and souvenirs, on the outskirts of Tel Aviv.

We sat around tea and cookies, but there wasn't really a discussion. Sana and Golda merely exchanged statements of their respective positions. Golda became agitated only once.

"As long as I have anything to say in this country," she declared, "we won't talk to the murderers of our children!"

It was only a few weeks after the massacre at Maalot, where Palestinian commandos had seized high school students on an outing and held them as hostages.

As if she had suddenly remembered something, Golda turned to Clara, opened her eyes wide — for the first time, we discovered that they were gray — and exclaimed, "And people who put Jews and Palestinians on the same level are wrong!"

She became a little calmer, then asked me, "Well, when are you going to take an Israeli to Cairo?"

"Soon, I hope."

"Who do you have in mind?"

"I've got a whole list."

"But who's on it?"

"I'm thinking especially of Amos Oz."

"Why Amos Oz? Always the same ones. . . . The only Israelis who interest you are the ones who criticize Israel."

"It's because his books are well known," I said. "The best thing would be to take you."

Golda smiled and shrugged her shoulders. She really did seem tired. The Yom Kippur War, her withdrawal from the government, and the Palestinian acts of terror had left their mark on her. Her smile was bitter, her face was sad. I wanted to tell her something nice before leaving her, but I couldn't think of anything. We kissed each other.

Then Clara, Sana, and I went to have dinner with the Ebans. It was the last time they would receive guests in the spacious residence that belonged to the foreign ministry. Its rooms were already half empty. Abba Eban, replaced in his post by Yigal Allon, had again become an ordinary member of the Knesset. He seemed to be greatly affected by it. He sharply criticized Golda Meir's policies and chewed his fingernails even more than usual. I didn't have the heart — he seemed so worried, so embittered — to ask him why he had so long defended the same policies he was now attacking; I preferred to let him go on talking. His wife realized he was probably saying too much, and asked us not to repeat any of our conversation.

Our tour of Israel was now over. Many Israelis had seen Sana and praised her for what she was doing, wanting to see her as the swallow that announced springtime. She seemed to have taken a liking to the part she was playing, probably a little more than would have been best in such an enterprise, but I attached little importance to that; to me, what mattered was that the first phase of the operation had gone well. Now it was time for the second phase: going to Egypt.

We went to Paris, intending to stay there only a short time before going on to Egypt, but I found my mother ill and we postponed our departure. Sana was relieved, as if she were afraid to return to Egypt. She immediately flew to the United States, from where she called me some time later to tell me that she intended to go back to Israel, without passing through Cairo. I was furious: she was going to discredit me politically and put our project in danger of being ruined. She told me I was right — and went to Israel anyway. She spent several months in an *ulpan* (a school for the intensive study of Hebrew) and never answered the letter I wrote to her.

That failure saddened me, and I talked to my mother about it one day. She saw it as confirmation of something she had always thought: I had been caught once again in the trap of my idealism. And she read me this passage from Baudelaire:

I once knew a certain Benedicta, who filled the atmosphere with ideality, and whose eyes diffused a desire for greatness, beauty, glory, and everything that makes us believe in immortality.

But that miraculous girl was too beautiful to live very long, and so she died a few days after I met her. It was I myself who buried her, one day when springtime was waving its censer over the cemeteries. It was I who buried her, tightly enclosed in a perfumed wooden coffin as imperishable as an Indian chest.

And as my eyes were fixed on the place where my treasure was interred, I suddenly saw a small person who bore a singular resemblance to the deceased. She trampled the freshly turned earth with strange, hysterical violence, burst out laughing, and said, "Here I am, a vile, shameless wench! And as punishment for your madness and blindness, you'll love me as I am!"

But I was furious and answered, "No! No! No!" And to stress my refusal I stamped on the ground so violently that my leg sank into the new grave up to the knee, and, like a wolf caught in a trap, I am still bound, perhaps forever, to the burial pit of the ideal.

26

Time Out

I don't know what feeling of urgency made me go to my mother's apartment much earlier than we had agreed. The night before, she had been pale and her hands had trembled strangely; a doctor had ordered some tests and I was going to take her to the laboratory.

I rang the doorbell without getting an answer, rang again, knocked. Nothing. Then I heard a faint sigh. I leaned down, looked through the keyhole, and saw my mother on the floor, trying to get to the door. I knocked again, frantic with fear, as though to tell her I was there, that it was I. She moaned more and more loudly and began calling for help. She couldn't raise herself high enough to reach the doorknob.

Some Turkish workmen, who had been working in the building, came to help. We tried together, but in vain, to break open the door. We were beginning to panic. The woman who lived across the hall suggested calling the firemen, and I called them from her apartment. Wait. They came in five minutes, went in through the window, put my mother on her bed, and opened the door for us.

Death was there, lurking in her bedroom. I recognized it immediately.

My mother was in a coma. I had her taken to a friend's hospital, where she stayed long enough for tests to be made. That evening, we knew what was wrong: internal bleeding, cirrhosis probably caused by jaundice that had been poorly treated, or completely untreated, during the war. We transferred her to the Franco–Muslim hospital in Bobigny — I had been told that Dr. Paraf's service was one of the best for that kind of illness. And it wasn't as far from Paris to Bobigny as from Kokand to Samarkand. I hoped I could throw death off the trail by going through that Arab-looking door.

Three months, three months of anguish, three months of hope, and mingled hope and anxiety. Whenever I convinced myself that death had changed its mind and gone somewhere else, I saw it reappear, indifferent. I was afraid to leave my mother alone. I had to fight with the all-powerful administration to see her outside of visiting hours; I had to argue with the supervisor, and make phone calls here and there, to get those visiting rights, even though I had been told at the ministry of health that they were guaranteed.

"This isn't the ministry of health," the supervisor told me, "this is Dr. Paraf's service, and I'm the one who decides!"

I had to call Dr. Paraf's assistant to get permission to come and sit beside my mother when she wanted or needed me to be there. Sometimes during the day, sometimes at night, sometimes night and day. The night nurses, overwhelmed with calls from their patients, often said to me, "It's lucky you're here."

The hospital. . . . Thirty patients along a hall, thirty patients without identities, quickly reduced to being only "Papa" or "Mama."

"How did you sleep, Papa? You peed in your bed again."

Two nurses for thirty patients. Objects to be drained and cleaned, rather than individuals.

In the morning, the place was like a beehive, and the supervisor was the queen bee ruling her army of trainees, nurses' aides, attendants, and assistant supervisors. The patient was only a means of promotion. One day a young nurse tried in vain to insert a catheter in my mother's arm, and butchered her so badly that she begged her to stop.

"I'm the nurse, and I have to keep trying till I do it!"

My mother snatched the needle away from her. The nurse became angry and stamped out of the room. My mother was then left for twelve hours without care. I tried to reason with the nurse. She said she didn't want to spend the rest of her life emptying bedpans, and that she had to succeed in putting that catheter in place.

A merciless, hierarchical society, all the more cruel because the patients are defenseless.

Three times a week the chief, dressed all in white, came in with his entourage: assistants, interns, externs, nurses. He hurriedly visited the patients and talked loudly in the halls, and his dazzled entourage drank in his words. It was always a great event for the patients when the professor wasted a few seconds of his precious time talking to them. It was he, that God the Father in white, who held the patients' lives in his hand.

"Professor! Professor!" my mother called out to him one day. "Save me! I don't want to die!"

The chief stopped a moment, turned his back on her without an encouraging word, and went to me in the hall, where I had been waiting, on the alert.

"There's not much hope," he said. "The course of her illness isn't encouraging."

A little later, in the elevator, the intern saw fit to tell me, "You heard the chief: it's not encouraging. There will be an accumulation of gas, then the last stage before death will begin."

On the first floor he left me without saying anything more. Why aren't doctors taught how to talk to patients and their relatives and friends? Don't they know that the right word can be as important as an injection?

A sense of humanity is most often found at the bottom of the social ladder. An old cleaning woman in the hospital, who began scrubbing the floors at six in the morning, always found a few moments to sit beside my mother.

"I'm praying for you, Mrs. Halter," she would say. "You'll get well, you'll see."

And they would both talk about their children.

During those three months my mother remained lucid. She was very weak, but she made me take her to the bathroom every day. She wouldn't accept the hospital humiliation of lying dirtied for hours and calling in vain for someone to come and change her. She knew she was going to die, but she was always ready to take anything as a sign that she could go on hoping in spite of everything. Three months. . . . I changed her, helped her to sit up, fed her, encouraged her; but there was nothing I could do to ward off the inevitable.

Yet I believed she would get well. I believed it so firmly that I bought a plane ticket for the United States, where I was expected. But on the day when I was supposed to leave, she relapsed into a coma. I stayed with her, powerless.

She died quietly. One more whose plans would never be realized.

When I went to the hospital one last time to identify her body, it became clear to me that I had gotten used to that life: going to the hospital, taking care of my mother, fighting with the nurses, calling the assistant, waiting for the chief to come by. . . . I could probably have gone on like that for a long time. Death is the only thing I can't get used to.

I was now an orphan. There was no longer anyone, any barrier, between me and death. I was like a reservist who had suddenly found himself in the front lines. How much longer did I have? Ten years? Two years? A few days? I was again gripped by my familiar anxiety at knowing that time was passing and that my will could do nothing to change it.

Everyone has either had that feeling or will have it some-day. My case, however, was more complex. In losing my mother, I had also lost the last person with whom I could speak Yiddish. I was doubly an orphan: I had lost my parents and a vanished civilization.

My inheritance: a few personal memories, an album of pho-tographs, some poems by my mother, and a few books pub-lished by my ancestors, printers from father to son since Gu-tenberg. Not much. Yet my parents had so often tried to share their memories with me, to explain the photographs, to put the family jigsaw puzzle together; but I had been too busy with my work, my friends, and especially my battles. I thought I could always find an hour or two to listen to my father and mother tell about the past.

Too late.

Now I could only accept oblivion or set out to reconquer memory. And since the dimmest ink is worth more than the best memory, I began to write.

There was, it is said, a rabbi in Poland whom the Jews re-garded as a genius, and, being from Vilno, he was called "the genius of Vilno." When a child had difficulties in school, he was told, "*Vilno vestu zein a gwen*," which means "Just will it and you'll be a genius." My mother used that play on words — *vilno* means "will" as well as being the name of the city — to educate me. She believed till her death that the human will has no limits.

But can one write a book if one has never written? Pierre Viansson-Ponté, the editor of *Le Monde*, thought so.

"You've already written dozens of articles for me," he said. "You can write a book too."

"But a book isn't an article!"

"Yes, it is, but it's a very, very long article."

So I began writing, and day after day, surprised and won-derstruck, I saw the successive periods of my two-thousand-year history rising from sheets of paper covered with inked letters.

"Not to share a human story with human beings," said the rabbi of Gur, "is to betray humanity."

Was the story of my ancestors and me worth the time I would devote to it?

Time! What was to be done with it, if not to organize it, fill it, pack as much into it as possible? Like a careful accountant, I drew up balance sheets and put my priorities in order.

Would I have to forget about peace in the Middle East? I had hoped more often than most, and I had always been disappointed, though it was true that circumstances and people hadn't given me much help. But — how shall I put it? — that struggle was part of my life. Kanafani was dead, Shamali was dead, and Ran Cohen, my friend from Kibbutz Gan Shmuel, had survived the inferno of the Yom Kippur War only by a miracle. I didn't want any more dying. But sometimes I was overwhelmed by the futility of my efforts and it seemed that human will counted for very little when confronted with the formidable machinery of history on the march.

Israel withdrew from part of the Sinai and, in exchange, Sadat's Egypt promised, through the United States, to adopt a policy of nonbelligerence. And when would there be peace?

In May 1977 I was in Washington to give a lecture when I learned of the most important upheaval in the history of the State of Israel: the Labor Party, in power since 1947, had lost an election and Likud had won. Menachem Begin, former head of the Irgun and the man who had told us that his heart was on the left, became prime minister. David Ben-Gurion had said of him, "If he ever takes power, he will lead the country to ruin!"

Paradoxically, it was the Sephardim who elected that Ashkenazi of Polish origin: they preferred him to Yitzhak Rabin, a sabra (native-born Israeli).

I went to Israel in early November, in search of documents and information to use in reconstructing the history of my family. The atmosphere of the country had changed. What was left of the pioneer spirit was being swept away by the whirlwind of the consumer society. But my biggest surprise was seeing that members of the Knesset now wore ties when they attended its sessions.

Dayan, however, hadn't changed: having become Begin's foreign minister, he still wanted to meet with Arafat as much as ever. Since Arafat was in Cairo, I went there for the third time, perhaps with a little less enthusiasm than before, but with more stubbornness. And while Lotfi El Kholi tried to arrange a meeting with Arafat for me, President Sadat gave me an audience on short notice.

He was going to give a speech before the Assembly the next day. "An important speech," he told me with a smile that narrowed his kindly eyes — the eyes of a peasant who, as he liked to recall, had been brought up on the banks of the Nile. "In politics," he went on, "you jump on a galloping horse and let the others catch up with you if you can. Well, I'm going to ride a rocket, not a horse, and you'll see all those wheezing old politicians running after me, begging me to let them catch their breath!"

At the time, I didn't understand what he meant. The next day, I listened to his speech on television, with a running translation. And his talk about a rocket and a horse became clear to me. Here is what he announced:

"I am ready to go to the end of the earth to save the life of one of my sons. I am ready to go to the devil. I am ready to go to the end of the world. . . . I am even ready to go to Israel."

The Assembly broke into applause. I saw them applauding. Arafat saw them too. But I was unable to meet with him and had to leave Cairo two days later. I went back to Paris excited and credulous.

Begin replied to the Egyptians on television: "We Israelis hold out our hands to you. . . . Let us make peace."

Things happened very fast. On November 13 the Knesset authorized the prime minister to invite the Egyptian president for a visit.

At that time, Anwar Sadat was in Syria, trying to persuade

Hafiz al-Assad to share his views. He failed. And when he returned to Cairo he learned that Syria had launched a vicious campaign of disparagement against him throughout the Arab world.

27

Peace At Last?

On the morning of November 19, 1977, I was awakened
by a phone call from Radio France: "Will you come to
the studio and do a live commentary on Sadat's arrival in Jerusalem?"

"Sadat in Jerusalem!" I exclaimed. "Then peace has come!"

A little later I saw them all on television, in front of the
Egyptian president's white plane at Lod airport: Begin, Dayan,
Meir, Peres, Rabin, Eban, Sadat, Butros Ghali. And my voice
faltered with emotion as I told my listeners about those people
who had played such important parts in the play that is my
life.

One question gnawed at me, however: did I deserve any
credit for that historic event? Had my words, our words,
touched those people's consciences? I would probably never
know. As for the politicians, they would need two more years
of negotiations before signing a peace treaty in March 1979 in
Washington.

But another terrorist attack in Tel Aviv, and the reprisal

bombing of Lebanon, reminded me that in spite of Sadat's gesture the war wasn't over yet. One evening I wrote to my friends who still held responsible positions on one side or the other. I told them that after all the deaths on both sides it was high time for the Israelis and the Palestinians to recognize each other, and for Arafat to follow Sadat's example. I added that we hadn't given up our dreams and were developing new plans.

A few days later Naim Khader, the PLO representative in Belgium, called me from Brussels.

"What's happening to you?" he asked with his usual familiarity.

"What do you mean?"

"I mean you're becoming a pessimist! If people like you lose their faith, there will never be peace in the Middle East."

"I haven't lost my faith," I said, "but I'm tired. Sadat has made a gesture that took great courage and has historic implications. But the Palestinians are disheartening: no initiative, no prospects . . ."

"What do you want them to do?"

"I want Arafat to follow Sadat's example."

"Why don't you tell him so?"

"I'm willing, but I don't even know where he is."

"Leave it to me. Salam, shalom."

"Shalom, Naim."

Beirut, it seemed to me, had changed. There were, of course, as many cars as before, and the display windows of pastry shops were still full of sweets, but I sensed a certain nervousness everywhere. I stayed at the Hotel St. George, as planned. No one was waiting for me there. It wasn't till one in the morning that someone named Fahti called to make an appointment with me for the next morning.

As usual in the Middle East, I had to wait more than two hours in the lobby of the hotel. Finally a young boy came up to me.

"Someone will come for you at noon."

At two-thirty I got into a big Mercedes and set off for my appointment.

Several armed fedayeen stood guard in front of what looked like a small suburban house. My driver, also armed, talked with them for a few moments, then parked the car while other armed men walked past.

I was taken into a living room where men were sitting on sofas. In the center stood Arafat, in fatigues, with a pistol on his belt.

"Welcome back to Beirut," he said in English, patting me on the shoulder. He continued in Arabic, translated by a plump Palestinian: "Well, how is peace coming along?"

"Better. Sadat has taken the first step."

"Sadat is Egypt, and Egypt wanted to get back its territory."

"What about you?"

"For us, it's Palestine that matters."

"All of Palestine?"

Arafat looked at me suspiciously.

"Israel must begin by giving back the territories it occupied in the 1967 war."

"To get them back, would you be willing to do what Sadat did?"

"Go to Jerusalem?"

"Yes."

"It's up to the Israelis to recognize us first!"

"Would you be willing," I repeated, "to tell the world that you'll go to Jerusalem for discussions with Israeli leaders?"

There was a movement in the room.

"Discussions about what?" asked Arafat.

"The occupied territories, and the possibility of your finally creating a Palestinian state in them. To be viable, I think that state would have to be federated with Jordan, but that's your affair."

Arafat sat down on a stool.

"And Begin the terrorist would be willing to talk with Arafat?"

"With Arafat the terrorist? Certainly, if you say beforehand that you're coming to discuss peace."

"What if he refused?"

"Then hundreds of thousands of Israelis would demonstrate in the streets. In a democracy, the government has to listen to public opinion."

"If I understand what you're saying, you want me to go to the Allenby Bridge and say to the Israeli soldiers, 'I'm Arafat, head of the PLO, and I'd like you to take me to Mr. Begin.' "

"No. I'm only asking you to make a public statement."

Coffee was brought to us. Arafat abruptly looked at his watch and stood up.

"My friend, I have to go," he said in English. And again in Arabic: "Keep trying, maybe someday you'll succeed."

"You could help me."

"I could? How?"

"Why not make the public statement I mentioned? After Sadat's trip to Israel, it would be like a bombshell, and you wouldn't be risking anything."

"Except my life."

"Your life?"

"If I made such a statement, Dr. Habash would kill me."

For the first time, I lost patience.

"If you're afraid, Mr. Chairman, to risk your life for your people —"

He angrily interrupted me: "I've never been afraid to risk my life for my people!"

A few men stood up.

"It sometimes takes more courage to talk to your enemy than to fight him," I said.

"Everything in its own time," he answered, evidently a little calmer. "For now, it's too soon."

That was not to be the last time I saw him, but it was the last time I saw Beirut intact.

28

Reconquering
Memory

Sadat was assassinated in 1981. So was my Palestinian friend Naim Khader. Sadat knew that by going to Jerusalem he would be risking his life, and he told me so. But he felt that peace was worth that price. Naim Khader knew that by advocating an agreement between the Israelis and the Palestinians he was running a risk of being killed. But he felt that peace was worth that price. Like Said Hamami, killed in London; Azedin Kalak, killed in Paris; and, later, Issam Sartawi, killed in Lisbon. Peace, like war, devoured its own children.

One day in Buenos Aires, when the military junta was terrorizing the country, I was visiting Eduardo Galeano, editor of the magazine *Crisis*. He was worried: he had just received death threats for the third time in a week. When we left the building where his office was, we saw five men across the street put their right hands to their hips and walk toward us. I grabbed Galeano, pulled him inside, and shoved an old lady back into the elevator as she was about to come out of it. We went up the eight stories and spent two hours at the window, until the five men disappeared. Had they only gone to wait out of sight?

Galeano took two pistols from a drawer and put one of them in his pocket and the other in my shoulder bag. We left and went to a restaurant, where I sat staring at the door with my right hand in my bag and a knot of anxiety in my stomach, unable to eat anything.

"Are you afraid?" Galeano asked me.

"Yes, I'm afraid. And besides, it would be stupid to come to Buenos Aires to be killed by a bullet that wasn't even meant for me. At least people who are fighting . . ."

Galeano half closed his hard blue eyes.

"You remind me of the Argentinian peasants who say that a glass of maté cures everything. Fighting isn't a remedy for melancholy."

Fighting. A temptation and a nostalgia for men of my generation. We are too young to have fought in the war against Nazism, and too old to have had a carefree childhood. We are just the right age to feel guilty about what others did and we didn't. We are unsettled, always in search of just causes, love, and the brotherhood of arms. To recover the irrecoverable, we will take any way out — and we find only disillusionment. I vainly tried to exorcise my anxieties and my dreams by throwing myself into the conflict between the Jews and the Arabs. My effort failed and I found no serenity in it.

I like to believe that the ideas we have sown will eventually germinate. Furthermore, Judaism has taught us to fight for the future of our children, our grandchildren, and our grandchildren's children. But all that is far off. For me, the future is today. I am impatient: life has not taught me to respect time and seasons. What I like about writing is the possibility of seeing letters and words come into being on paper, here, now, immediately, under my fingers and before my eyes.

For three years I had been engaged in reconquering my family memory and I still couldn't see the end of my project. *The Book of Abraham*, the book I was writing, was enriched every day

with new characters, unexpected events, and unknown stories. I lived in a state of constant excitement mingled with
doubts caused by my lack of documentation. Whenever the
doubts became too strong, I would set off across the world in
search of scholars, unknown archives, and rare libraries.

And so I was in New York in August 1982. One evening
Stanley Hoffman told me that Israel had just invaded Lebanon.

"Operation Peace in Galilee," which Ariel Sharon presented
as being intended to protect Jewish localities in Galilee against
terrorist attacks, was quickly transformed into a siege of Beirut. And in one of the ironies of history, that siege enabled
Uri Avnery and several other Israelis to be received by Arafat
at last.

A few years later, in Paris, Ariel Sharon tried to justify himself by saying that he hadn't been allowed to finish the war.
But, as a statesman, shouldn't he have known that he wouldn't
be allowed to finish that war as he intended? It was a war that
caused deep uneasiness in the Diaspora. For the first time,
Israel hadn't been fighting *b'ein breira*, for lack of choice. And
even though most Jews understood the reasons for that war,
they were unable to find a justification for it.

Yet in spite of my personal opposition to the operation in
Lebanon, I was troubled by the anti-Israeli hysteria it aroused.
It was as if hatred of Jews, long held back by an invisible dam,
had suddenly burst out through lack of vigilance by the Israelis themselves, carrying away in its torrent those who still
hesitated and those who were disappointed in a country to
which only yesterday they had attributed all sorts of good and
noble qualities.

Believing so much in the power of words, I couldn't remain
inactive in the face of the threat that loomed behind words,
and so, with several other people, I tried to oppose words
with other words: I initiated debates and wrote articles. I was
writing one for my friend Martin Peretz's *New Republic* when
a nearby explosion rattled the windowpanes. I went out into
the street. A police car sped past with its siren howling. Peo-

ple were running toward the Rue des Rosiers. The Jewish quarter!

So I was one of the first to arrive in front of Jo Goldenberg's restaurant on that morning of August 2, 1982, just as policemen were bringing out on stretchers the first victims of one of the bloodiest anti-Jewish assaults in recent years.

Jewish dead. Again and always. . . . I trembled with emotion. I couldn't control my body or my memory. And it was hard for me to answer questions from reporters.

Blood on the paving stones of the Rue des Rosiers . . . it had once been an Ashkenazic street; then it was emptied by the Nazis, and repopulated with Sephardim in the 1960s. Confronted with that blood on that street, the anti-Zionist campaign was toned down a little. But in Israel, Menachem Begin was violently jolted by that bombing in Paris. He felt as if he had gone back to the black days of Polish pogroms in his childhood, and he called on French Jews to arm themselves.

In a democracy, can one part of the population be allowed to exercise its own system of justice? I don't think so now and I didn't think so then. And I didn't accept that concept of Judaism based on the sword. The sword, yes, but only as a last resort, after having exhausted all other means, beginning with speech. And so on August 15 I published an open letter to Menachem Begin in *Le Monde*. Two days later it appeared in the Israeli newspaper *Ma'ariv,* and the next day Begin answered it.

Letter from Marek Halter, in Paris, to
Menachem Begin, in Jerusalem:

Dear Mr. Prime Minister,
    I would never have addressed you publicly if you had not publicly claimed to speak in my name. A Jew like you, I was born, like you, in Poland; like you, I was persecuted by the Nazis; like you, I found myself

in Central Asia. But I was then too young to follow the road that led you to the land of our ancestors, and too young to take part in the struggle against the British. In adulthood, I believe I have done no disservice, through my work or my life, to the cause of Israel and the Jewish people. And even though we belong to two different generations, you will agree with me that, as the Midrash Tahumot says, "All the generations of Israel were present at Sinai, and the Torah is given each time a man receives it."

But mainly, Mr. Prime Minister, we belong to two antagonistic currents of thought that have always stirred our people: that of the Zealots and that of the Pharisees. The Zealots wanted to be the secular army of the Almighty; the Pharisees wanted to be His word and His voice. The former relied on the sword and the stone, the latter on the pen and the book. I must acknowledge that while the stone did not save the people from exile, the book did not protect them from barbarity. For there is no salvation if one of those two principles triumphs to the exclusion of the other.

For any state, in a world filled with violence, and especially for Israel, which cannot survive a defeat, determination and strength are firm guarantees of existence. However, Mr. Prime Minister, they are not the only ones. In the schools of Yabneh and Usha, and in the school of Sepphoris, where Judah ha-Nasi compiled the Midrash in A.D. 189, and in the academies of Tiberias, where the Talmud was completed in the fifth century, the Tannaim and the Amoraim, the scribes and the scholars, built around the Law a stronghold in which the Jews were able to place their collective destiny. Freud called that stronghold, conceived in Judea, "the invisible edifice of Judaism." Today it is as necessary to Israel's existence as secure borders. Yet you seem not to know that, Mr. Prime

Minister, judging from your recent statements. In the spirit of the Torah there are no triumphal arches, and a victory should give rise neither to pride nor to self-confidence. After defeating the four kings — the four main ideologies, according to the Maharal — Abraham came back worried instead of rejoicing: he was afraid he might have killed a righteous man among the combatants.

I know, Mr. Prime Minister, that Israel is a democratic state and that you were democratically elected by its people. By a very slight majority, it is true, and largely because of the hatred and fear engendered by the PLO leaders' statements, their acts of terrorism and their stubborn refusal to take the hand held out to them so long by those Israelis who understand their cause. But the fact remains that you are the prime minister of the State of Israel and I respect your office. It does not permit you, however, to speak in the name of millions of Jews who did not elect you. And it certainly does not permit you to be discourteous to the president of the French Republic, who is, moreover, a friend of Israel.

There are times, I know, when a man considers it permissible to violate conventions and rules. That is not possible for a head of state, and it is forbidden to a Jew. The Hetsia treatise in the Talmud tells us that "if someone makes his fellow man's face turn white in public, it is as if he had killed him."

I was, Mr. Prime Minister, among the first in France to protest publicly against the way the media reported on events in Lebanon, against their lack of objectivity and the part they played, no doubt unintentionally, in the deterioration of the image of Jews in this country. Like nearly all of the French Jewish community, Mr. Prime Minister, I am firmly committed to Israel's existence and security. And my com-

mitment would not falter even if Israel should someday depart from the principles that for centuries have
made us Jews, for a brother who has a flaw is still a
brother. But I would then be worried about Israel's
future. History teaches us that the Almighty armed
His people because they were the people of the Law,
but that He warned them against transgressing the
Law, "lest the land vomit you out, when you defile
it, as it vomited out the nation that was before you"
(Leviticus 18:28).

And in conclusion, Mr. Prime Minister, let me quote
a passage from the First Book of Kings, which I am
sure you study often, and which enlightens us on the
realism of the wise man: "Then on the seventh day
the battle was joined; and the people of Israel smote
of the Syrians a hundred thousand foot soldiers in
one day." The rest fled. Their leader, Ben-Hadad, took
refuge in the city. "And his servants said to him, 'Be-
hold now, we have heard that the kings of the house
of Israel are merciful kings; let us put sackcloth on
our loins and ropes upon our heads, and go out to
the king of Israel; perhaps he will spare your life.' "
They went to the king and said, "Your servant Ben-
Hadad says, 'Pray, let me live.' " The king replied,
"Does he still live? He is my brother." Ben-Hadad
came and the king took him into his chariot. "And
Ben-Hadad said to him, 'The cities which my father
took from your father I will restore; and you may establish bazaars for yourself in Damascus, as my father did in Samaria.' And Ahab said, 'I will let you
go on these terms.' So he made a covenant with him
and let him go" (I Kings 20:29–34).

Wishing peace for all of Israel, I remain,

Yours truly,
Marek Halter

Letter from Menachem Begin, in Jerusalem, to
Marek Halter, in Paris:

Dear Mr. Halter,

I am glad to know that you were able to escape
from the German Nazis, but I regret that, having become an adult, you have remained in exile in spite of
everything. You could, of course, have come to live
in Israel at any time after May 15, 1948. Since then,
there has been no need for "certificates," and any Jew
who wants to return to the land of our common
ancestors can do so. You evidently prefer to live in a
foreign country rather than "in the historic homeland
of the Jewish people," to use the words of our heroic
brothers in the Soviet Union. So much the worse
for you.

But you want to lecture us from abroad, and furthermore you want to do it with the aid of verses and
maxims of our wise men. You recognize that I was
democratically elected to head the Israeli government, but then you note that it was a close election,
won "by a very slight majority." (Is not a slight majority a majority? In a democracy, is the great minority entitled to manage the state's affairs?)

And you continue: "By a very slight majority, it is
true, and largely because of the hatred and fear engendered by the PLO leaders' statements, their acts
of terrorism and their stubborn refusal to take the hand
held out to them so long by those Israelis who understand their cause."

How did you learn that, my dear Mr. Halter, living
as you do in Paris, the beautiful City of Light? You
deny me, the prime minister of the democratic Jewish
state, the right to say anything about or to the Jews
of France, yet you arrogate to yourself the right to

say why, in a country of which you are not a citizen, one of its citizens was elected to head its government.

I will now come to my main point. I have not been, as you claim, discourteous to François Mitterrand, president of the French Republic. The simple truth is that our friend François Mitterrand — for I continue to call him a friend — has committed a terrible, atrocious sin against the whole Jewish people. I have heard the words he spoke in Hungary: "I have not accepted Oradours* in France, and I will not accept them in Lebanon."

Oradours, Mr. Halter? Being Jewish, you must understand that the odious anti-Semitism now rampant in France, as it was at the time of the Dreyfus affair, is a result of those terrible words about "Oradours in Lebanon."

François Mitterrand should have asked forgiveness of our people, and of the French people, for those unfortunate words. He has not yet done so. Who, then, has been discourteous?

You became frightened, Mr. Halter, when you heard me say that "if the French authorities do not protect French citizens from such Nazi manifestations as the murder of Jews killed for the sole reason that they are Jews, I will not hesitate, as a Jew, to call on the younger generation of our people to defend the lives and human dignity of Jews."

I repeat that, without taking back a single word of it. I am not speaking in your name, my dear Mr. Halter, or in the name of Jews who, like you, live in France. I am speaking as a Jew who has lived, grown old and seen with his own eyes what has been seen by the generation of destruction and rebirth. I have

---

*On June 10, 1944, in reprisal for acts of sabotage, a German SS division killed all but ten of the 652 inhabitants of the French village of Oradour-sur-Glane. (Translator's note.)

left to the French authorities the option of putting an end to such neo-Nazi acts as the murder of Jews because they are Jews. But if those authorities cannot or will not do their duty, what do you think young Jews should do, after what our people suffered in the nineteen-thirties and nineteen-forties — in France also?

I will go on saying, whenever an opportunity arises, that the murder of Jews killed because they are Jews is not an "internal affair" of any country, wherever it may be. It is the affair of the whole Jewish people, of the Jewish state, and of men of good will all over the world.

You are a writer and a scholar, my dear Mr. Halter, and I greatly respect your learning, but allow me to give you this advice: you should reread, or read if you have not yet done so, Ahad Ha'am's article on "Servitude in Freedom."

Assuring you of my fraternal feelings, I am,

Yours sincerely,
Menachem Begin

The world press mentioned that singular debate between a prime minister and a writer living in a foreign country.

Jewish memory is made up of superimposed events; in the media, however, one event drives away another. So the victims on the Rue des Rosiers in Paris were replaced only a month later by the Palestinian victims in the Lebanese refugee camps of Sabra and Shatila. The Israelis hadn't taken part in slaughtering those hundreds of people, but, by letting the Lebanese Christians do it, they set off another wave of anti-Israeli feeling all over the world.

"What happened to Jewish principles in Israel?" Lotfi El Kholi, staying briefly in Paris, asked me.

"It's odd," I said, "that Israel is expected to preserve principles that no other country respects."

"Wasn't it in the name of those principles that the Jews came to Palestine?"

"That hasn't stopped you from fighting those Jews for thirty-five years. . . . And I've never claimed that Israel represents absolute good. Evil is in each one of us. What distinguishes people from each other is the extent to which they're able to restrain it."

"So in Israel —"

"You shouldn't judge a nation before seeing its reactions."

A month later, on September 28, 1982, more than three hundred and fifty thousand people demonstrated in the Square of the Kings of Israel, facing the Tel Aviv city hall, to show their opposition to the war in Lebanon.

The next day, I happened to meet Pierre Mauroy, the French prime minister at the time.

"I don't approve of the war in Lebanon," I said, "but it's rare for ten percent of the population to demonstrate against a war that, rightly or wrongly, their country is fighting. Imagine the same percentage of American citizens getting together to protest the war in Vietnam — it would have been a demonstration of more than twenty million people!"

Sometimes a chance meeting with a politician can change the content of his discourse: in his speech before Parliament, the French prime minister paid tribute to Israeli democracy, and the media echoed that theme.

Later events showed that we were right. On September 28, 1982, the Israeli government decided to form a committee to investigate the massacres of Sabra and Shatila, and the committee published its report on February 8, 1983. Israel withdrew from Lebanon, but the war didn't stop. There was a series of massacres perpetrated by the various Arab factions. Arafat, driven out of Syria, settled in Tunisia. Menachem Begin, last of the founding fathers of the State of Israel, feeling responsible for the failure of the war in Lebanon, and especially for the deaths of hundreds of young soldiers, humbly withdrew from the political scene. The new elections showed no decisive choice between the left and the right. A national-unity government was formed, with Shimon Peres and Yitzhak Shamir sharing the post of prime minister. Peace still remained to be conquered.

29

Hope in Spite of Everything

One day in December 1986 I was again in Israel. With Senator Ted Kennedy, I was presiding over a ceremony commemorating David Ben-Gurion's hundredth birthday, at Kibbutz Sde Boker, where he had spent his last years. On that ocher hill, overlooking the rocky Negev Desert, there were nearly all members of the Israeli government, foreign diplomats, and friends and relatives of Ben-Gurion. We were all deeply moved. In my speech, I referred to my last conversation with Ben-Gurion. We had talked about the Palestinian question.

The Palestinian question? At that moment, ceremony or not, Ben-Gurion's son and daughter launched into a vehement argument. Within a minute, the guests and the government ministers were all embroiled in the debate. In all circumstances in Israel, even at a solemn commemorative ceremony, even in front of diplomats, in a city or in a desert, the Palestinian question is always there, stirring up passions.

A few days later, a military airplane brought Ted Kennedy and me to Jerusalem. It was winter, and raining.

A phone call.

"Marek Halter?"

"Yes."

"My name is Albert Aghazarian. I'm a spokesman for the Bir Zeit Arab University and I'd like to meet you."

"I'm willing. Where?"

"In a little Armenian café in the Old City, opposite the Jaffa Gate."

It was only a week after violent anti-Israeli demonstrations in which a young Arab had been killed. The atmosphere was tense. Hasidim in dark clusters quickened their pace on the way to the Wailing Wall.

Like many Palestinians, Albert Aghazarian knew Hebrew perfectly, but we talked in English and French. He invited me to give a lecture at his university.

"It's important that you come," he said. "The world must realize that we don't only use violence, that we're also ready for dialogue. We're going to invite the international press."

"I feel honored," I said, "but I'm not an Israeli, and a debate between you and me would be pointless."

"No, it wouldn't," Aghazarian insisted. "We all know your views, your commitment to Israeli–Palestinian peace, your struggles for peace in the Middle East."

"Well, what of it?"

"Your position should be stated."

"Which position?"

"Your idea that a Palestinian state should exist in peace beside Israel."

"Do you agree with that idea?"

"Most Palestinians do."

"Then say so!"

"That's impossible."

"Why?"

"Because it's up to Israel to take the first step. Otherwise, our extremists wouldn't understand . . ."

"Why?"

"Because we have no land. And recognition of Israel is all we have to give in exchange for recognition of our national existence. It's the only card we can play."

"But most Israelis already recognize you. Even Shimon Peres."

The spokesman of Bir Zeit University finished his fourth cup of coffee and gave me a stubborn look.

"It's up to the Israeli government to take a public position."

"And who will respond to that gesture?"

"The PLO."

"Will Arafat agree?"

"Yes."

"Then why doesn't he say so?"

And for the thousandth time I gave an explanation that seemed to me both simple and obvious: if Arafat promised to stop terrorism and declared himself ready to discuss peace with Israel, no Israeli government could refuse to meet with him.

"Maybe," said Aghazarian, "but Arafat can't do that."

"Why?"

"Because our extremists would kill him."

Several young tourists invaded the café. I said nothing. I was sad. Twenty years. . . . For more than twenty years I had been carrying on that absurd dialogue that led nowhere. Meanwhile the world was experiencing the fourth technological revolution in human history and rushing toward the year 2000, men had long since walked on the moon, governments had been succeeding each other in both the East and the West, and here, in this land that had known so many miracles, nothing had changed, in either words or acts.

Yet that evening, on the terrace of the Mishkenot Sheananim, as I contemplated the Old City shimmering in the golden fog that spread over the purple mountains, I felt myself escaping from despair. Was this the miracle of the Holy Land? Or was it simply that I belonged to a people whose hope had survived all catastrophes? "Houses and fields and vineyards shall again be bought in this land," said Jeremiah. And Isaiah prophesied, "In that day there will be a highway from Egypt to Assyria, and the Assyrian will come into Egypt, and the Egyptian into Assyria. . . . In that day Israel will be the third with Egypt and Assyria." And at peace.

30

The Tunis Affair

W ho would have believed that, ten years after our last meeting, Arafat would invite me to see him again, this time in Tunis?

It was at the beginning of August 1988. I was working on the sequel to *The Book of Abraham*. Raymonda Tawill, passing through Paris, told me that "the Old Man" would like to see me as soon as possible. "The Old Man" was what the Israelis had called David Ben-Gurion in his time, and now it is what the Palestinians call Yasir Arafat. One more proof of the Palestinians' fascination with the Israelis.

Arafat invited me to see him in Tunis on August 15. I didn't want to leave Paris before finishing my chapter. We agreed on the date of August 20. Clara and I arrived in the evening at the Hilton Hotel, on a hill some distance from the center of the city.

Many Palestinians stay at the Hilton, and those I saw in the lobby or in the restaurant near the pool, gathered for a conference on the question of funds for the PLO, reminded me of their Zionist counterparts in America, Germany, France, Britain. . . . While a Tunisian orchestra played in the background, they commented on the latest developments in the Palestinian uprising in the occupied territories and discussed the coming Israeli elections. Among them was Ghassan Kanafani's brother, Marwan, who lives in Washington, and the poet Mahmoud Darwish, who lives in Paris. We were a long way from the warlike atmosphere of Beirut. Here there was no Rambo, no paratroopers' uniforms, no hand grenades hanging from belts. Time had marked people and ideas.

In the office next to Arafat's, we found some of the PLO leaders we had met years ago in Lebanon. They had aged. In their shirtsleeves, with tired eyes, they were rereading the latest draft of a declaration by PLO headquarters. Pages strewn over the table quivered under the pulsations of an electric fan.

Arafat himself had changed. His beard was turning white, and when he put on glasses to sign something that a fedayee had brought him, he said apologetically, "It's old age. . . ."

We were left alone with him. Since his English had improved greatly, we no longer needed an interpreter, and so, for the first time since we had met, our conversation took a more personal turn. More outspoken, too, with humor-tinged interludes. I think that, for him, our meeting was a welcome change from his usual political interviews. When, after two hours of discussion, he told us that he had to leave us and go to a dinner, scheduled long in advance, with Bettino Craxi, head of the Italian Socialist Party, I wasn't surprised to hear him say that he would like to see us again afterward.

At about eleven in the evening, a car came for us at the hotel. Our first meeting had taken place in the suburb of Carthage; the second one took place in a house in a residental quarter of Tunis. For security reasons, Arafat often changes residences — and headgear: in the morning, he had worn a military hat; in the evening, he wore the traditional kaffiyeh.

Though he was now more open and conciliatory than he had ever been before, he still made the same errors of judgment regarding Israeli society. In his view, the Israelis are children of Western rationalism, which leads to demanding everything, while madness, which leads to understanding and excusing everything, is a disease — or the prerogative — of Middle Eastern societies.

"Madness is a universal disease," I said, "and the Jews, or the Israelis, are no less likely to have it than anyone else, but it can never be used to justify unjustifiable acts."

As we were about to leave him, late at night, I told him that our conversation could not remain confidential, because otherwise it would be sterile.

"All right," he said, "but remember: this isn't an interview. I agreed not to give any interviews before the meeting of the National Council in Algiers, a month or two from now."

I answered that, being a writer, I would find an acceptable form in which to make his commitments known.

"I trust you," he said, and he then suggested that we have some pictures taken as souvenirs of our meeting.

Back in Paris, I described our discussion in the form of an open letter to the chairman of the PLO. On August 30, 1988, it was published in *Ma'ariv* in Israel, in *Le Monde* in France, and in the *New York Times:*

> Mr. Chairman,
>
> You invited me to Tunis and for several hours there we had a thorough and brisk conversation on Aug. 20. You told me you were surprised by the number and brutality of my questions. Yet those are the questions raised not only by Israelis but by every Jew in the world, and by many people who are not involved in the Arab–Israeli conflict. And you know it, too.
>
> Never before, you said, had so many preconditions been put for settling a war. And you are right. But you are at war, and in this war, in which you are a protagonist, you pretend the opponent does not exist.
>
> You assured me that things would change — you said they already are changing — but, when I asked,

you said you could make no public statement before the meeting of the Palestine National Council in a few weeks.

You know I am not a diplomat, but a writer. I feel, to be honest with myself and respectful to my readers, I must put my questions publicly. You will have to answer them just as publicly sooner or later.

You also know I am a Jew, and this was no doubt one of your reasons for inviting me. I am a Jew born in a world that was destroyed, whose memories and values I am trying to preserve. You know that for me Israel is the heart of this effort, and that I am viscerally attached to its existence.

So, Mr. Chairman, do you endorse the recent declarations of Bassam Abu Sharif and Abu Iyad? Mr. Sharif says the Palestine Liberation Organization is ready to start talks with the Israeli government, whether it is run by Shimon Peres or Yitzhak Shamir. Abu Iyad speaks of a Palestinian state alongside Israel and at peace with her.

You told me that nothing happens within the PLO leadership without your consent, but you also told me that you would not take a position on this issue until after the Palestine National Council meeting.

George Habash, chief of the Popular Front for the Liberation of Palestine, has declared his opposition to any peaceful settlement. How will you deal with all these verbal or armed hostilities emerging each day in the name of the Palestinian people?

Hasn't the time come for you to impose a single authority and policy on the PLO, while preserving the internal democracy you say is so important? Would the plan for a Palestinian government-in-exile, drafted by a man you said is so close to you, be the answer to the preceding question? Would you endorse this plan?

In Yiddish, one says a man is what he is, not what he was. But I would like to know the reasons behind your change toward Israel.

You remember we first met 20 years ago in Beirut. You and your friends seemed surprised by what I said. I simply proposed a dialogue between Israelis and Palestinians.

As for me, I was horrified by what you said. The goal of the PLO then was "the destruction of the Zionist entity in Palestine" and establishment "of a lay state" where "Jews, Moslems, and Christians would live together." There was even talk of expelling the Jews who came to the Middle East after 1947.

If I remind you of this, it is on purpose. You must understand, and I believe you do understand, that such a brutal switch from rejection to acceptance provokes distrust.

And you know nothing can be done in politics without a minimum of confidence in the adversary's good faith.

So, how can you say, Mr. Chairman, "We want a Palestinian state next door to the Israeli state" if your national charter's goal is still the destruction of Israel?

You explained to me that PLO decisions made after the charter was written annul these provisions. But you also told me, that we, Jews and Arabs, are both people of the Book and that we believe more in what is written than in what is said. You even told me that, according to Arab tradition, God ordered the Book written so man would at last believe in His existence.

Fundamentalists in Gaza are eroding your authority. You said this worries you. Israeli society is hardening and you said this preoccupies you. But you also said the "fanatics and extremists" — these are your words — whose importance is spreading in Gaza and the West Bank, are just filling the gap which you left by not proposing an acceptable, realistic goal.

And you said Israeli society is hardening because it feels threatened. I ask: Will a tiny Palestinian state survive? Will it not always want to expand at the expense of Israel? Will it not cause interminable wars in the region? The choice Israelis make at the elections in November will depend partly on your answers.

You said you conceive of not just another tiny state but a Jordanian–Palestinian federation "with or without King Hussein." The Palestinians are more than 70 percent of the Jordanian population. You told me this federation plan has been an integral part of PLO decisions for several years and there is no reason to change it. Don't you think such a statement should be made publicly today?

My last question was whether you are ready to announce publicly and solemnly your intention to sign peace with Israel. Are you ready, as a sign of your sincerity, to pledge the end of all terrorist actions and strikes in the occupied territories, and straightforward annulment of the PLO Charter? You know this is the price for starting to remove the distrust brought by so many years of rejection and hate.

You promised me you would say these things in your statement to the United Nations Assembly in November. Will you do so?

This article set off an avalanche of comments, both in Israel and in the Arab press, where it was published in its entirety. One phrase in particular stirred up a violent controversy between Yasir Arafat and King Hussein. Referring to the prospect of a Palestinian–Jordanian federation, I had quoted Arafat's comment: "with or without King Hussein." Some Arab leaders, including first of all King Hussein himself, regarded that statement as an incitement to murder. Facing their indignant outcry, Arafat asked me, as a favor, to declare publicly that neither in his mind nor in mine were his words a call to murder, but were only meant to convey a political expectation for the near or distant future. My declaration was published on the front pages of the Arab press.

That was when the Palestinian extremists took a hand in the situation. They had also just discovered Flora Lewis's incisive article in the *New York Times*, published the day after mine, in which she commented on my conversation with Arafat. That article had irritated them.

Bassam Abu Sharif called me from Tunis on September 3 and said bluntly, "Because of pressure from our extremists, we have to revise some of the points you raised in the press. Arafat apologizes, but you must understand —"

"No, I don't understand, and I'm going to say exactly what I think about it," I answered angrily.

And that was what happened. The PLO statement was published in France on September 7, 1988, in *Le Monde*, under the headline, *The PLO Denies Yasir Arafat's Conciliatory Remarks to Marek Halter*, and below it was a statement by me, with a headline of equal size: *But Halter Stands by His Report:*

> After a week of hesitation and, it seems, confrontation within the leadership of the PLO, the policy of expecting the worst has prevailed, for, in denying Yasir Arafat's words reported in my article, PLO headquarters appears to be saying:
>
> 1. That the PLO is not willing to engage in peace talks with Israel;
>
> 2. That it has no intention of renouncing the PLO Charter, which states the objective of destroying Israel;
>
> 3. That it rejects the idea of a Palestinian–Jordanian federation;
>
> 4. And that it has not resolved to set up a provisional government that would sign a peace treaty with the Jewish state.
>
> All this will not be heartening to those who feel that the only thing the PLO has never denied is its determination to destroy Israel.

"It's starting all over again," Clara said to me sadly.

I was beginning to regret our trip to Tunis when a phone call calmed me a little: Arafat was sorry about that misunderstanding and promised not to disappoint me in the future. And in fact a meeting in Aqaba at the end of October, among Egyptian President Hosni Mubarak, King Hussein, and Yasir Arafat, made official (once again) the plan of a Palestinian–Jordanian federation, and announced the PLO's willingness to conclude a peace agreement with Israel. But just before the Israeli elections a murderous act of violence in Jericho, which killed a young woman and her three children, put everything in question again.

Will the Palestinian leader keep his promises completely, in spite of everything? Will more suffering and death be necessary before the Israelis and Palestinians consent to live side by side in a world at peace? Then we will be able to say, with the prophet Amos:

"Are you not like the Ethiopians to me, O people of Israel?" says the Lord. "Did I not bring up Israel from the land of Egypt, and the Philistines from Caphtor and the Syrians from Kir?"

For the time being, all I have left is this stack of pages that I spent years blackening. When I began, I didn't know where it would take me. Now that I've finished, I think I know: to write one's story is to stop it a little.

I have an urge to be in action again, but I need a pause, a time out. The experience is so new to me that I don't know how it will turn out. Will I be satisfied with only being a spectator? Can I do without the vain satisfaction I had when I felt I was taking part in the life of the world among famous and influential people? Will my friends still like me?

It remains true that everything is in motion, that one event is always followed by another. Maybe someday it will finally be possible to keep the moon in a bucket of water.

It is said in the Zohar that the first step in the ascent toward God is prayer; the next step is singing; an even higher one is a cry; the highest is the memory of that cry — and that is this book.

Index